MAKING
THE
ROUNDS

ALLAN WEISS

EDGE SCIENCE FICTION AND FANTASY PUBLISHING
AN IMPRINT OF HADES PUBLICATIONS, INC.

CALGARY

Making The Rounds
Copyright © 2016 by Allan Weiss

This is a work of fiction. Names, characters, places, and
incidents are the products of the author's imagination or
are used fictitiously and are not to be construed as real.
Any resemblance to actual events, locales, organizations, or
persons, living or dead, is entirely coincidental.

The following stories appeared previously in On Spec:
"The Missing Word" (Summer 2001); "Making Light" (Spring 2007);
"The Whole Megillah" (Summer 2011); "A Little Leavening" (Fall 2014)

Edge Science Fiction and Fantasy Publishing
An Imprint of Hades Publications Inc.
P.O. Box 1714, Calgary, Alberta, T2P 2L7, Canada

In-house editing by Brian Hades
Interior design by Janice Blaine
Cover Illustration by Marija Vilotijevic

ISBN: 978-1-77053-116-1

EDGE Science Fiction and Fantasy Publishing and Hades Publications, Inc.
acknowledges the ongoing support of the Alberta Foundation for the Arts and
the Canada Council for the Arts for our publishing programme.

Canada Council Conseil des Arts
for the Arts du Canada

Library and Archives Canada Cataloguing in Publication

CIP Data on file with the National Library of Canada

ISBN: 978-1-77053-116-1
(e-book ISBN: 978-1-77053-115-4)

FIRST EDITION
(F-20160227)
Printed in Canada
www.edgewebsite.com

DEDICATION

To the Cecil Street Irregulars, who made all of my stories
better, and especially to Theresa Wojtasiewicz, who insisted I
write more than one Jewish wizard story.

· ✡ ·

CONTENTS

· ✡ ·

THE MISSING WORD

IT WAS A typical late afternoon in the desert, and Eliezer nearly fell asleep in his saddle after a day of seeing nothing but the featureless horizon shimmering around him. For hours, there'd been no sign of a village, or distant oasis, or caravan stretched along the brown sands. Even Melech seemed ready to doze as he lethargically planted his hooves on the packed sand.

So, did every day have to be interesting? Was God an entertainer?

As it was only four days after the summer solstice, the evening came slowly. Eliezer loved the dusk, because every moment promised deeper and richer night that revealed more and more of the five-pointed stars of this world. It was God Who made the stars shine… but who was responsible for the black spot that now suddenly appeared on the western horizon? The spot grew, gained definition, until he discerned a horseman leading a band of pedestrians, the entire crowd heading straight for him. He halted Melech and pulled himself erect, moving only to stroke his beard. It was never a mistake to adopt an appropriately intimidating appearance for such encounters.

The horseman, he now saw, was swathed in fine white and gray robes, his head wrapped in a *kaffiyeh* that flapped in the wind. "A big shot," Eliezer suggested to Melech. Melech nodded. "Might be trouble, too," Eliezer added, and shrugged: what else could a big shot be?

"Greetings!" the leader called in a Gentile tongue; his little troupe held tightly together behind him as they nervously watched Eliezer— maybe afraid he'd impulsively turn them into birds or something. "I'm sorry," the man continued as he halted his horse; "*shalom!*"

Eliezer maintained his silence, which never failed to impress. He appreciated the unnecessary shift in language, but knew it wouldn't last. The *goyim* never bothered to learn more than a polite word or two of the language of the Book.

After a minute the horseman tried again. "Can you understand me? I don't know your tongue very well!"

Eliezer nodded. Melech said, *Speak up already; the people look scared silly.* To come to him like this, out in the middle of the desert... *They must be desperate,* Melech suggested, stating the obvious. Eliezer waited for the usual comment about the irrationality of humans, but the horse preferred to be uncharacteristically restrained.

Using one hand to hold down the bottom of his *kaffiyeh* while awkwardly clutching his reins with the other, the horseman said, "Are you Eliezer Ben-Avraham, the wizard we have heard so much about?" His entourage peeked around, above, and under his black steed, but avoided getting too near the animal, as if it were some unEarthly creature.

"I am," Eliezer said at last. "And who is asking?"

"I am Kala-Wek, of the rockcity of Al-ayar. We need your services. Can you follow us?"

"Well—" Eliezer said, stretching the word out to an absurd length. For his part, Melech refused to offer an opinion. Some helper he was being! "What is the nature of the task you wish me to perform?"

"It's hard to explain—"

"Transformation? Something with your herds? You have crops?" In this desert? Not likely. "A good harvest I can try, but I'm not as young as I used to be." That was true; it was also irrelevant; but it often excused him from interfering too much with God's will.

"Please, come with us. The priests will explain."

Melech shook his head in distaste. He hated mysteries, surprises; he was always so cautious... if he had his way they would avoid anything that was even remotely interesting. "I'm sorry," Eliezer said, "but if you can't explain your problem maybe it's not so serious."

"It's very serious, Wizard."

"You interrupt me as I do my rounds, and won't even say why? Give me an idea at least."

Most of Kala-Wek's face was hidden by the headdress, but the strain was apparent. "A word is missing," he said at last.

As soon as he said that the people raised their right hands toward the sky, and made a bizarre sign across their foreheads — something from the Sun-Maker religion, no doubt. Maybe his ancient brain had misinterpreted what the man had said. But Melech must have heard the same thing; his ears twitched, and his eyes blinked rapidly — not, it seemed, from the effects of blowing sand. *Sunstroke*, Melech joked, then half-said, half-asked, *I guess we have to go?* Eliezer nodded, and while he wasn't all that eager to deal with crazies he knew that he would hate himself forever if he didn't find out what this was all about.

"Please come," Kala-Wek begged (a shame to see a man acting so), as he gestured with his free hand. The reins in the other slapped against the horse's back; Melech said how much he pitied a mount burdened with an incompetent rider. The man was no youngster; in all his years had he never ridden a horse before?

Eliezer spread his hands in surrender. His curse required him to help anyone in need, and his curiosity wouldn't let him pass up this opportunity. "All right, all right. But if this takes long others who are expecting my services may suffer." Always a good idea to add a little guilt.

"I understand," replied the gentleman, obviously relieved. "Thank you, sir."

The rider turned in a wide circle, his horse straining to obey almost contradictory commands of hands and legs, and the people walked beside, glancing back at Eliezer and Melech. Eliezer made sure to follow at a safe distance.

They led him into a strange part of the desert, one he'd believed uninhabited, and climbed up the jagged ridge of what proved to be a crater. Melech stepped carefully through the pass the people crossed, and on to the downslope of the crater. In the crater's bowl was nothing but sand and a central outcrop of rock. Melech shot a look at Eliezer that meant, "Whatever happens, this was your idea." *So!*

The central protrusion proved to be larger than he'd thought, and holes dotted its surface. Heads poked out of the holes, watching his arrival. What, had they never seen a stranger before? And then Melech raised his left front hoof in derision (a very annoying gesture!) and waves came from his mind of disbelief that Eliezer hadn't figured out already that they were a race of cave-dwelling hermits. Kala-Wek dismounted and led the way into a small opening at the base of the little mountain. Eliezer

3

found himself in a well-lit warren of tunnels. *Bat-people*, Melech sneered (sometimes he was such a bigot). "Be fair, my friend," Eliezer said aloud; "God makes all kinds. Is it so much better to have no home at all?" Melech answered in a half-serious affirmative as Eliezer dismounted, his ankles and knees communicating their unhappiness with their renewed burden.

Two men led the horses away, and Eliezer told Melech to keep him informed of his condition. "We've heard tales about you, Great Wizard," Kala-Wek began as he removed the headdress, "and we know your powers." Despite being a desert-dweller he had pale skin; his long, curly hair and thick beard were gray — not the gray of age, but of the iron around him, as if he were not merely a resident of the mountain but part of it. "Our problem is serious, Wizard, and only one such as you can help us."

"Your confidence in me is very flattering, but I just perform my deeds with God's power and indulgence." And because he had no choice.

"Come." Kala-Wek led him through a series of tunnels illuminated by smokeless torches, upstairs and down (Eliezer felt every ascent and descent in his legs), until they reached an arched doorway covered by a curtain of thin, opaque material, hanging from rings set into the very stone of the arch itself. Kala-Wek pushed the curtain aside, revealing a high-ceilinged room, its walls gleaming with polished stone tiles and lines of tiny jewels curling in elaborate designs. Kala-Wek motioned him to enter, and Eliezer did so, blinking as the jewels flashed in the light from the round windows above his head.

Four men in fancy robes and tall, bulbous hats glimmering with yet more jewels knelt on low benches before an even lower table, on which lay a huge black tome. The priests focused entirely on the book, not deigning even to look at Eliezer. This was why he came so far out of his way, to be shown no hospitality? On the wall behind them, high over their bent heads, was a sun of beaten gold; seven pointed beams radiated from it, each ending in a blood-colored ruby. Such wealth! But if you lived in a mountain you should expect to find a few nice stones lying around… Eliezer waited before the priests. *Nu?*

Without looking up from the book the priest on the far left said, "If you wish, you may sit on the floor, Heathen."

'Heathen'! God should only —! "I'll stand, thank you."

"As you wish. It is difficult to speak about these matters with barbarians and unbelievers."

With WHAT? "Then I won't dirty your temple!" Eliezer turned to leave, but the second priest called him back.

"Please, Wizard!"

Eliezer stood before them again. "Unfortunately, it's my God-given duty to use my powers to help His Adamic brood, no matter how far from His path they stray." 'Unbeliever'! 'Barbarian'! Through gritted teeth he said, "Tell me what you need me to do."

The first priest spoke again, but never raised his eyes from the book. "You see before you the Ma'arim, our Holy Text. Each day we read from the Great Beacon's word, and praise His Name."

The four priests, in unison, bowed forward and mumbled something like, "Blessed be His Name."

"But three manifestations ago," the first continued, "we looked within and saw that a word was missing."

Again the same story? Eliezer waited for more explanation, but none came. "A word is missing," he repeated, trying to sound interested, not incredulous.

"Yes," the second priest said. "There was a horrifying space where a word would be. It was gone."

"My friends, you'll excuse me, but a word can't just get up and walk away."

"We think it did."

Oy! Crazy, the lot of them. When Eliezer had played with fire, and violated the Code by delving into those off-limit secrets, he had been obliged to wander the world for all time, and use the powers he'd gained to assist any who needed his help. He'd thought it a good bargain at the time, given the possible alternative punishments... But this! Okay, so he'd learned a few things! So he'd maybe stuck his nose where it didn't belong! But did that mean he'd have to deal with *meshuggeneh goyim*?

"My friends, I've heard many stories in my travels, but yours... well, so how can I be of assistance?"

"It is obvious, Wizard," the first priest said, as if Eliezer were stupid not to see. "Please find it."

"Of course." He struck a thoughtful pose, but really he was calling to Melech, who replied that everything was fine, he'd been led to a stone-walled stall full of feed and water, so not to worry. *You heard?* Eliezer asked him, and Melech replied, *Yes, I did, and I'm sorry I didn't insist we run.* Eliezer changed his posture to suggest to his audience (as if they were looking!) that he'd come up with an important point. "It would help, naturally, if you would tell me what the word is."

"We can't."

Eliezer let that sink in. "I see." But then, what did it matter? You find a word running around the desert, it has to be the right one— how many could there be? "Can you at least give me the context? It might help me know where to look."

"No heathen may know the Holy Text."

Eliezer sighed. "God granted me many powers as I studied his Word. But he did not make me like Himself; I cannot do the impossible. I'm sorry." He once more turned to go.

"Wizard," the second priest said, "without a pristine Text, our world is doomed. Without our Words, we are nothing."

Eliezer considered a moment. That was understandable, certainly— especially to one whose religion was based on the Book, the Word. And these people were desperate, or they'd never have dared leave their rockcity, en masse, to wander the desert looking for him. Help them he couldn't, that was plain; to *try* to help them would definitely qualify as a *mitzvah*. "At least tell me how to start. Give me some idea."

Priest Number One raised his left hand. "The Great Beacon will guide you."

"Thank you." Eliezer gave the bowed heads a look he was glad they couldn't see. "My fee, as you probably know, is shelter and nourishment, as much as I want."

"We know. A meal is being prepared by one of our women— may we never be cursed as they."

Eliezer wasn't so sure he agreed with that sentiment, but only said, "Goodbye," and walked out through the doorway. Kala-Wek awaited him in the corridor, smiling questioningly. Eliezer nodded and shrugged that he would help if he could, and Kala-Wek burst out with a cry of joy.

"Bless you, Eliezer Ben-Avraham!" he cried, clapping his hands twice. "My people have prepared a fine welcome for you."

"Are you in charge here?" Eliezer asked. They wound through the mountain interior, passing many doorways veiled with curtains ranging from plain to very fancy. That made sense; how else to show off your wealth and status in a cave?

"I am the Prince." Kala-Wek didn't stop for bows, as most sheiks and kings would have.

The walls around them shone, not with dampness but with skillful polishing. Which got him wondering what these people did about water. His question was answered when he saw pipes curling up the walls of the tunnel. "Quite a city you have here," Eliezer remarked.

"Yes. We have lived here for uncounted centuries."

They came to a huge doorway covered by a curtain embroidered with scenes of merriment: people eating, drinking wine, laughing like fools. The curtain was parted by two very shy girls who glanced up at Eliezer briefly then lowered their eyes. Kala-Wek's world was one where the females were kept in suitably secondary roles, at least; the Kabbalah was strict about such things, since only men — and only those of a certain age — could explore its mysteries. Inside, a long table reached almost from one end of the room to the other, topped with all manner of foods: meats, poultry, dates, you name it. Two full silver wine goblets stood opposite each other. And all, as far as a glance could tell him, seemed, if not perfectly *kosher*, reasonably unobjectionable.

"We will dine and talk," Kala-Wek said. "Then you will rest, and begin your search tomorrow."

"It's a bargain," Eliezer said, eyes magnetically drawn to the abundant dinner before him. A wonderful sight; so he'd put up with a little craziness!

· ✡ ·

"Where, may I ask, did you get such delicacies?" he asked Kala-Wek, as they sat eating the last of the dates.

"We have special chambers where we grow our food, and sometimes we trade." Kala-Wek ordered his maidservants about with hand gestures, seldom needing to say anything beyond "You!"

Trade? An isolated place like this? Eliezer stroked his beard. "With whom, if I may be so bold as to ask?"

"With wandering people like yourself."

"And what do you offer in return, that would draw people to your stony market?"

Kala-Wek laughed. "Look around you." Of course: the jewels were useful for more than just decoration.

"Are you not afraid of thieves?"

"No," Kala-Wek said dismissively, but didn't elaborate.

"Yet for all your wealth, you still grieve the loss of a few letters, eh?"

Kala-Wek sat back on his ottoman, clutching the table to keep himself from falling altogether. A precarious position. "You speak truly, Wizard," he said somberly.

"Does anyone know how such a thing could have happened?"

"Is it not obvious, Wizard? You of all people should understand. It is a *word*."

Light flooded Eliezer's stupid old brain. And he a "master" of the Kabbalah! So it wasn't only his circulation that was slowing down! He lifted his goblet and downed a little wine, to cover his embarrassment. "You shame me, Kala-Wek," he said at last. "A great Wizard I thought I was, but no man should forget his roots."

Kala-Wek looked at him with a puzzled expression — and maybe a little disappointment? "Of course. The power of the letters, the sound… why do you think we sought out a student of the Kabbalah, for is that not a system based on the magic of words, the ultimate guide to logomancy?"

"So it is." He called to Melech, who heard and (he had to admit justifiably) laughed. In self-punishment he refused to touch the small orange cake placed before him by a silver-robed maiden. "Forgive an old man."

Kala-Wek simply shrugged, granting absolution for whatever sin Eliezer might feel guilty of. "Who else but a Kabbalist would understand the power of language and know how to recapture and restrain a word?"

"A word has powers, true," Eliezer said; "indeed, words are the basis of *all* magic, not just that of Kabbalah, but I have to admit I've never heard of one… becoming mobile."

"I think that when a word is believed in as our words are, it must gain even more power. Under the Beacon's glow, who knows what such a word might become able to do?"

"Of course you are right, Your Highness," Eliezer said.

As Kala-Wek was served more wine, Eliezer asked Melech how he fared. Melech replied he was very comfortable, and in fact enjoyed sole residency in the stable. *Doesn't it seem strange,* he continued, *that these people have a stable, although they have no need of a horse, since they never travel beyond this mountain?*

Eliezer considered for a moment. Our host has a horse, he reminded Melech.

Then where is it?

Melech's question hung there between them, in the mental silence, as Eliezer sucked the last morsels of fruit from the pit.

In another stable? In another part of the mountain. How was he supposed to know? Why should he care?

Because this stable is brand-new.

You're sure? Eliezer mind-asked.

Eliezer felt waves of exasperation coming from the horse's head — as if he couldn't tell!

"Wizard, are you well?"

Oy! Another sudden burst of recognition.

The Prince seemed to see something in his eyes. "You have questions," he said.

"You have magic."

The Prince froze briefly, then swallowed what was in his mouth. "Of course. Not in your league, but, yes, we do."

"Why do you need me, then?"

"For your specialized skills."

"You can create living things, am I right?" Eliezer recalled the taste of the many foods he'd eaten: bread, meat, fruit. Delicious — but not natural. "The prerogative of God."

"Do you not exercise control over the forces of nature?"

As if there was no difference! "Over all but life itself. Some things only the Lord can or should do." When he'd gained his powers through such unlawful studies, that had been one of his decreed limitations: he must not use his powers to create or destroy life. The other was that he must never use his powers to perform immoral acts — and he had to be sure that that wasn't a risk here. The power to create living beings was the kind only granted by the Black Demons (God forbid!) for evil purposes.

Kala-Wek said nothing for a while, as his servants poured coffee into a tiny red cup and helped him wipe his royal mouth. At last the Prince stretched his legs, adopting a more relaxed pose as he rested a forearm on a raised knee and waved the rest of the food away. Eliezer was able to grab another clump of bread before it disappeared. Maybe "disappeared" was just the right word.

"Wizard," the Prince began, "our powers were great — great enough to let us live in a desert, with only our underground sea and ingenuity to keep us alive. And this mountain," he said, looking around as if able to see it all, "is uninviting to the Bedou who roam the sands looking for new homes. But it is our home; we *are* our home; we are here, alive and prosperous, thanks to the bounty of the true God, his gift of water, and our faith."

So. "And your faith gives the words strength."

"Until now, yes." Kala-Wek spread his hands. "What happens, then, if the words gain a life of their own, if our Holy Text flits away, word by word?" He motioned toward the walls, the tapestries, the jewels. "No more. We ourselves would become Bedou." He said that with a shudder, and Eliezer nodded. To become nothing more than a wanderer, dependent on the hospitality of others, or God's blessings on an unknown land! A life to be wished on no one....

"It would truly be a regrettable fate for a God-fearing people," Eliezer observed— generously, for these were *goyim*. "And your own priests—"

"—are useless without what you can return to us. Even now, our power wanes, and we do not know how much longer we can continue to feed ourselves. Let alone you."

A chill coursed up his neck. Eliezer was obliged to stay until he'd helped them, but their power to keep flesh on his bones was fading. Would he end up starving with all the rest? Should he fail, what then? If only he hadn't pried into God's forbidden secrets!

"So, where do I begin?"

"I cannot tell you, Wizard."

It was utterly exasperating. "You won't tell me what word it is I'm to look for, nor its context." Kala-Wek shook his head. "So! I'll see what I can do, then."

But no ideas came, even as the maidservants led him to a small bedchamber. He had undeservingly been given a smooth stone bed topped with a straw-stuffed mattress, and a pillow filled with the finest sand for his thick head. Before sleeping he tried calling Melech again, but at the sound of his mind's voice the horse merely snorted, and Eliezer shut him out.

· ✡ ·

The next morning, after an equally sumptuous breakfast of magically produced foods, he mounted Melech once more just outside the rockcity. Melech looked fine, but was not talkative.

Kala-Wek stood in the entranceway, surrounded by a crowd of his people, who cowered in the darkness like moles; others looked on from their windows. "Good luck, Wizard," he said, beaming up at Eliezer as the sun beamed down. "Only you can save us all!"

All! Eliezer included. "Is there nothing you can tell me?"

"Only that we pray God may shine on your quest."

"Thank you." A heart-warming sentiment. "Don't worry. It couldn't have gotten far—" he automatically added. How quickly *did* a word travel? (*If it isn't a rumor, that is?* he thought with an internal grin.) He always liked to offer the client encouraging words, but… "It's in God's hands, not mine." That was the easy thing to say, but it also happened to be true. Eliezer patted Melech's neck. No better companion in the world; but a silent one now. So, let him be like that!

"Your steed is magnificent," Kala-Wek enthused, as if Eliezer (and Melech!) didn't know it already. "We had only the poor specimens of a few foolish thieves to use as models for our own creation." Kala-Wek regarded Melech closely. "He'll carry you far and well."

"Yes," Eliezer agreed, "if only we knew in which direction." Eliezer checked his hip for his little velvet pouch with the *Mogen David* and Holy Name embroidered on the front. The crater floor stretched featurelessly all around, right up to the craggy rim.

Let us assume, Eliezer thought, *it has not gone beyond the rim*— for if it escaped that far, it could be anywhere in the whole world, and even Eliezer wouldn't live long enough to search the entire globe! He rode a short way from the city.

"The priests said to tell you to remember their words," Kala-Wek called after him. "May God be with you!" He bowed and led his people out of the hot and dry into the cool and watered, the city with its diminishing supplies of food and magic. *Mazel tov*, Eliezer silently wished them.

"So, Melech, are you speaking to me?" The horse returned a definite *Yes*. "And have you more insights?" On that, Melech was less forthcoming. "The day the word was found missing was the eleventh of Tammuz. But it could have — 'departed' — before that."

I don't like this, Melech complained.

"Could you be more specific?"

Why hide their magic?

Eliezer shrugged. "A private people, in their own world."

Melech nodded— a habit he'd picked up from lowly humans.

"So, let's see, what did the priests say? 'The sun will guide you.' Maybe they were trying to tell us something." Eliezer looked up into the sky. "All right, then, we'll go west." Melech had no better suggestion, so he faced away from the morning sun and walked slowly across the sands. "Keep your head down, and look carefully on the ground for anything unusual. I'll keep an eye on higher things." As was appropriate for the one with the soul, he mused, and allowed himself a smile.

Melech assured him he'd use his lower equine — and younger — eyes to full advantage. Meanwhile Eliezer scanned the crater rim. A word has power — the Kabbalah was based on that fact — but without knowing the specific word what could he do? He couldn't employ the numerology needed to work the magic without knowing the letters and therefore the word's numerical value. So frustrating! The sands blew around Melech's feet, and Eliezer shaded his eyes with his free hand. Melech stopped suddenly.

"What is it?"

Look for yourself, Melech replied.

Eliezer stepped down, his legs sore but steady; despite the grumbling of his joints he squatted in the sand. Peeking through the blowing dust, never moving but blinking in and out of sight, was a black spot— so small only the sand's fineness and uniform color made it visible at all. What kind of crazy thing—? It was like a tiny hole in the desert that the sand couldn't fill, a little black void that refused to be denied. They said nature hates a vacuum— but was this nature, or something beyond?

Eliezer knelt in the skittering sand and bowed over it like a *goy* in prayer. Up close it looked even blacker, almost a supernatural black, like the creatures Eliezer had once accidentally called up in his early days of conjuring. Bravely, he put his finger into the blackness, and raised the finger to his eyes. A dot of the black clung to his fingertip. He smelled the stuff, touched his tongue to it, and closed his eyes.

"*Oy!*" he moaned, covering his face with his hand. "*Oyoyoy!*"

Melech stared at him quizzically.

"May God forgive me for past transgressions!" he wailed, swaying back and forth on his haunches.

So, what is it already? Melech asked.

Eliezer gave him a sick look. "Ink!"

·   ✡   ·

At least he knew he was on the right track; for that he could be grateful. They kept moving westward, but no more of the "trail" appeared. That one spot, clinging tenaciously to the ground, remaining visible through the drifting dust for however many days, showed one thing: the word had tremendous power of endurance, it was a word of such importance that it magically asserted itself despite everything.

Eliezer couldn't figure out why any word would run away, and follow the sun in its course across the sky, and Melech could offer no suggestions, either. They reached the foot of the crater wall, and Melech kicked at the loose sand sprinkled at the foot of the rise. Eliezer dismounted and brought his eyes close to the ground, to no avail. He tried further up the wall, above the edge of the sand blanket covering the crater floor, past the ring of pebbles to the bare stone, to where the tooth-like peaks jabbed up at the sky. Blown sand pattered on his upper cheeks, and found its way between his teeth, so that he crunched with every movement of his jaw. Melech idly nosed pebbles around.

Eliezer grunted his way up the twenty feet or so of gently sloping cliff. "Do we keep going west?" he asked as he stood on top of the jagged crater wall, not expecting an answer. Beyond the crater was sheer desert, more blankness than Eliezer had ever seen from any vantage point. Such a desolate place— no wonder these crazy people loved their home so much; what beauty! So what were they afraid to leave behind here? Nothing but dust-towers, parallel lines of dunes, sand and more sand, as far as the horizon. And within the crater, just the rockcity, and, between the city and himself, a few odd shadows cast by sand-whips or some such phenomenon snaking across the ground.

The city was right in the center, the exact focus of the perfectly circular wall. The whole thing reminded him of something, but he couldn't quite say what. Three hours of riding, just for the view!

Eliezer descended once more, and as he did so — careful to keep from jarring his God-forsaken knees — he heard warning noises coming from the back of Melech's mind. Nothing definite... but something amiss. Eliezer stood beside the horse and asked him what was going on. Melech hemmed and hawed (such an annoying habit!), then said, *I think we're being followed.*

"Followed? By whom? Our employers?"

What came next from Melech's mind was a wave of pure sarcasm: the gist of it was, *who else?* "All right, you don't have to be that way about it." Melech's nose was sufficiently reliable to forestall doubt. Someone was trying to keep down-wind and far enough away to prevent Melech from becoming skittish. But of course whoever it was didn't know Melech had other ways of communicating discomfort to Eliezer.

Eliezer sat on some smooth rocks, resting his back against the cliff, and searched for those no-longer-mysterious shadows in the desert. He ate a little of the bread Kala-Wek's people had supplied him with. It would serve his followers right, whoever they might be, to have to sit and watch him stuff himself while they went hungry and thirsty. Eliezer took a sugar cube from his provisions bag and Melech lazily lipped it up. "Enjoy."

The hot sun beamed down on them, almost straight overhead, but Eliezer's circulation was such that he didn't mind at all. "What we do now, Melech, I honestly don't know." After brushing breadcrumbs from his robes, Eliezer pushed himself up and remounted, deciding to scout the cliffs' inside base. Melech reported that the pursuer or pursuers followed in step. Well, what would they do to him? Nothing— at least, until he found their word.

Look below, Melech advised, and Eliezer, too tired to step down, asked, "What?" The horse replied that while his eyes were not perfect, he was sure another spot lay beneath his feet.

"Are you joking?"

Melech replied negatively, his tone showing his displeasure at the question.

"Then let's continue in a clockwise direction, and see—"

What did you say?

"Weren't you listening? I said, we'll continue in a clockwise direction, and—"

Melech repeated the question, and Eliezer nearly slapped the horse's neck. "So now you've gone deaf? *Ach*! All right, I'll spell it out: we... will... walk... in... a... clockwise... direction...."

Clockwise.

Eliezer smacked his forehead, ready to burst. *Of course*! Such a stupid, useless head! Was this, then, the ultimate in God's curse? To be at the world's beck and call, for countless years, without enough brains to do the work? He looked over the crater once more: a giant circle with a protrusion in the middle whose shadow swept around the desert floor. *Stupid!*

He steered Melech back towards the city, one eye on the sand behind. He heard a slight rustling as his pursuers scrambled to change direction. Eliezer threw a few Hebrew words back at them, and both he and Melech turned their heads to see the results of the spell: four robed moles huddled in the sand, attempting to dig through the fine dust to find a home beneath.

Before long they arrived at the base of the outcropping. Eliezer looked up its sharp slope, and shook his head. "A senile old man I am," he said; "a fool I'm not." With a couple of words whose letters added up to 55, the same as in *nesher*, he metamorphosed into an eagle and soared aloft. He passed the open windows of Al-ayar, through which fine curtains billowed, and young maidens (if only *he* were so young again!) looked out over the desert and combed their hair. They watched as he sailed ever higher, to the mountain's summit. There, he transformed back into his human shape, rubbed his aching arms, and stood unsteadily on the peak. Melech waited below, occasionally glancing up but repelled by the glare of the sun directly above Eliezer's head. Here he was, on the highest visible point of land sticking up out of the desert floor. And all around was the crater, looking remarkably like...

A sundial, of course.

Eliezer stroked his beard, and, saying a short prayer for strength and stamina, got down on his ancient knees on a narrow ledge of rock. If he ever got up again it would be a miracle. He pushed aside some pebbles and brushed away wisps of sand. Sure enough, huddled against the sunward side of the mountaintop was a little black formless mass.

"Hello," Eliezer said, with both relief and amazement. "You've caused quite a commotion, eh, little noun?" The word cringed, recoiling from Eliezer's appalling Unbeliever-hood, but Eliezer was not to be denied. "Don't be such a trouble-maker. Come." He reached out his hand. The word slunk back, leaving a tiny black speck on the rock. It couldn't afford to lose much more of its life-blood.

"The strongest belief makes the most powerful word," Eliezer said to it, knowing it couldn't understand. "Only one word in their language attracts so much belief it could gain enough power to get up and go for a stroll. Fortunately," he continued, pointing straight up to what its worshippers called the Beacon, "you *aren't* what you designate, or you'd be too hot to handle. *Oy!*" he moaned, as his knees scolded him. "In Hebrew your letters would add up to 55, too. A nice coincidence, eh? It's now noon. If I say the Holy Name in my head 55 times, would you stop aspiring to be what you signify? Would you stop following your original and begin following me?"

Eliezer passed his hand over the timid letters, blocking out the sun's rays and influence, and pronounced the Name. The letters relaxed, expanded, separated to form a true word. Eliezer averted his eyes so he wouldn't actually see the full word (something that was not for his "Barbarian," his "Unbeliever"'s eyes!). He put his hand beside it so it could crawl up on to his palm. Such a frightened little thing— terrified of its new-found power, mobility, freedom. And who wouldn't be frightened, suddenly torn from home because of new powers, to wander the Earth in search of—? But the analogy was stretched, and — more importantly — a waste of time. He felt the wet thing slither along his palm, fortunately for both of them without leaving a trail, and transferred it into his pouch.

Eliezer became an eagle once more, and flew down to the window of his own room. He made sure his curtain was closed, and reassumed human form in private so that none should know his mysteries; he was every bit as jealous of his magical secrets as Kala-Wek. Eliezer stepped out into the corridor, and made his way undetected to the priests' chamber. The fools had not trusted him with their secrets; didn't they realize he of all people would know the Magi's Code, that you don't encroach on another's secrets, or — worse — tell tales about them? What had they planned to do with him after learning his secrets?

The black tome lay still open at the day's reading. He stood on the wrong side of the book so that even at best he could only see the text upside down, then crouched so that his view was even worse— all he saw was a series of blurred, parallel black lines. He flipped back four pages, and sure enough found in the left-hand page a glaring white spot, like a tiny sun itself interrupting the surrounding blackness. He took his pouch from under his belt and pulled open the puckered mouth, then lay the pouch on the blemished page.

"*Nu*, go home," Eliezer said; "and don't go touring around again." He repeated the Holy Name twice, and added a few words of incantation. The word peeked out of the bag meekly at first, then waggled its capital boldly. With a hop the whole word — letters all in proper order — leapt *on to* the page (such a switch from the usual!). It slithered through the ranks of its fellows, elongating and squeezing as needed, until it found the blank space awaiting it, the one it had left behind when it had been drawn by the climax of the real sun's rise through the sky five days ago, the solstice. The word settled in, resuming its place, and only its slightly lighter shade — the effect of its ink-losses through injury and maybe evaporation — kept it from blending completely into the lines of text. Someone would have to get out a pen and touch it up.

Eliezer returned the book to its proper page. "Now, little friends," he said, "how can I convince you to stay where you belong?" It wouldn't take much for another word to get it into its — head? capital letter? — to run away like its fellow. "Your power is great, but must flow to others, not remain in yourselves." He waved his hand over the book and chanted a few words, then drew the letter *aleph* in the air above it. "All words are one, and they are the words of God, as is everything. Become again what you are meant to be: the source and symbol of the faith of those who read you. No longer aspire to be that which you merely represent." The words hit home in his own head and heart, but he merely sighed and said, "*Omain.*"

Satisfied, Eliezer stretched up to full height once more, and his arthritis punished him for his audacity. At that moment came a barked, "What are you doing here?" Eliezer turned and saw Kala-Wek standing in the doorway, feet wide apart and hand on his ceremonial dagger.

"What you asked me to do," Eliezer replied.

"What?" Kala-Wek scanned the room, his expression bearing none of his earlier amiability. "Where are the priests?"

"By now, making a home under your sand-moat." Eliezer congratulated himself on his *bon-mot*; Melech, listening in, groaned softly to make his feelings clear. "They followed me, thinking to steal my knowledge — for the city's benefit or their own, I don't know — or kill me should I learn theirs." He shrugged. "Whatever their scheme was, whether they were doing so on your orders or were acting on their own, that's none of my business. They'll be back soon — after the spell wears off — and you can take it up with them, either for the attempt or their failure in it."

Kala-Wek said nothing for a second or two, then asked, "And the word, Wizard?"

"It shines once more from the page, and should stay there from now on. And I have not sullied your sacred words with my" — he turned the sarcasm on full-strength — "*heathenish* vision!"

Kala-Wek relaxed and even cracked a smile, removing his hand finally from the dagger. "Well-done, Wizard. You have lived up to your reputation, and you have saved my people and my home."

And your Princely station, Eliezer added silently (may God forgive his cynicism, especially if he was wrong). Eliezer bowed. "My horse awaits outside."

"So I noticed. But how did you find the word? *Where* did you find it? What—?"

Eliezer cut him off with a wave. "Please, so many questions! It's so simple even my horse could figure it out. Your belief made the little wanderer think it had *become* what it merely *meant*, and followed your 'Beacon' around." Such a term for God's first creation! "Then, at the solstice, it naturally climbed as high as it could — higher than *I* could, with just these old bones — reaching for its source." Enough explanation. "My job is done, and I must go. Lead me out, and I'll be on my way."

"As you wish." Kala-Wek silently led him through the stone hallways, past gawking women and children, and men with apparently no work to do. A paradise — all they needed with little labor — so no wonder they feared being thrown out into the world to search for a few pieces of bread, a little water, a place to lay one's head. It was understandable, all right.

Downstairs, Eliezer mounted his horse, whose bridle Kala-Wek unnecessarily held for him.

"Thank you, Eliezer Ben-Avraham!" Kala-Wek said. "You are indeed a great wizard!"

Eliezer shrugged dismissively. "It is God's power, not mine; and God's will if I succeed or fail."

Melech nodded — a little *too* enthusiastically, perhaps — at Eliezer's formulaic farewell. Then they turned their backs on Kala-Wek, Al-ayar, and the whole strange adventure. Neither said anything until they'd crossed the crater rim through the pass they'd earlier traversed. At last, as they re-entered the Desert of Alakhar, and turned toward the path of their rounds, Melech said something about their need to be more selective in choosing their assignments, and avoiding strange people who had extremely strange problems.

"Not another word," Eliezer said. "Please, God, not another word!"

UNSPEAKABLE

"YOU SHOULD MAKE a golem," the Mayor said.

Eliezer rolled his eyes. "I'm not going to make a golem."

The Mayor surveyed the blasted room. Smashed furniture, gouged walls, shredded carpets— as the Mayor swiveled his globular head from side to side to take in the damage, Eliezer mirrored his motions. Such a mess. "I really think you should make a golem. Isn't that what you people do?"

Gevalt. "Haven't you ever heard of the word 'amok'?" Eliezer made suitably sympathetic *tut-tut* noises. "Be careful what you ask for," he advised.

But he could understand. Such a simple solution: create an irresistible avenger to track down and slay the nemesis. How often had the People yearned for such a champion!

"It's appalling," the Mayor declared. "My own office." He then turned his rotund form a full half-rotation and waddled down the hall, shaking his head. Although quite short, he weighed nearly as much as Melech— who was himself no lightweight for a horse.

So, my friend, Eliezer subvocalized, *shall I do what I am bid?*

Melech's reply was a firm, *Of course not!*

Then, of course, the question was: what to do instead?

The City of Doron was in the midst of a terrible crisis: disintegration. For nearly a week now, things had quite literally fallen apart; pieces of buildings had broken off, chairs collapsed beneath even not-so-Mayor-like citizens, a road reverted to gravel before the eyes and wheels of horrified travellers, and street lamps decided to suddenly, and without logical reason, douse themselves and then turn to powder. People's homes looked as if they had been vandalized, but the Police had asserted in no uncertain terms that no vandals were at large. No one had been seen. Things had just spontaneously collapsed.

"Melech," Eliezer vocalized. "I think we're going to have some trouble here."

· ✡ ·

Eliezer had been summoned two days ago while in the midst of a somewhat painless duty: providing magic entertainment for a horde of children in a distant commune. The semi-religious, semi-political compound shared everything— property, the responsibilities for raising children, and a smug and probably deserved sense of superiority. The written message delivered by a young, breathless, dishevelled-looking man put Eliezer in something of a quandary, for by his curse he was obliged to use his ill-gained magical powers to perform whatever tasks he was asked to do, but even he could not be in two places at once. Or at least not really— he transformed a goat (much to Melech's amusement) into a pseudo-Eliezer, and gave it the ability to channel some of Eliezer's powers. The goat seemed to be sufficiently adept at magic to amuse the children (who were noisy and inattentive and smelly, anyway), and so he was not missed when he absented himself to answer a more pressing call.

The Mayor's letter, filled with pretentious diction and subordinate clauses, barely conveyed any real information about what was happening to Doron. All the Mayor and his assistants knew was that much of the city's infrastructure was collapsing without discernible cause. It was as if someone had turned off the forces that glued reality together, and that was reason enough to worry. A chair or a house you could nail back together if you had to— but the stuff of matter itself?

Eliezer scanned the Mayor's Office for clues, saw none, and was escorted by members of the Police back to his room in the rear of the Hall. At times, he got extremely lucky when it came to the room and board he required in payment for his magical efforts, and he was able to enjoy the hospitality of princes and Mayors. So he'd hoped to sleep in the lap of luxury — so to speak — but the room the Mayor had given him was little more than a closet with a bed in it. Of course, he was in no position to complain, but still… "Melech?"

The horse was safely ensconced in a City Stable somewhere behind the building, in rough but adequate equine quarters. Melech replied with a vague acknowledgement of Eliezer's call.

"You are well, my friend?"

Melech sent him the telepathic equivalent of a shrug. Melech was *always* in a position to complain.

"Let me know if there's trouble." Now, the horse responded with a snort as if to say, *What do you* think *I'm going to do?* "And if you hear anything...." But of course there was no need to complete the sentence.

The problem was the Mayor himself. He must have known something, if only who his enemies might be. But he refused to speak, treating everything as a complete mystery, and whenever Eliezer tried to press him the Mayor would shrug and find some utterly compelling matters of state to attend to. He would, of course, have no reason to hide what he knew, unless he was implicated somehow.

Make a golem: what an idea. If there was a way to make the situation worse, that would be it.

"I'm going for a fly," Eliezer said. "A waste of time, but do I have anything better to do?" When Melech didn't answer, Eliezer mentally dismissed him and began the process of turning into a bird. Nighthawk: that would suit. He opened the smudged window, then recited the Hebrew word for nighthawk the correct number of times, and winced when his arthritis once again stabbed the base of his wing.

He flapped his way above City Hall and saw, this time from above, the orphan marble staircase on which he had nearly bumped his head the first time he approached the building. The Mayor had explained that he'd planned to construct a magnificent monument, a palace of sorts to enrich the citizens' lives in unspecified ways, but had run out of money after his workers completed the staircase. "Fabulous, fabulous," the Mayor said of his proposed structure, "but the fools on my Council won't let me do the walls, those spendthrifts!"

Eliezer knew then that he could anticipate hearing no logic from his new employer.

He flew up the nearest residential towers. Cracks in the buildings' walls were only the most outwardly visible signs; he peeked into the uncurtained windows and was greeted with scenes of minor and not-so-minor destruction: piles of splinters that had once been benches, shards of glass that had once been lamps. It was as if an army of demons had invaded, spreading decay everywhere they went while not touching the humans themselves. But once the four-storey buildings began to collapse around their inhabitants, the danger to life and limb would be immense.

Without knowing more about the cause, he could only guess at the cure, or at least at some measure of temporary relief. He shaped his mouth back into something resembling a human's, grotesque as his appearance might have been to anyone unfortunate enough to see, and with a few incantations cast a stability spell on the city's structures. Such a spell was temporary even under the best of circumstances, but it was all he had to offer. The stones that comprised the houses and towers glowed a hearty orange in the evening light, indicating that his words had had some effect; to be certain, he checked around, and noticed one granite block hang precariously but in defiance of gravity from the top layer of a building still under construction.

The scenes all over the city were distressing. Pieces of civilization lay scattered among the structures that still stood in defiance of whatever was pulling the city apart. A cart resembled a sick sheep, with its wheels splayed out to the sides and its "head" slumped to the ground. A shop's windows looked as if they had been smashed with a sledgehammer— not in one blow, but in several to ensure no piece larger than a coin remained. Part of the city wall had been reduced to pebbles.

A mess? The word didn't come close to describing it. What could have wreaked such a cataclysm? (And imagine what a golem might contribute to the destruction!)

Melech, who couldn't resist reading Eliezer's mind whether invited or no, sniffed in agreement. Then he said that he'd been listening to the grooms and the bypassers, something that did not surprise Eliezer in the least.

"So, Mr. Busybody, can't mind your own business even when it comes to other people, eh? Nice. So what do you hear?"

Melech's reply was as curt as it was unnecessary: *That the Mayor is an idiot.*

"And what else is new?"

Melech went silent at that. So be it. Eliezer reshaped his mouth into a beak once more and continued to fly around the city, detecting nothing that would suggest a military or demonic invasion. He tried to train his senses on the outer reaches of the detectable world, feeling for a tale-tell sign of the supernatural, of something that wasn't normal. But all he felt was a curiously pervasive normality, as if the disintegration was not an anomaly but the reverse, the way things were supposed to be. If somebody asked, he wouldn't be able to explain the sensation.

Keep listening, my friend, he said to Melech. *Let me know if you hear something I don't know.*

With what remained of his energy — and it wasn't much at this hour — Eliezer extended his survey beyond the main conglomeration of buildings to the outlying areas. All he saw was more of the same: rubble where a house used to be, bronze shards where a statue once stood, a gaping hole where a short bridge once spanned the river that provided the city with its water supply. At least the city walls were largely intact, apart from the one breach, and the shelters of various size and shape that huddled against the outsides of the walls still stood, for the most part, except for one mound of splinters.

The city lay in a valley overlooked by two nearly identical ranks of jagged mountains to the east and west, while at the north end stood one grand peak. It was as if the city were in the grip of giant jaws that would never snap closed, forming bastions rather than threats, while that one uprising fang dared anyone to approach. What a place to build a city! But for all its ugliness, the setting ensured the city's safety. Or had.

That tallest mountain formed a near-perfect cone, rising smoothly and symmetrically to a pointed summit with a lovely snow-cap, the white coating gleaming in the waning light of dusk. As Eliezer gazed upon God's magnificent handiwork, so vastly superior to the Mayor's bizarre efforts to add to the world's skyline, a spark burst into life right at the tip, as if the mountain were a candle and someone had suddenly decided to light it.

Eliezer glided toward the mountain to get a better look, and saw that sure enough it *was* a fire, small but bright, a tiny yet defiant burst of illumination in the darkness that was swallowing the world. It flickered in the midst of a circular plateau at the very top of the mountain, one so flat it was as if someone had sliced off the last few feet of the peak with a razor. He descended slowly toward the blaze, testing the air beneath his feathers to determine the fire's exact size and intensity. It was too limited to be volcanic; and as he got closer he saw that it was unquestionably man-made. But what man lived at the very top of a mountain? and for what purpose? Surely not to transmit fiery signals, for who could see such a small fire so high up, except birds and the Lord Himself? Eliezer wanted to land and regain his human form well away from flame, so as to give himself time to see what or whom he was dealing with, but the small diameter of the plateau — just barely room for the fire and its attendant — made that impossible. Whoever was up here, then, would find himself the sudden host of a very unexpected guest.

Eliezer swooped down — plummeted, more precisely — and just missed landing in the lap of a seated elderly man, who would have been almost invisible to human eyes in the deepening dusk. The man was staring into the fire and didn't seem to notice Eliezer's arrival. There was hardly room for Eliezer to become human again, without stepping on the old man or into the fire. A fierce wind whipped his feathers, but seemed to affect neither the old man nor his flame.

And what an old man! With his nighthawk's eyes Eliezer could see every detail. His face was skeletal, and from its cheeks and chin stretched a white beard parted in the middle whose two sides flowed off his lap, along the ground in opposite directions, and down the mountainsides. Eliezer — still unseen, apparently — peered over the closest side of the mountain and could see no end to the whiskers. Impressive! His hair was equally long and white, and meandered its way down his back and off the mountain on a third slope. The fourth side, if one could say "side" of a cone, faced the city; so did the old man, who would be looking straight down at the Mayor's domain if he wasn't entranced by his fire.

To warn the old man of his presence, Eliezer let out a hawkish squawk. The old man's only response was to turn his head in Eliezer's direction, squint a little, then return to his previous employment of watching the fire.

Fine; if that was how he wanted to be… Eliezer transformed, rose to his full height, and felt the most appalling attack of vertigo as he realized how close his heels were to the edge. The wind hit his expanded bulk even harder, and he feared he would be instantly blown off the mountain before he could regrow his wings and save himself. Eliezer constructed a shield of power that anchored him to the rock. Question: how was the old man able to sit there, untouched and unmoved right down to his white follicles?

"Hello," Eliezer said, in a soft voice, so as not to startle the gentleman. But his greeting evoked no reaction. In a slightly louder voice, he said, "Sir?" Nothing— such rudeness he'd seldom encountered. *Oy*, he thought, why must everything be a struggle? "Are you deaf?" The old man's expression changed slightly, indicating he'd heard well enough. "Blind?"

The old man turned to face Eliezer, or rather Eliezer's knees, then lifted his gaze up Eliezer's body to his face. In a voice of surprising power from such a frail-looking head, the old man said, "You're ugly."

"So you're not blind."

The old man turned back to the flame, and refused once more to acknowledge Eliezer's existence.

"Hungry? I see no food, no water. No shelter. Come to think of it, nothing but yourself in this inhospitable environment. Aren't you cold?"

After a few moments of patient waiting, Eliezer was prepared to speak again in order to provoke some sort of reply, even a rude one. But the old man inhaled deeply and said, "I have nothing to say."

"Such a paradox!" His sarcastic tone went unappreciated.

"I say nothing."

"All right, so you're not in a mood to *kibbitz*. Maybe I'll join you in your evening's entertainment." But seating himself before the fire was easier said than done. He tried to lower himself to the ground, but without more room to maneuver his bad joints, he could find no way to do so. Finally, he turned himself back into the nighthawk, settled on to the stone, and watched the flames dance and writhe.

For a good half-hour.

With a human mouth, he said, "I may be ugly, but you're very dull. And a poor host besides."

"I have nothing to say."

"So you say." Eliezer waited a bit longer. "For someone with nothing to say you won't shut up about it. Say, am I better-looking as a bird?" Nothing. "All right, I can take a hint. Shall I return tomorrow? Want me to bring you anything? A biscuit? Some fruit?" At the old man's persistent silence, Eliezer spread his wings, flapped away from the summit, and glided down. He would return, all right, but he'd be a poor guest and come empty-handed when he did.

Back in Doron, Eliezer first consulted Melech, hoping to benefit from his equine set of extra eyes and ears. But the horse had nothing to report beyond the painfully obvious: that the citizens thought little of their current Mayor, and compared him most unfavorably to his predecessors. *They have nothing good to say about him*, Melech told him. That was not at all surprising; Melech had never been to Doron before, but he had heard stories about the wonderful leaders the city had had in the past, forward-looking and -thinking men who'd built a very advanced place for their citizens to inhabit. Melech advised him to talk to the Mayor as soon as possible.

"More unhelpful communication," Eliezer said; "I was going to do that, anyway."

He went in search of the Mayor or some official who could summon him. Instead, he found himself wandering the Hall, lost among the chambers, offices, and broken chunks of plaster. Giant cracks formed black, dry rivers along the corridor walls and ceilings; wind whistled through split glass in the windows. Yet the orange glow remained, cementing the building's remains in place until he could come up with a more permanent solution to the problem.

He managed to locate the residential portion of the Hall at last; the Mayoral Bedchamber lay down a glistening white hallway guarded by two Policemen. They recognized him at once and smiled warmly. "May I speak with the Mayor, please," he asked the closer of the two.

"No." The refusal came with a truly friendly and helpful air.

"But it is urgent. I must ask him some questions."

"I understand, Great Wizard," the Policeman said. "But His Honour left strict orders not to be disturbed."

"But—"

"By Mayoral custom, bed-time is just after sunset."

"Custom!" This was ridiculous. "This is no time for custom! Is it customary for the city to fall to pieces?"

"His Honour is a strict follower of custom. Except—" At a grunt from the other Policeman he choked back whatever he was going to say.

"At least tell him I wish to speak to him. Tell him it is urgent."

"I can try." The vocal Policeman spun and marched down the hallway, while the other, still at attention, smiled and cast at Eliezer what he could only interpret as a sympathetic look. The helpful Policeman returned from his errand almost immediately. "I regret that His Honour is occupied and may not be disturbed."

"*But!*"

"He did ask about the golem."

Eliezer proceeded to tell the Policeman in Yiddish — a language he knew none of these people understood — about a possible fate for the desired golem, and stormed back to his bedroom.

"Melech!" The horse took a few moments to reply, and seemed to be somewhat sleepy-headed. "*Melech*! The Mayor is a *goyische kopf*! The Mayor is an *idiot!*"

Melech then asked him, in somewhat abrupt terms, if Eliezer had awakened him just to tell him this.

"*Ach!*" Eliezer let his heart slow to a more acceptable rate before trying to go to bed. As he tossed and turned on the thin strip of leather that constituted his mattress, striving to control his rage, he had visions of constructing the golem after all, and sending it down the hallways of City Hall....

· ✡ ·

He was awakened by a loud *crack!* followed by a sprinkle of powder on his face. He focused his bleary eyes on a portion of the ceiling directly above his head that seemed to be — no, was — sagging toward him. A thin, ragged line curled through the sag, widening even as he watched... he threw a renewed stabilizing spell at the drooping bulge and that seemed to hold it. *Oy vey oy vey oy vey...*

He pulled on his robes and stomped out of his bedchamber, aiming himself straight at the Mayor's residence. Or at least in its general direction— the labyrinth defeated him again. He finally found the corridor, but no Police officers stood guard, and that suggested the little fool was perhaps not still sleeping. "Where are you?" he muttered. "You fat little *putz*, where are you?" He stumbled upon the more public portion of the building, and from there he was able to wend his way to the Mayor's Office. The idiot's secretary, a man as thin and shrewd-looking as the Mayor was the opposite, was nowhere to be seen. But beyond the secretary's desk was the open door of the Office itself. Eliezer, unconcerned with protocol, barged right in. The Mayor was standing at his desk, or rather at what used to be his desk, staring at splinters and sawdust.

"Hello!" Eliezer nearly shouted.

"Oh, it's you." The Mayor's distraction was painful to see. "Terrible, terrible." He finally looked up at Eliezer. "Yes? Oh, did you find the culprit?"

"Mayor. The world is full of fools. Who is the one at the top of the mountain?"

The Mayor started. "What? Oh no oh no oh no." He prepared to plunk himself down in his chair, then realized how impossible that would be. "No," he said, "no, that's impossible. I'm sorry, but that's not possible."

Eliezer thought at first he was talking about sitting down, but then recognized the truth. "So you know of him? What do you know?"

"No, Wizard, I'm sorry, but what you're saying is absurd. I was thinking: can you make something *like* a golem, but not as dangerous?"

"Will you stop with the golem already?" Eliezer looked around but saw nothing they could rest on. Then he recalled the staircase, and thought it might as well be put to some use. "Come, let's have a chat."

"Oh, I don't know…"

"I'm not surprised. Well, *I* do."

Eliezer headed out the door and motioned for the Mayor to follow. As he led the way outside he called out to Melech, who grunted in reply. *Still well, my friend?* With a brief flash, Eliezer was able to see through Melech's eyes. The stable in which he'd been housed had disappeared. All that remained was jagged sticks. *The man is an absolute fool,* Eliezer told him, only to have Melech mentally mutter something about the human race in general.

In the square before City Hall, Eliezer lowered himself to the most convenient step and directed the Mayor either to join him on the useless structure or to stand, as he wished. The Mayor chose to stand, or couldn't figure out how to sit down— it wasn't entirely clear. "So?"

"Well, what you're saying is silly, Wizard. But there's an ancient legend…"

"The best kind."

"About the first Mayor."

"Incidentally, what was his name?" Eliezer realized he didn't know this one's name, either.

"First Mayor! I don't understand the question." After a pause, he continued, scrabbling in his mind for words. "Yes, well, the first Mayor — First Mayor — founded the city. Before that, the city didn't exist, you know." *Oy!* "Anyway, he appointed a City Poet, whose job it was to make up poetry to honor the city. Praise it. Praise him. The Poet was supposed to make the city known throughout the wide world. What happened to the Poet I don't know."

"I see."

"You don't think…"

"No, Your Honour, I'm not the one who doesn't think." The Mayor shot him a puzzled look. "Is that the man on the mountain?"

"I don't know. That's impossible. That was hundreds of years ago."

"I see." Eliezer's empty stomach growled at him. *Shush!*

"I don't."

"I know." Eliezer bowed and said, "If you will excuse me, I must have some breakfast, then I must fly. In the meantime, please evacuate your buildings. I do not know how much longer I can keep things from turning to dust." At the look in the Mayor's eyes, Eliezer said, "And no golems."

· ✡ ·

Eliezer renewed the stabilizing spell, then had a quick bite to eat in the City Hall dining room (undercooked eggs!), at a split table that caused his plate to sit at a thirty-degree angle from the horizontal. All around him, bureaucrats struggled to keep their food from sliding off their dishes, or their dishes from sliding off their tables, and on to the floor. A few glanced his way, perhaps wondering what he would do for them, or how much the city was paying for his services. It would shock them to hear that he had no idea what to do for them, and that they were watching him consume his payment.

Listen to it, Melech broke in, startling Eliezer so much he dropped his fork. It skipped over the tablecloth and off the far edge before Eliezer could stop it. Too lazy to bend down, and too certain he might not be able to get up again if he tried, Eliezer used a little of his magic to retrieve it. Neighboring diners gasped as they watched the fork levitate and float into Eliezer's hand. He inspected it: clean enough.

"Now," he said out loud. "You were saying?"

The neighbors returned to their elusive meals, ignoring the crazy old man talking to himself. So, is that crazier than talking to a horse?

People are talking. Listen.

His horse's sensitive hearing had caught something. Fine. What Eliezer heard was a series of comments that Melech had overheard and committed to memory, spoken in the exact voices of the people who had made them, both male and female, young and old— a full city of human tongues:

"A fool who can't do anything straight."

"We have to get rid of him."

Eliezer rolled his eyes. "So?" he asked. But the horse just kept going.

"Wasting our money on his ridiculous schemes and leaving the place to rot!"

"How could we have been so stupid? He can't even perform the most basic ceremonies properly."

"The man is unspeakable!"

Then Melech repeated the final example in a higher volume, as if — or so Eliezer interpreted — this was the most common complaint.

The Mayor: he was a public joke. And yet, he was the embodiment of the public that had elected him. The city was run by its own joke. Eliezer had no sympathy, for a fool in power is merely the outward sign of a wider folly.

"Unspeakable" — so what was there left to say? "Ah. Melech, I think I understand." For both politics and magic were powered by language, and so a city and a wizard were equally sustained by it.

Eliezer drained his tea. *"Nah*, my friend, so there's no point in further consulting His Honour. I must talk to a higher fool." Or not a fool, perhaps… Satisfied at last, Eliezer pushed himself away from the table, only to see it finally surrender to entropy and, despite his spell, collapse, bringing the cloth, the dish, the fork, and the teacup down with it. Such is politics!

He transformed this time into an eagle: a regal beast and one revered throughout the Bible as a symbol of royalty, of leadership. It took no time for him to make his way back to the top of the mountain, where the old man, the Poet, sat in eternal watchfulness, surveying his artistic domain. How many years had he sat there, witnessing the splendor and shame of the city's history? How many words had he spoken in honor of the city's achievements, keeping them — and, through them, the city itself — alive?

The white cap below him gleamed in the sunshine, and would grow ever longer, year after year, as long as the city itself grew.

Eliezer the eagle landed so that he faced the old man, the now-cold fire-pit between them. How appropriate, for it seemed the light of inspiration had been extinguished, too. He shielded himself from the winds with a brief incantation once he'd constructed a mouth. "Good morning."

"I have nothing to say," the old man said again.

Eliezer's first impulse was to be exasperated, but he reminded himself what he was speaking to: not a man, but a manifestation, an embodiment of the people, a being of thoughts and language with far too much power.

"I know, I know," Eliezer said. "You don't have to speak, just listen." Eliezer folded his wings, and tried to find a position for them that would not aggravate his arthritis. "I know all about the power of words, for my magic, the Kabbalah, is built on such a force. You know who I am, eh?" The old man's expression didn't change. "Because you see everything that goes on down there. For that, my sympathies." It proved impossible to shrug wings, so he went on. "My faith is the faith in the Word, the Creating Word; I made the mistake of delving a little too far into that power, and that's why I'm here, helping your city. Call me an old fool. I'm paying for it now.

"You, too, are cursed with the power of the Creating Word, but you are also cursed with the power of the Uncreating Silence. We have a book called Genesis; I'll bring you a copy one day so you can read it. But you have to read it the right way, from right to left. Too many people get it backwards, eh?

"Listen, I know what you're going through. There are times human beings make me speechless, too. When this idiot became Mayor, you sank into silence, maybe because he was *unspeakable*. How can you praise the unpraiseworthy? But your power is a dangerous power, especially when you don't use it. *Fershteyn*? By speaking the city you kept it alive; by stopping, you're killing it. I don't know what power the first Mayor gave you, but you must be sorry to have it. How long are you supposed to stay up here, anyway?" Eliezer pointed his thumb down the slope to his right. "Till the whole mountain is white? Till time ends? Till you run out of combinations of words to lend the city its immortality? But there is no immortality, not for us. Thank God."

A power and responsibility like the Poet's was unimaginable. He could not afford to be a man of few words; too much depended on him.

"Well, I don't blame you for having nothing to say. But we are slaves to our obligations, eh? The city will endure, for as long as God wills; the idiot will be gone soon. Don't speak of him. Speak of what endures."

The Poet finally met Eliezer's eyes, and even blinked. "What can I say?"

"Of the Mayor? It's very simple, my ancient poetic friend. You've been saying it all along."

And so the Poet recited a poem, something transcendent and impossible to write down, about how much nothing he had to say. It was a double negative in verse, and Eliezer didn't understand much of it. But then again, he'd never been much for secular literature.

"Nice. At least it rhymes," Eliezer said, although he wasn't entirely sure even about that. The Poet then commenced what sounded like an epic, or anti-epic: something the opposite of what it should be, in any case. Eliezer restored his beak, silencing himself, and took flight down the mountainside, down past the glowing white to the hard stone below. As he descended, the city expanded with every moment, the details more crisp, and he could see a wondrous sight: this human creation restoring itself, as buildings rebuilt, carts reconstructed, and even glass reglazed.

Order again: for now, at least.

Eliezer called Melech forth as soon as he returned to City Hall, and the horse managed to get through the front wall of the stable before it entirely reintegrated itself. Melech twitched his head back and forth as Things went back to normal, or at least their normal magical abnormality. The Mayor watched as Eliezer achingly climbed into the saddle, and seemed mesmerized by Eliezer's compulsive tapping of various objects on his own person and the saddle to ensure all his possessions were with him.

"It's a miracle!" the Mayor cried. "How did you do it?"

"Spoke to a fellow wordsmith," Eliezer said. "I think your legacy is secure for a long, long time."

"And you managed to do it without... well, any help?"

Eliezer shook his head, not so much in reply as in disbelief. "But if you would like, I would be very glad to make you a golem."

"Oh, yes!"

But Melech chuffed violently in rebuke, and Eliezer let out a heavy sigh. "Fine, my friend. Mr. Mayor, no golem for you today, but if it ever proves necessary, I'm sure I can accommodate you."

"Oh, thank you!" the rotund little idiot said. "I'm looking forward to that!"

"So am I," Eliezer said as he turned Melech around to face the wide world beyond the stairway to nowhere and the city's gates. "So am I."

MAKING LIGHT

FOR JUST A few minutes, Eliezer's brain fooled him into thinking that he was a healthy man again. The eastern horizon glowed with what looked for all the world like the dawn, and Eliezer knew — *knew* — that he had not yet awakened that night to answer the call of nature. Could it really be, then, that he had slept for seven or eight hours without interruption?

"A little thing," he said, "but a miracle nonetheless."

He walked a short way from his camp and relieved himself, careful to keep holy thoughts from his mind even as he yearned to praise God for such a gift. But his brief stroll took him past Melech, who stood dozing atop a rocky dune, and on his way back to camp Eliezer made the mistake of saying, "A long sleep like that may foretell other nights when I actually get some rest."

In reply, Melech neighed drowsily and advised him to look up.

"Up?" One glance at the stars made his heart sink. Such hope! And so quickly dashed! The constellations had hardly moved; as far as he could tell, it was only a little past midnight. "Such a shame." Melech made it clear he wanted to go back to sleep, and shook his mane gently as he lowered his head. Still, Eliezer couldn't resist asking, "Then why is the sun trying to rise at the same time as old men suffering old men's problems?" The horizon shone with a flickering light, and Eliezer nodded. "The desert blazes even at night, eh? But what can burn?"

Melech said he didn't care.

"A horse can afford not to care. A human must help." *Especially me*, he thought; there was his true curse. He'd been condemned to spend eternity doing *mitzvah*s; but was it a *mitzvah* if one is forced to do it? That was a theological question he would consider in the morning; right now, he had no choice but to investigate.

"Someone may be injured. Someone may need our assistance."

And someone else may be around to offer it, Melech suggested, although clearly not convincing even himself. With a snort Melech lowered himself just enough to let Eliezer climb on to his back. Only now did Eliezer notice the stabbing pain over his left kidney, from sleeping on a hard, cold ground in a bad position. Winter was coming: Chanukah would begin tomorrow, and the solstice was not far away.

"We'll need some shelter soon," Eliezer said, and added with a shrug, "What better reason to find some work?"

So they rode down the hill, following the light that beckoned in the east (thus re-enacting the legend of the *goyim*, may they learn the truth someday). Melech kept his pace even but frustratingly slow, as if to make it clear he did not appreciate having his slumber disturbed. Eliezer knew of no town in that direction, nor of any caravans whose leaders were so foolish as to travel at night. So where could the light be coming from?

"*Nu?*" Eliezer asked. "What do you think?"

Melech remained silent. But then his head jerked up, and he stared off at something Eliezer's age- and sleep-bleared eyes couldn't discern.

"What? What is it?" Melech stopped, and Eliezer climbed down. "*Oy.* Or do I want to know?" It didn't take him long to find the source of the glow. On a low rise in the distance, something metallic rose above the desert sand and stone, reaching toward the sky like a man with arms stretched to the limit. As he trudged through the grit toward it, he let out a low, stunned, "*Gevalt!*"

Melech recommended that they withdraw, return to their camp, and leave the thing alone.

"You know better. Shush."

There was no question what it was, but there were plenty of questions about it:

What was a giant menorah doing standing in the middle of the desert?

Who had made it, and why?

And who had lit the one giant candle at its top, whose towering yellow and blue flame blazed steadily even in the night breeze?

"A nice mystery, Melech. How can you not want to try to solve it?"

Melech had some uncomplimentary things to say about mysteries— based, it was true, on plenty of experience. But whether they pursued the matter wasn't up to him, as he knew full well.

A giant menorah: eight empty candle-holders the size of village wells, and one holder towering over the others bearing up the king of candles, its wick a rope the diameter of his (admittedly ropy) arm. And the menorah was a rich gold, a fact that explained how it reflected the candle's light into an all-encompassing glow that made it difficult to imagine how brightly the thing would shine with a full complement of candles.

"It's a beauty."

"It's a beauty, nah?" a scratchy voice suddenly declared, in perfect Hebrew, and Eliezer nearly lost the little heart function remaining to him.

From the base of the menorah rose a strange, twisted little man, his beard a fluttering fan of streamers. He wore a loose robe tied with a series of rope belts, each a different shade— perhaps a different color, although it was hard to tell. Despite the darkness, his eyes shone with a light that appeared to come, most disturbingly, from within. Again, and even more forcibly, Melech counselled retreat. He loathed the odd, especially the humanly odd.

"And who might you be?" Eliezer asked, ignoring Melech's cowardly advice. Melech pawed the ground in high annoyance.

"A keeper of the flame, maybe?" the old man said. "Someone you should talk to with respect." The keeper aimed a gaunt forefinger at Eliezer. "Look up!"

"All right, my old friend." *Older than me*, Eliezer thought with wonder, and Melech nodded mischievously: *that would be a wonder, indeed*. Eliezer raised his eyes to the single blazing candle. "And what am I seeing?"

"Fire!"

"Thank you for the infor—"

"Distant fire! No chance to move its cursed weight, not with these spindly arms!"

"Ah!" Now it was clear; he needed help to light his menorah during the eight days of Chanukah.

"During the eight days of Chanukah, nah? Representatives."

"Yes, of the eight days that the oil—"

"Of the eight days of Creation!" The old man stood motionlessly, finger pointing (so rudely!) at Eliezer's eyes.

"Forgive my presumption for saying so, my old" — *old* — "friend, but perhaps you are not fully familiar with the Holy Word. For there were seven days of creation. Well, to be exact six—"

"Eight!" the old man interrupted him again. "Six days of Adonai's labor, one of rest, one of creation every day."

"All right," Eliezer said slowly, soothingly. "Eight." And indeed it was true that in some branches of Kabbalistic thought there was talk of eight days, seven of physical creation and one of spiritual transcendence. Yet this ancient soul looked like no scholar.

"Rest, nah?"

That was certainly the proper exchange. "Perhaps you have heard of me, then," Eliezer said. "Ever since I transgressed the proper boundaries of knowledge" (*forgive me, already!*) "my curse has been to wander the world, assisting all who seek my help with the magic I learned. And in return, I ask only room and board."

"It's a curse to do *mitzvah*s?" He'd echoed Eliezer's earlier thoughts so closely, it was uncanny. Very uncanny.

"If it's done under duress."

"God does not 'duress'!"

Little do you know, Eliezer thought. Melech seemed in no mood to take a position one way or another.

The old, old man said, "Sounds like punishment to me."

"If you say so." Eliezer certainly felt that way.

"But it was your choice, nah? You chose to go where you weren't supposed to? And so, the consequences: doing good."

The keeper had offered him rest, but there was no shelter anywhere in sight, and as thin as the old, old man was, there appeared to be no food anywhere nearby, either. Melech responded to these obvious observations with an obvious plan: leave.

Be nice, Melech, Eliezer "whispered"; *he's mad*.

The horse merely stated that that was precisely his point.

"The ground is warm," the keeper said. "Lie and eat."

Eliezer moved to where the keeper pointed: a patch of ground that seemed lighter in color than the surrounding sand. Sure enough, it radiated heat, making blankets and a tent perhaps unnecessary. But as for food—

"As for food," the old, old man said, "manna!"

Oy, Eliezer thought. This was real trouble. Yet some of the sand wasn't sand; it was smooth-surfaced mounds that rose from the dirt like bubbles. Eliezer picked up a beige bubble and raised it to his lips. Melech declared that now Eliezer was the mad one, but Eliezer tongued the opaque bubble and found himself utterly smitten. It was the sweetest delight he'd ever tasted! He knew the taste but could not place it: creamy and sweet. He ate an entire bubble, which was full of air and substance all at once. His stomach sang songs of praise.

"No *brochah*?" the keeper asked. "A gentile?"

"Forgive me." Then Eliezer chanted the blessing of thanks for the food. *Baruch atoh Adonai elohaynu*. Blessed art thou, O Lord our God. *Melech ha'olam*. King of the Universe.

"King of all!" And the keeper pointed up, at Heaven or the candle, it wasn't clear.

When the blessing was done, Eliezer said, "So, you want me to light your other candles for you. Just one problem, my old friend."

"Where are the other candles, nah?" The keeper laughed. "Where are the other candles? See the light!" Then the old man disappeared, sinking away into the base of the menorah as if he'd melted into it.

"I guess that means wait till morning. What do you think?"

But as he turned to face Melech, he noticed the horse had fallen asleep, a light coating of bubble painting his equine lips.

"So be it." Eliezer lay on the warm ground, wrapping himself in the glow and instantly dropping off.

· ✡ ·

"Come on!"

Once again, Eliezer nearly jumped out of his skin, this time from a position still deep inside sleep. He opened his bleary eyes to see the keeper standing over him, face in full shadow as the sun glared beyond his head. "*Oy*," Eliezer commented, "you."

"Tonight's the first night!"

"I know." Eliezer lifted himself off the ground and began to brush the sand from his clothing, as slowly as he could in order to annoy the old, old man. Surprisingly, his joints didn't raise their usual litany of complaints; the warmth of the ground must have done them good. Above, the lone candle in the menorah raised aloft its steady flame, and there was no sign that the candle had shrunk to any degree. Eliezer made the keeper watch as, with exaggerated care, he gathered his robes around him. "You'll excuse me." He went behind a distant rock to relieve himself;

along the way, he spotted Melech in the distance, munching on a patch of something.

"Bubble?" he asked the horse, half-verbally.

Melech horse-nodded and kept on going. What *was* that flavour?

"You finished?" came the harsh voice of the keeper.

"It is not permitted to interfere with the functions of the body!" Eliezer called back. *Does the man know none of the Laws?* A sorry soul.

"You must begin!"

"I'll begin when I'm finished." That was a truly Kabbalistic paradox— maybe he was going to manage this after all, if his head was working so well. Except for that one insoluble problem. He returned to the menorah to find the keeper standing with arms crossed, one hand fingering the end of a rope belt.

"*Nu?*" the keeper asked with an impatient lilt.

Eliezer drew himself to his maximum height. "My old friend," he began, "I will help you as far as I can. But I cannot perform miracles." A half-truth— no more. "I cannot light candles that aren't th—"

"Get them!"

"And where may I do that?" He had visions of entering into a lifelong quest, across the desert sands and into oasis after oasis, village after village, just to find eight giant candles. "Is there a caravan loaded with eight-foot-tall candles coming through here soon? Do you know of a shop?"

The keeper leaned toward him, breaking into a manic grin as he stuck his face in Eliezer's.

"*BEES!*"

Eliezer could only stare at him. Such madness was ludicrous and sad all at once. He stifled a sigh and calmed himself by licking his lips. That was when he noticed that he was neither thirsty nor — even more amazingly — hungry. Those bubbles....

The keeper straightened himself once more, then unwound one of his belts from his waist. He held the rope out to Eliezer. "A wick, nah?"

By now, Melech had come to witness the discussion, and muttered something offensive. *I won't listen to such talk*, Eliezer told him, *such* beastly *talk*. "Thank you. Thank you very much," he said as he took the rope, which turned out to be well over eight feet long. Where did it all come from? Yet the old man's waist was still encircled with other belts.

"Bees!" the keeper repeated, and laughed. He reached down to the base of the menorah, from which he never moved more than a few inches, and lifted a brown, well-glazed jug from somewhere below. "Nah!"

Eliezer took the jug from him and lifted the earthenware lid. Inside was a sweet white liquid. Nectar.

He understood now what the keeper wanted him to do, which was just as well since the old man had disappeared. "Come on, Melech," he said, "let's build a candle."

Melech was now more certain than ever that Eliezer's own brains were addled, and felt it necessary to remind him that there were no bees in the desert.

"So who am I to argue?" Eliezer replied. Then, to himself, he muttered, "What bird, then, Melech?" He opened the jug once more and lowered the end of the rope into it; twirling the rope in its descent, he was able to immerse it entirely in the nectar. "An eagle? Perhaps an owl? Something with strong talons."

Melech made some facetious suggestions involving barnyard fowl; he seemed determined to be no help whatsoever. Eliezer shrugged and withdrew the soaking rope from the jug. It was now a feast for bees— the only problem was finding bees in a wasteland like this. Yet the old keeper seemed to know what he was about, so Eliezer decided he would simply exercise some faith. Faith....

"You don't think... that the old gentleman is... no!"

The Lord had His many avatars, perhaps, but none could be so patently absurd. The glowing figure who had come to tell Eliezer of his punishment was somewhat more dignified than this old fool.

"Then again, go figure the Lord's ways! So: an eagle? Maybe a hawk." Just to be on the safe side; he was good at hawks. He spoke the letters of the word for hawk, repeating the word as many times as their numerical value. Now — though more slowly than ever before (he *was* getting old!) — came the metamorphosis. His arms became wings; his robes became, and his body sprouted, feathers; his mouth elongated to a beak: the usual story.

Grasping the dry end of the rope in his right talon — the one without arthritis — he flew up the front of the menorah. Saturated as it was with nectar, the rope was terribly heavy, and his every joint complained at the load. Looking below, he could see no sign of the keeper, just the gleaming gold base of the candelabra.

Melech glanced up at him, then returned to nuzzling the ground looking for more bubble. Food fit for a horse as well as a man: not bad. Careful to avoid the flame of the *shamas*, the servant candle, Eliezer flew over the rightmost candle-holder and suspended the lower end of the rope into its very center. So there was the wick; now he needed a candle to go around it! With a few words he'd learned from a rope-charmer, he stiffened the rope till it stood erect without assistance.

He wanted to ask Melech if he knew any bee-calls, but could easily imagine the sort of unpleasantly sarcastic answer the horse would make. He flew back down to the ground and began the metamorphosis once more, unable to resist stealing a look at the foolish wick that stood shiny with nectar, but otherwise naked, above the holder. Maybe Melech was right; maybe this was all sheer madness.

"Nice!"

The keeper stood below the candle-holder with its towering wick, shielding his eyes from the sun.

"Adam Cadmon, human All: the jug and the crackpot and you are one, Eliezer ben-Avraham! Speak the voice, nah?"

"What are you, crazy?" The keeper wanted him to tap into the deepest part of the Kabbalah, the *En Sof*, where all unity — as represented by the human figure Adam Cadmon — could be found, and call forth with the voice of the One. "You want me to spend all eternity…?" Well, in the Jewish version of Hell (that terrible *goyische* concept): in the void. He'd already violated the boundaries of forbidden knowledge; he didn't need to press his luck any further.

"You won't be pressing your luck, nah? You'll be making light!"

"Stop reading my mi—"

"One with the light, and one with creation." Then the old, old man let out a shriek, a kind of yell that pierced Eliezer's ears and brain and reached down to his very core. It triggered Eliezer's own spirit, and almost without any effort on his part the cry went out to the world at large, at a level no one could hear but everyone and everything could feel. "Stop worrying," the keeper said. "Baby!"

A black dot appeared over the northern horizon; it grew into a cloud, a pitch-black cloud that wavered and roiled. The cloud expanded, and ahead of it as it approached came an answering call to the cry, a steady, heavy buzz. In seconds the bees swarmed them: Melech, Eliezer, the keeper, then the menorah, swallowing everything in a deafening, blinding mass. They poured through the air right up to the candle-holder, and began to drink the nectar from the bottom up. In their wake, honey flowed off the holder into the desert; and as the swarm moved its way up the wick, a pale, translucent candle rose behind it, inch by inch. Eliezer watched as the bees jostled and swirled and danced their bee-dance.

"So, eat!"

Eliezer looked down and saw that the honey was generating bubbles in the sand. In the bosom of Mother Earth. Now he knew what the bubbles had reminded him of: milk and honey. He made eye contact with Melech, who gave him a pitying look. "So we're here," Eliezer called out, his voice barely above the din of the buzzing masses above. "We've made it home." Home: the most precious of words for a wanderer like himself. He'd meant it as a joke, but... he shook his head to clear the dreams away.

Yet he couldn't help thinking, or maybe just feeling, that this was a place he'd been to before, a starting point.

As the bees did their work, Eliezer sat and tucked into some of the bubble, enjoying it like a starving man. Was it addictive? All he knew was that he could not get enough of it, at least till his stomach groaned in dismay. *So?* he told his belly; *you've made me suffer enough over the years.*

"Do you know the story of Chanukah?" the keeper asked.

Eliezer rolled his eyes. "Such a question for an old man like me. What am I, a five-year-old *putz*?"

Yet the keeper told him the story anyway, about the miracle of the lamp with oil enough for one day but that lasted for eight. By now the bees were high enough up the candle that the two men could speak without shouting. Eliezer nodded his head as the old, old man declared, "And so, in honor of God's miracle, we light a candle every night for eight nights, not far off the solstice!"

"Eh?" Well, that wasn't the usual ending to the story. But it seemed that the keeper was finally silent, and Eliezer said, "*Mazel tov*; you know your festivals. You must be very proud."

"And the circle is complete, nah?"

"So, you talk in riddles, is that it? And I'm supposed to figure out what you're talking about. Fine, I'll play your game. Later." It was time for a nap. At the rate they were going, the bees would be working for another couple of hours turning nectar into beeswax, and he could take a little snooze.

"Games? You want games?" From somewhere in his robes the old, old man extracted a gold dreidel. On the nearest side, the raised letter "shin" was intricately carved.

"All right; I get the picture, I see what you are. But a wise fool is supposed to be *wise*!"

To Eliezer's dismay, the keeper bent down and, with a flick of its stem between thumb and forefinger, spun the dreidel a couple of inches above the ground. So now they were going to play children's games? The point of the dreidel touched down on the desert and stood rock-solid, its four flat sides blurred into a perfect cylinder like that of the rising candle. The stem's position was so steady, and its rotation so fast, it seemed motionless. And what would they use as counters, to be won or lost depending on how the dreidel fell? He tried to remember what the four letters on the sides of the dreidel represented.

"'A great miracle happened there'!" the old, old man cried.

"I know that!" As if he needed such lessons! "In the *game*!" One letter meant you won the pot, another meant you put something in... Melech expressed astonishment that Eliezer would even consider becoming involved in such silliness, but Eliezer needed to keep the keeper happy and calm. Who knew what craziness lurked within?

Eliezer waited impatiently to see which side the dreidel would land on. But it didn't slow down at all; it maintained its momentum far beyond what would be reasonably expected, and even began to create its own miniature tornado as it drew desert sand into its tiny vortex.

"Nah! Always turning!"

So that's how it was. Not only did the dreidel carry upon it the four initial letters of that phrase in honor of the holiday, it also symbolized the passage of time. Or some such mystery — everything the keeper said was a riddle, like the Kabbalah itself. Eliezer stretched himself out on the deliciously warm ground. The days were nearly as short as they would ever be, but the sun here was every bit as bright as during the height of summer — yet the heat of the sand radiated from within, not above. He could watch in comfort as the candle stretched toward the sky behind the black and gold swarm, as the dreidel spun at the foot of the menorah. At times the hypnotic spin of one and buzz of the other made him doze off, but he snapped awake again, fearful he would miss something. The keeper did his disappearing act once more, and Melech was silent, preferring to keep his opinions to himself for a change.

· ✡ ·

Toward evening, the bees completed their work; they reached the dry top of the wick, and with nothing more to eat they rose en masse and returned to their distant home somewhere in the north. So now a second huge candle stood in the menorah, but unlit. One was supposed to light the eight candles of Chanukah with the servant (thus its name), but how was he to move that wax-and-flame giant? His arms were not that much less "spindly" than the keeper's.

"Nah! Good work!"

Eliezer's heart recovered from its flip. "*Oy*, do you have to sneak up on people?" He gestured at the new candle. "Thank you for the compliment, anyw —"

"I was talking about the *bees*!" The keeper seemed to be trying to align the candles with his bony hands, as if measuring them for some great portrait or act of engineering. As if *he* was the one who'd be doing the work! "Now you have to light it."

"Yes, thank you again for the information. But how?"

"With the king!"

"You mean the servant. A servant isn't a king." The old, old man knew nothing, yet kept trying to teach Eliezer about Chanukah!

"The source of light is the king!"

"If you say so." Melech did the horse equivalent of a roll of the eyes. "But," Eliezer repeated, hoping for some greater clarity, "how?"

"You are the spark, nah?"

Thank you again, Eliezer said, in as sarcastic a mental tone as possible. He hoped that the old, old man could indeed read his mind. "Perhaps you can offer more practical advice?"

"Let there be light!" the keeper cried. "You have the spark. Every day: the eighth day."

"Ah! So every day is a new creation, like an eighth day, yes?" No answer. "And the 'spark'?" Maybe life itself. Every day there is life, the world is born anew. "You see, Melech? It all makes sense, in a way."

Melech was not so sure.

"One question, my ancient friend. You're the keeper; why don't you have this 'spark'?"

"I never said I was 'the' keeper."

Melech, with his better memory, confirmed it. In Hebrew there is no indefinite article, only the definite. And the old, old man had not said, "*Ha*" to denote "the" when he identified himself. So what was the significance of that?

"You're a keeper, too," the old, old man continued.

Melech neighed, right out loud, manifesting some sort of worry he could not specify.

"Make some fire, wizard! You have the spark, you are the spark!"

Life: that was what Eliezer had, and maybe the Keeper didn't, or no longer had in sufficient amount to light the flame. Life: the candles themselves were symbols of that fire. Light symbolized life, and the extra, ever-burning candle—the one normally called the servant—represented the King giving that light and life to the others. "As only the Lord can create life, so only the king candle can provide the spark for all the others." *Melech ha'olam.* "You see, Melech?" he said to his coincidentally named horse. "It all fits." *And what are you so afraid of, silly one?*

But Melech couldn't answer, because he was still trying to work out what was bothering him, what made him want to run. Eliezer could not afford to be so cynical, so skeptical. He had to do what he'd been asked to do.

And what he'd been asked to do was a great honor: Eliezer was the means to bring light unto the darkening world. As the winter solstice approached, and night reached its greatest power, this menorah would light the darkness, and call Light back to the world. "Chanukah, Melech: the Festival of Lights."

"So get busy!" Keeper said. "The night falls!"

"All right! Be patient!"

At that point Melech cried out into Eliezer's mind. A keeper. Did that mean there would be another?

Oy.

"So that's it," Eliezer said to Keeper. "I'm to be your successor? *Nah*?" And he would spend eternity, or a good portion of it, stuck here in the desert lighting candles. "What did you do last year on Chanukah? How did you manage? Was it you then? Were you the lighter of the candles? And now you're weak, and you want to find someone to take your place. If I—"

Keeper burst out laughing, so raucously that Eliezer couldn't hear himself think. The old, old man doubled up, slapped his knees and stomach. Finally, the laugh gradually subsided, but then he looked at Eliezer again and started laughing even harder, if that was possible. He waggled his bony fingers at Eliezer, opened his eyes wide, and appeared to be trying to say something, but couldn't get it out. Eliezer crossed his arms and waited patiently for the old, old fool to finish. *Thank you for the warning*, Eliezer said to Melech in the meantime. *We were almost permanent residents of this place.* Although, with all the wandering he'd done, the idea of a home did have its appeal....

Keeper did his eyes-wide, waggling-fingers nonsense again, but this time was in sufficient self-control to finish the thought. He twisted his face into a mock-monstrous expression, and said, "Boogoo boogoo!" That just set him off again. It was getting very tiresome. "Boogoo boogoo!"

Melech suggested they leave immediately, but Eliezer could not, for a variety of reasons. Did his punishment mean that he would have to help Keeper even if it meant his own imprisonment in a task of no definable duration? How could he help others if he was stuck here, attached to the menorah like this fool till his flesh melted away and his own fingers were as skeletal as these?

"Conspiracies!" Keeper cried, in a bogeyman's voice. "Plots and conspiracies!" And, accompanied by yet more waggling, "Boogoo boogoo!"

"Explain yourself or I will go on my way." It was an empty threat, but—

"An empty threat, Eliezer ben-Avraham." Then Keeper finally became serious, or something approaching it. "You think I'm the only keeper? Or you are? Who do you think you are, nah?"

"So all living things have it. The spark."

"All living things have it. All are the flame. You can help the most."

"Who helped you last year?" An answer to that would be a help. "Who lit your candles on Chanukah?"

"I was a younger man then. Not so close to the dark."

"To the dark," Eliezer repeated. The solstice. Because he was so close to the solstice he was older and weaker. Was that it? Melech was still skeptical, but Eliezer decided something: he had no choice, either because of God's punishment that required him to do such *mitzvah*s, or because he would not call Keeper a liar without proof, or because, quite simply, it was a *mitzvah*. A good deed.

And because he had to have faith, or he might as well be in darkness forever.

"Fine, my ancient friend. No more talk of plots and conspiracies." He turned to Melech. "So, any thoughts?"

Melech came up with an intriguing suggestion: a phoenix.

"A mythical creature? And not even one of ours?" Eliezer thought about it a moment. "Certainly appropriate, but I'm not sure I can do that. I can't create life, but can I create a nonlife?" Too absurd.

"I like the phoenix!" Keeper declared.

"So shall it be."

Eliezer could imitate life's many forms using the life within himself, but had only a hazy idea of what a phoenix might look like. He transformed himself into a large red bird. The sun set just as his metamorphosis was complete, and he glowed in the final golden rays of dusk-light. He flew up to the king candle, and felt no heat, no burning pain, as he lowered himself into the heart of its flame. Its fire touched the fire inside him, joining with his very soul and spark. He rose once more, all aflame but not burning, and prepared to land—to *alight*—on the candle representing the first night of Chanukah.

"What, again no *brochah*?" Keeper called up from below. "Do you know nothing?"

In his mind Eliezer began the words of the blessing, and he was joined in his recitation by Keeper's voice and the "voice" of Melech, too, who seemed to enjoy the opportunity to participate in a religious ceremony for a change. So what if he had no soul?

Baruch atoh Adonai elohaynu....

Blessed art thou, O Lord our God....

Melech ha'olam.

King of the universe.

And they recited the blessing till the very end:

Vetzivanu l'hadlik nehr shel Chanukah.

And commanded us to light the Chanukah candle.

Eliezer flew on to the other candle, clutched the wick between his talons, and it caught the flame with enthusiasm. As he lifted himself into the air again, Eliezer noted that the fire stayed behind; he was as free of flames as the two who waited for him below. He descended and reversed the transformation.

When he was done, he rubbed a new ache in his back as they all recited the other two blessings for the first night, then said as one, "*Omain!*"

Keeper followed with a final, satisfied, "Nah!"

· ✡ ·

The candles burned all night, and all the next day, with no discernible shortening. The wax simply refused to melt. It was a miracle… or something close to it. Even after a long, rich night's sleep — uninterrupted by his bladder! a real miracle! — he found them still burning, still the same size.

And the dreidel still spun.

And so, for seven more days and seven more nights, Eliezer repeated the procedure. Keeper would hand him another rope belt and jug of nectar, the bees came to do their duty, and Eliezer lit the new candle. On the eighth night was the solstice, but at the darkest time of the year the desert glowed with blazing light from nine giant, stubborn, never-say-die candles. Now that all were finally lit, the golden menorah shone like something God himself must have fashioned.

"Maybe this is what the Lord uses to see in the dark, eh?" Eliezer joked to Melech, who cautioned him against blasphemy. "Come, don't take everything so seriously."

"You may go!"

Keeper was waving his hand sharply, as if wantonly dismissing them. Or perhaps he was trying to prove that they were free, that they would not be held captive here. Melech's paranoia had never completed dissipated, but he was calm enough not to need such reassurance. Eliezer turned briefly to the horse to flash him a look signalling that a little faith was not a bad thing, even in an animal.

"Keeper—" But the old, old man was just now disappearing into the base of the menorah. Did he sleep under it? Was he part of it? While looking at the ground, Eliezer noticed some bubbles rising to the surface. "Well, no reason we can't stay till morning, no? After all, we're entitled to another night's room and board, even in the absence of a room."

Melech hesitated to agree, but then nuzzled one of the bubbles at his feet and gave in.

The next morning there was no sign of Keeper. The sun was peeking over the eastern horizon. Eliezer looked up at the menorah, and saw what he should have expected to see: only the king candle remained standing and ablaze. Thin trails of smoke rose from where the other eight had stood. There was not a sign of melted wax or charred rope. But that one flame never wavered, never flickered, never dimmed, even in the sun's glow.

"Good magic, my friend," Eliezer commented.

Melech nodded and urged him to get ready to leave. The horse always wanted to go on, find someplace more comfortable. What could be more comfortable than here? But he knew better than to expect he could stay. Keeper could — was obliged to — remain here forever; Eliezer's role was quite the opposite. Melech made a vague, and predictable, comment about mirror-images, even hinting at a physical resemblance between them.

"God forbid, Melech."

Eliezer's eye was caught by a glimmer on the ground. The dreidel had landed at last, and the letter that stood on the top-most side was the "Nes": the initial letter of the word "miracle."

After a brief visit to the other side of that boulder, he mounted Melech and rode toward the rising sun. As Melech's feet clopped on the ground, Eliezer thought he heard the old, old man's "Nah!" coming from behind him. Oddly, it also sounded like a baby's cry, a "Wah!"

"Maybe we're all going in circles," Eliezer said. Melech had no reply. "What if we come here every year, and don't even know it afterward? Hmm? Maybe we forget, and come and light the candles all over again."

Melech now made a poor joke about being in the dark when it came to such questions.

"Shame on you."

THE WHOLE MEGILLAH

1

NOW IT CAME to pass in the days of Ahasuerus (this is Ahasuerus which reigned, from India even unto Ethiopia, over an hundred and seven and twenty provinces)

That in those days, when the king Ahasuerus sat on the throne of his kingdom, which was in Shushan the palace,

In the third year of his reign, he made a feast unto all his princes and his servants; the power of Persia and Media, the nobles and princes of the provinces, being before him...

Now in Shushan the palace there was a certain Jew, whose name was Mordecai, the son of Jair, the son of Shimei, the son of Kish, a Benjamite;

Who had been carried away from Jerusalem with the captivity which had been carried away with Jeconiah king of Judah, whom Nebuchadnezzar the king of Babylon had carried away.

And he brought up Hadassah, that is, Esther, his uncle's daughter: for she had neither father nor mother, and the maid was fair and beautiful; whom Mordecai, when her father and mother were dead, took for his own daughter.

When the young armed guard asked, "Who are you?" Eliezer wasn't sure what to answer. As Melech impatiently scraped ruts in the hard-packed sand with his hoof, Eliezer considered his words and said, "I am he who was summoned."

Beyond the two guards — who both wore thin red eye-masks that failed to hide their beardless chins — Eliezer could see the city's glow above the vast iron gates, rivalling the dusk's purple gleam. Lions of Judah, crowned and roaring and wielding swords at each other, stood out in shallow relief against the black gates. So typical: fighting with each other.

"Summoned?" the other guard demanded. "By whom?"

"Your masters, sirs!" Eliezer replied, standing in as haughty a posture as he could, given his arthritis. *Oy, the arrogance of youth!*

Melech made a comment about the arrogance of age, but Eliezer ignored him.

"We know of no summons."

"Listen," Eliezer said, slowly and with a degree of restraint that was costing his blood pressure dearly. "I am Eliezer ben-Avraham." He waited for recognition to dawn on their faces, despite the dusk. "The *wizard!*"

"Ah!" "Oh!" the young fools replied. "Enter and good *yom tov* to you."

"Good *yontif*," Eliezer said, in his preferred pronunciation, and watched the gates swing open before him. They revealed a city blazing with lamps. Eliezer didn't deign to look at the guards as he passed through. Melech recommended they first find the stable. "You know better." His blue pouch with the *Mogen David* stitched in gold on the side nearly slapped the *pisher* on the right as it jounced against Melech's side. Eliezer suspected the horse had swayed just enough to cause that.

The whole city glowed with fire, its highest towers wreathed in swirls of smoke. Melech's steel shoes clanked against the cobbles, the sound barely audible against a distant, steady roar. Suddenly, there rose the burr of noisemakers like a cicada's call; it faded just as quickly. Haman's name was abroad! Yet the reading of the *Megillah* should not have begun yet; maybe these people had a different Purim service from others. Eliezer, though it was a dirty habit, spat on the ground— his own, private, and silent condemnation of Haman, the Evil One. "May he roast for eternity in the *goyim*'s hell," Eliezer said, and Melech nodded. Eliezer steered them between high flat buildings of sandstone that seemed ready to crush them in a giant's vice. He followed the sound. The *graggers*, wielded by what sounded like thousands of children, burred again. Why weren't the worshippers in *shul*, listening respectfully to the recitation of the *Megillah* like proper Jews?

He'd passed this city frequently in his rounds, but no one had ever summoned him inside before, to perform a task or even just offer some accommodations. It would have been a *mitzvah* to provide food and shelter — basic hospitality — without asking for assistance from his magic. Few, however, were that generous: usually, he had to work for his supper, doing the little tasks only magic (or more hard work than the lazy souls were willing to invest!) could accomplish.

They found the people at last, jammed into the town square— circle, really, of ancient-looking buildings. The eastern curve was dominated by a pile that could only be a palace: three storeys high, with massive doors. Thousands of masked and costumed men, women, and children stood crushed together, facing inward, yelling all at once.

"Condemn him!"

"Tear him to pieces!"

"Blessed is the saviour Queen, for she is our lamp!"

"Kill him!"

Such un-*yontif* sentiments coming from the masked horde. A hundred Mordecais, a hundred King Ahasueruses, a hundred Queen Esthers, scattered Chamberlains and Harem Supervisors, and with them a few non-Purim figures, screamed in rage and devotion. "Have they gone mad?" Eliezer shouted above the din. Melech expressed an opinion about humans in general that wasn't at all helpful in this particular situation.

"How dare such a beast roam our streets?"

"Drive Haman *out*!"

At the name, the *graggers* burst into life, and Eliezer covered his ears. It was like the sound of a million bees — *dear God, let us not have that again*! — and Melech shook his head violently, at the deafening noise (or maybe the reminder). The children spun their *graggers*, filling the air with their cacophony. It was one thing to show your displeasure with Haman; it was another to deafen the world!

He had no space to ride through the crush, so he dismounted and allowed Melech to sniff out — literally and figuratively — the stable. Meanwhile, with a few simple repetitions, he transformed himself into a sizeable but otherwise inconspicuous moth. He manoeuvred toward the palace through the torches' smoke-streams. A balcony protruded from the second storey, its railing elaborately carved in the shapes of various animals: lions, asses, camels. And the doors! These lions were even more elaborately carved, and wore gilded crowns.

Before the doors stood another guard, this one far more fully disguised than his city-wall brethren. Eliezer could not identify the disguise, but he *could* recognize a bulbous paunch. Shameful! He metamorphosed back to human on the steps of the palace, and immediately his stomach growled— as if it had transformed into a lion itself. The guard, leaning on his ceremonial spear, nearly fell over at Eliezer's sudden manifestation. Good— a little surprise never hurt his efforts at impressing.

"I am Eliezer ben-Avraham," he said; then, given his experience of these people's intelligence, added, "the wizard, come to see thy master." A snort tickled his inner left lobe: Melech being amused at the heightened language.

"W-I'm honored!" the guard said, regaining his balance. "Your reputation precedes you." Eliezer gave him a meaningful look, the meaning being, "And who are you to express an opinion?"

"Please," the guard continued, raising his voice to be heard above a renewed outcry from the noisemakers. "Be welcome within!" He pressed somewhere between the doors and they swung open, seemingly of their own accord.

"Thank you so much!" Eliezer said with all the sarcasm he could muster at this impertinent *putz*, to no avail. Thick, dense, practically stone: a head like that on a human body! Two more guards, their breastplates gold and engraved with Stars of David, escorted him through a short, barrel-ceilinged lobby toward an arched opening in a jewel-encrusted dividing wall. Very nice! And far better than so many of the places he'd been required to sleep: barns, attics, sometimes the fields themselves. At least here, he wouldn't be disturbed by mice; they were the bane of his sleep, as he had an irrational loathing of the things.

Beyond was a round chamber — the throne room, he quickly recognized — decorated in brightly colored tapestries, hanging jewels, and gold-leafed festoons; bronze doors were set in the walls to the right and to the left, while stretching beyond the throne was a long hall that seemed to be for dining. Not bad! Fit for a King or Prince or....

Woman?

May God have mercy ... may God *explain* ... for there, upon an ivory throne, in flowing gown, maskless (but with painted face, bejewelled hair, glittering ears), in the midst of guards and attending women and lean courtiers, sat what was unmistakably a *woman*. From the depths of his mind, Eliezer pulled out a relevant *brochah* — the one on seeing a freak of nature — and recited it in a rushed whisper. *Baruch atoh adonai elohaynu...*

"Welcome," she (*she*!) said, "to the City of Shushan. We are Queen Hadassah." Otherwise known as Esther. A coincidence? "To whom do we speak, and to what do we owe the pleasure?"

"Your— *Majesty* [the word stuck in his throat], I am the wizard Eliezer ben-Avraham, come to do your bidding." Her expression changed: puzzlement beneath the paint. When she offered no reply, he said slowly, "As you are no doubt aware, I must wander the world using the powers I so foolishly gained, to aid all who request such help." Still no word. "This is my penance for..." no interruption, no sign of recognition "...my explorations of forbidden knowledge. In exchange, I receive room and board" and let it be a great deal of board! "as my only and full payment."

"Your reputation is well known, great wizard," the woman said, "and it is fortuitous that you have come, for we have evil in our midst."

"'Fortuitous'?" What was *she* talking about? "I am glad as well as obliged to help, but I come in response to your summons."

"But, great wizard," replied the Queen, her tone matching the bewilderment in her face, "we did not summon you."

"You—" Eliezer's lips froze in the position of pronouncing the word. Somewhere in the distance, audible in the back of Eliezer's mind, a horse laughed.

"Mysteries on mysteries," the Queen said. "Who summoned you? How did you know of our plight?"

Tell her! Melech cried in his "ear."

Tell her what? Use an old cliche? Yet, like all cliches, it possessed a grain of truth; and, in this case, far more. "I received a vis-ion." He had been about to say, "visit" or "visitation," but thought better of it. Until he understood the matter himself, it was best to exercise discretion. Melech chortled — if a horse can do such a thing — and waves of insulting skepticism flowed from the beast's mind.

When he had told Melech about the gleaming white dove that stood upon the rock above Eliezer's awakening form, and carefully enunciated the summons in accented Hebrew — "Please! Help! Come to Shushan!" — Melech had made half-joking insinuations about Eliezer's sanity, and reminded him of such things as "dreams." But could it have been only a dream? The bird had cried, "Oh!" then flown like an arrow in the direction of this city. Such magic— so much like his own.

"Wizard?"

"Excuse me, Your Majesty." And since when did Jews have queens? Even in the days of the ancients…. "Forgive an old man's confusion."

"Let us speak of this later," she said soothingly. "For now, you must partake of our feast. We have dined already, but you should have food and wine." She made signs to her minions, who scattered down various corridors. Her entourage all looked distinctly *wrong*: the military men were unfit, and the servants (females in their proper role) exhibited an ill-disguised sense of being too good for the job. So why hire such people? Unless the employers were as crazy as the employed….

"Yes." Food and wine. "My horse seeks accommodation, too." Melech reported success at last. "He is at your stable now."

"Our men shall find him and make him comfortable. So, great wizard," she said as her servants returned with a chair and table, and platter after platter, beaker after beaker of lovely refreshments, "tell us how you come to be here," the Queen said.

"It is difficult to say, your 'Majesty,'" he answered as he dug into the plateful of delectable roast fowl before him. *Embarrassing* was more like it. "Strange magic, abstruse mysteries to be solved. But enough of that." He raised a silver goblet to his lips and drank some wine: delicious! "You said something about needing my assistance." He bowed his head as low as he could bring himself to, considering.

"Yes, great wizard." Only now did he notice the specks of dirt beneath her fingernails. *What—?* "You see, Haman walks—"

At the sound of the Enemy's name, the entire congregation of guards and lackeys put their tongues between their lips and blew rude noises. Eliezer nearly jumped out of his skin.

"—among us."

"*Haman?*" he cried, before he could stop himself, and dropped his cutlery. Sure enough, the hall resounded again with the grating noise. He covered his food with his hand. "You have Ha— the Evil One in your midst?" And now he remembered that of all the costumes he had seen outside, there was not one of the great villain. Usually, children loved to play the part of the bad guy, if only to provoke their parents. "Let me see if I understand this. Someone has dressed up like Haman—" *Oy!* The *phhhtt*s filled the hall, echoed from its high ceiling, pierced his eardrums. For once, he wished he were *more* hard of hearing. "You're upset because someone chose a costume representing you-know-who? Is such a costume not acceptable among you?"

"This is no costume, wizard. He is here."

Eliezer chewed some fried yam (exquisite!) slowly to look thoughtful, but all he could think was that he had encountered yet more lunatics. *So many sick people in this world....* "So, he has risen from the dead." The Queen nodded. "King Ahasuerus had him hoist on his own gibbet for counselling the slaughter of the Jews, but he woke up and decided to visit your fair city." The Queen nodded again. "I see."

Melech, who was eavesdropping from his stall, recommended a hasty, if polite, exit. Eliezer reminded him that it was not possible— that it was never possible. A task is a task. "Your 'Majesty,'" Eliezer said, "forgive my skeptical nature. But—"

"Trust us, great wizard. Haman—" Loud, disgusting, *wet*, the appalling racket burst forth again. "—lives." She rose from her seat and was surrounded by her officious minions. "We must go to services, for the rabbi is about to begin the reading of the *Megillah*. All night, as we read from the Book of Esther, we will watch for the presence of the Enemy. But we ask that you join us — no, finish! eat! — and go forth, find him, and remove him, use your powers to free us from his vile presence." Melech, meanwhile, reported he was doing well, although his groom had very soft hands. *So?*

"This Ha-hateful being of yours— how can you believe he is real?"

"Our people have seen him," she said, "and they are frightened. It was not one lone soul who saw him, but many, and they say he is evil incarnate. You are a devotee of Kabbalah," she said. "We know of this power. Please use it to help us."

"If I can." Eliezer rose, out of courtesy, with a grunt and a shooting pain down his leg. "Your 'Majesty,' may I ask a question?"

She smiled with undisguised impatience. "Please."

"Forgive my impertinence; but as you know, I am curious to a fault." That was how he'd gotten into this situation in the first place. "As far as I know, our people have never been ruled by a female monarch, except as the wife of a king. How is it, then, that your people come to be ruled by a Queen?"

"They are not. Good evening."

And with that, she walked toward the door on the left, followed by almost her entire entourage. *S'gehert?* he asked, directing the question partly to Melech and partly to Heaven: *Did you hear her?* Unbelievable. Just before she reached the door she turned around and smiled. "Great Wizard," she said, "now may I ask you a question?"

"Of course."

"What is the name of your horse?"

"Melech."

"'Melech.'" The Queen smiled, and Eliezer stiffened. *Nu*, what was so funny about naming a horse "king"? "Tell me, wizard. Does your 'king' rule you, then?"

"It is only a name—" Eliezer said, then instantly knew that he had put himself on very shaky ground, philosophically.

"And since Adam himself, names have carried identity and power. Not so?"

"Of course." *Stupid old head.* For such power of names and words was the very source of his magic.

"An animal ruling a man— such a *reversal!*"

Oh. *Oy. OY!* "Your *Majesty* is wise," he said, humbly.

With a charming smile, Queen Hadassah — or whoever she was — nodded her acknowledgement of the (most deserved) compliment. For this was the festival of inversions, the Jewish carnival, when everything was topsy-turvy, and nobody was who he — or she — seemed. In this city, they had chosen to take the principle to its logical extreme, turning everything upside down. *Nu!*

One servant remained to provide for his needs, and she waited with another platter resting awkwardly on soft hands. "So now," he said, "I go find Haman." Mercifully, the girl did not make any noise, or withdraw. "When I'm done eating, of course." Purim was a time of enjoying sensual pleasures, those of food and drink, and Eliezer was determined to relish his full share.

The Story of Esther — disguised Jewess in the harem of King Ahasuerus of Persia — began to float in, narrated in a rich baritone that competed well against the never-ending hubbub. The long, rambling tale would dominate the night, and then be repeated the next morning. He'd heard it so often that he didn't need the refresher; but it was his duty as a Jew to listen, and so he did as he chewed and drank, dabbed his chin, and ordered the solitary girl to refill his silver plate and his goblet. It was even considered acceptable to become drunk this one night of the year. Right now, that seemed like a very, very good idea.

When he was done, he was escorted by the girl to a lush room: bed covered in silks, low stools upholstered in velvet with gold embroidery, a delicate porcelain-coated bath-table for washing one's face and hands, the usual royal accoutrements. Not bad. Outside, the blessing on the holiday was being said, thanking God for letting us celebrate Purim and the Jews' deliverance from certain slaughter. Eliezer sat on one of the stools and put aside his pouch. His stomach urged him to get up, but his joints insisted with equal force that he remain in blissful sloth. He collapsed backward, his head sinking into pillows lying at the foot of the bed before it began to swim—

Melech's voice entered his spinning head, saying, in an equine-accented imitation of Eliezer, *A little birdie told me so.* The horse then practically roared with laughter.

2

After these things did king Ahasuerus promote Haman the son of Hammedatha the Agagite, and advanced him, and set his seat above all the princes that were with him.

And all the king's servants, that were in the king's gate, bowed, and reverenced Haman: for the king had so commanded concerning him. But Mordecai bowed not, nor did him reverence...

And Haman said unto king Ahasuerus, There is a certain people scattered abroad and dispersed among the people in all the provinces of thy kingdom; and their laws are diverse from all people; neither keep they the king's laws: therefore it is not for the king's profit to suffer them.

If it please the king, let it be written that they be destroyed...

In the first month, that is, the month Nisan, in the twelfth year of king Ahasuerus, they cast Pur, that is, the lot, before Haman from day to day, and from month to month, to the twelfth month, that is, the month of Adar.

Something plopped onto his chest, just below his beard, and yanked him from a rich snooze. *What the—?* He blinked away the grit and fog and looked past the gray hairs at his chin... and found himself staring into the eyes of a mouse!

Oyoyoyoy! The mouse's snout didn't tremble, as it ought; instead, the horrid creature stared into Eliezer's eyes, its gaze steady, its ears perked up.

"Thank God you've come," the mouse said, in excellent Hebrew. "Please help me!"

"I—" But he couldn't get out another word. All his instinctive abhorrence of the beast fired through his body like lightning. If only he could reach his pouch... catch it, smash it, throw it out the window....

"I need your help, O wizard! Please, before I become—"

Melech, Eliezer subvocalized, in the mental equivalent of a squeak— a human squeak—

"Oh!" The mouse's eyes grew wide, as if it were beset with some unspeakable horror. "Find me!" Then it scampered at full speed off Eliezer's chest, off the bed, and a gorilla jumped out his window.

Melech! MELECH!!

Eliezer blinked over and over till his eyes teared. He tried to rise from the bed, but the night's imbibing was turning his gut to water that sloshed and undulated. A drowsy, guttural whinny tickled the back of his mind. To Melech's groggy inquiry, Eliezer told him what had just happened.

The horse was silent for some moments.

"I know what you're thinking," Eliezer said aloud. "It wasn't *that* much!"

Finally, Melech said something uncomplimentary that Eliezer put down to his having just been awakened. *Tell me again about the gorilla?* Melech continued, and Eliezer waved sharply in the stable's direction out of sheer frustration.

There's something wrong with the smell, Melech then commented.

Eliezer reminded him he was in a stable, and the sound Melech made in response was unclassifiable. *A mouse?*

"*Nu?*" In the sense of: well, isn't that what I said?

Gorilla? A headache burned behind his eyes. *Something doesn't smell right.* Melech's equine sense of smell would have naturally surpassed that of any human, even without his enhancements. Not that he could read other animals' minds, exactly, but maybe just a little of their noses.

"So, what's your thinking?"

Melech said he was thinking of going back to sleep.

Steeling himself, Eliezer raised himself off his awkward near-bed and stood up. He summoned Melech, then dressed, and snatched up his pouch brusquely, as if it had deliberately positioned itself beyond his grasp during the mouse invasion. Gathering his robes around him, he wound his way through the corridors; outside, the party went on, its sounds thrumming in the very walls like the heart of Adam Cadmon Himself. Through the open windows came the sounds of the reading of the Book of Esther — the *Megillah* — and the cries for vengeance, the outrage, the humble prayers. He descended the steps past the fat guard who had first addressed him, and who now nodded at an angle; that was deference? Ignoring him, Eliezer plunged deep into the roiling mass of humanity, his body shoved and prodded, his robes brushed and slapped by costumes and caught on whirling *gragger*s. All was yellowed by torches whose flames guttered and shot off brief-lived sparks. The "Queen" stood upon the balcony, listening to the long-winded Story of Esther recited by the black-suited, *talith*-bedecked rabbi at the center of the mob.

"Blessed is she who saved us from slaughter!"

"Praise the Lord for His Mercy!"

"Kill Haman!"

GRRRRRR! the noisemakers cried, driving a nail in his head.

In the midst of the reading and the shouts of fury, a dance had broken out on the eastern rim of the congregation. A few Mordecais and some Ahasueruses and tall, masculine Esthers skipped around in a distorted circle whose sides were warped by the press of bodies.

Eliezer made his way as best he could through the crush, looking for clues, for answers. And looking for the black-bearded being who might have convinced these mad people that the ancient Persian adviser (let his name be wiped out! if only for the sake of Eliezer's ears!) had actually resurrected.

Meanwhile, a gnat tickled at his neck, and even bit him once, and Eliezer slapped it away. His eyes teared from the smoke, and his ears and his skull were ready to burst. Their Festival: a time for making a racket; a time when courtiers made soft-handed grooms and fat guards, while dirty-fingered servant-girls acted as Ladies of Misrule! The gnat returned, buzzing around his ears; then, before Eliezer could send it to an early grave, it disappeared. A cat slipped between his calves, nearly upending him. It was a city full of aggravations.

The mouse had inspired him: an owl! He should survey the city from above. He counted the numerical value of the letters in *"yanshuf"* and spoke the word that many times, all the while tapping into the Spirit of the One. His arms turned into wings, his eyes grew round, and his mouth became a tiny beak in a flat face. He flapped his wings and soared above the people, till the mostly empty city spread out before him. Thanks to his superb night-vision he could observe the city while his sharp ears would allow him to hear the recitation of the *Megillah*. Whoever the boogeyman might be, he wouldn't be in the Town Circle. He would hide in the shadows: he'd be alone— and easier to spot.

Eliezer flew back and forth across the city. Did Evil Ones have a distinctive scent? Did they make certain sounds as they moved through the streets? And what did an Evil One really look like, anyway? Sadly, like everyone else....

But no human moved among the buildings, or at least no human sporting the traditional features of Haman: the black beard, the aristocratic robes, above all (so to speak!) the triangular hat that had inspired those tasty *hamantaschen*. Oh, for one of those wonderful pastries now, like the ones his mother baked centuries ago! and prune, the best flavour for old men. He spotted only a dog here, a hunch-backed child there, a tiger over there.... Eliezer blinked his owl eyes and the tiger was gone.

Maybe a talking tiger— either Eliezer was losing his mind, or magic of some mysterious kind was abroad tonight. He spotted a school, attached to which was a different sort of building: low, unadorned, as if trying to hide from the public eye. This city was full of secrets. *Mysteries on mysteries....* He swooped down for a closer look and saw over the narrow black door the words, "Beth Ari." House of the Lion: another reference to the city's beloved mascot, the Lion of Judah. But no mouse. To solve those mysteries he would have to be lucky, depend on the whims of chance: the way Haman threw the lots that would tell him on which day to order the slaughter of the Persian Jews. For Mordecai (the story went) had refused to bow before Haman, the king's adviser, and in his prideful wrath, Haman counselled King Ahasuerus to massacre the Jews. Only Queen Esther, Mordecai's cousin and goddaughter, prevented the King from carrying out the genocide, for she was his favorite among all his wives.

Tell the story a thousand times in all its meandering detail, as the rabbi was doing in the Town Circle; none of it would explain why these people thought Haman, who had been hanged on the gallows he had erected for the Jews, had managed to stand up and wander around this appropriately-named city.

Any answers to that *riddle?* he asked Melech. No reply.

A failure. *Where are the* sefirot, he wondered, *that would guide me to such a one?* Perhaps he was missing something in the Carnival; perhaps it was the duty of the false monarch to tell false tales, as the real King was obliged to tell the truth. In a world of inversions, anything was possible.

Maybe he needed to change his approach: instead of better eyes, he needed a better nose…. He asked the horse to meet him not far from the Circle. The rabbi was winding down; the last words of the *Megillah* echoed through the streets. Eliezer listened to the *brochah*s. Finally, the evening services were over— but the congregation did not disperse; instead, they took the opportunity to raise their voices again, and shout the Abominable Name again, and set the cursed noisemakers in motion again.

"*Oy*, they're going to kill me with their *noise!*"

"Wizard!"

The "Queen" stood before him, in all her ersatz "majesty," like one of the *goyim*'s phony stone gods. With a sinking heart Eliezer bowed down to her. "My Mistress," he said, in what he hoped was Purim-suitable mock-reverence.

"Can you help me?"

"I don't think I can." He patted the pouch at his side, and let his fingers stray over the smooth gold threads of the *Mogen David*. "With this power, I can solve a few of the world's problems. Only God Himself can do the rest."

"You must! I know what you can do. Please! I—"

The rabbi began a prayer, and Eliezer bowed his head, but when he looked up once more she was gone. Such rudeness! Melech commented, *She didn't train very well for the role, did she?* Without elaborating on that, Melech bent his knees to ease Eliezer's mounting— though in this chilly night, with his arthritis acting up, and that merciless headache, it was no easy task.

They skirted the crowd, in which a dozen dances had begun, and rushed from the Circle when someone screamed the Unholy Name. "Follow that mouse."

3

Then called Esther for Hatach, one of the king's chamberlains, who he had appointed to attend upon her, and gave him a commandment to Mordecai, to know what it was, and why it was.

So Hatach went forth to Mordecai upon the street of the city, which was before the king's gate.

And Mordecai told him of all that happened unto him, and of the sum of the money that Haman had promised to pay to the king's treasuries for the Jews, to destroy them.

Also he gave him the copy of the writing of the decree that was given at Shushan to destroy them, to shew it unto Esther, and to declare it unto her, and to charge her that she should go in unto the king, to make supplication unto him, and to make request before him for her people.

Melech used his nose, and Eliezer used his aged eyes, but still the city offered up no secrets. Bleak, empty streets, a couple of masked people rushing on some errands. And then:

A small child raced out of the darkness, hysterical, clutching a mask in her hand— such suffering innocence Eliezer had never seen. She tore down the street toward Eliezer, running as if she'd seen the manifestation of every nightmare and boogeyman haunting her young life, and flew past.

It's wrong, it's all wrong, Melech said, then headed into the darkness from which the child had fled.

Around the corner, they found him.

He stood half in the shadow of a building, a towering figure. He wore the black beard, and on his head was the triangular hat. This was no mask, this was no costume, for below the point of the infamous hat were eyes that blazed with evil. No makeup, no special devices to fool gullible souls; Eliezer was looking into a blank soul; there was nothing beyond that gaze.

"Who are you?" he asked.

"Haman, great wizard."

Melech shied away, but he also shook his head in a gesture of puzzlement.

"Where have you come from?"

"Risen from the dead, wizard. Help me. Help us."

"Help you?" What was this? "I don't know what sort of demon you are, but if you are evil, what makes you think I'll help you? *Feh!*" And using the royal "we" when it suited him, as if he were the King of Hell— Eliezer dropped his hand to the pouch, and drew his copy of the *Sefer Yetsirah* from it. "This is my power, my guide, my link to the Torah!" The knowledge and strength of Kabbalah stood in proud rows of letters on its pages. "Evil spirit, demon, whatever you may be, this is the way—"

"The way into the Words of Creation. For the Torah is the language of God and the Words of Creation. And the *sefirot* are the ten symbols, and there are twenty-two paths."

The devil himself speaking the words of wisdom, of *Hochmah*! *Disgusting*! How dare this *thing* throw the Kabbalah's own words back at him!

"And above it all is the *Keter*," Haman continued, "the crown, the kingdom and the Kinghood and the Godhead. I don't need your lessons in Kabbalah, wizard. I need your help."

"You were the one who summoned me."

"Yes."

"To do your evil bidding."

"To do good to an evil one."

This smells wrong, Melech said, and offered a thought about a lack of fire and brimstone.

"You are not what you seem," Eliezer said, understanding Melech's point at last. "Who are you?"

"Do you want to know my name?"

Would he give it? For that would grant Eliezer power over him, as anyone who knew the Kabbalah would also know. "Yes, demon, or whatever creature lies beneath this façade."

"I am Yacob ben-Ari. Ari is the name of my spiritual father."

It became clear, now. The strange building he had seen next to the school, Beth Ari: it was not named for the animal, or even the Judaic symbol, but for Isaac Luria, *the* Ari, the great Kabbalist, the spiritual Father of the whole system. Beth Ari was itself a school. "You are a Kabbalist, too."

"Yes. And more foolish even than you, wizard."

Eliezer's eyes widened. *Now you insult me?* "Explain yourself," he said, exercising all his restraint; right now, he was tempted to turn this thing into a succulent gosling to be eaten by a sow!

"I followed your path, wizard. I learned to tap into *Yesod*, the Foundation. I gained the power to metamorphose."

"That certainly was foolish, indeed." As Eliezer knew better than anyone. For learning such magic, for becoming a creator himself out of curiosity, he had lost his home, his right to even *have* a home. Now he wandered; and so, apparently, did this much younger seeker of abstruse knowledge.

"More foolish than you know, wizard." Haman had not budged an inch; he still stood in that half-shadow. "I did not learn how to control my changes. I shift and change without will or choice, and I have nothing left except this nothingness, this blank." *Of course!* Eliezer thought; to be everything is to be nothing. "Eliezer ben-Avraham, you can become what you want; but I become what chance decrees, or what others do *not* want."

That left even Melech speechless. Eliezer thought about the implications. To be a slave to chance — the throwing of the universe's lots — or the source of fear or loathing. On Purim, to be Haman, the opposite and bane of innocence; and, for a wizard with a hatred of mice, or a desire to avoid the "Queen"… "Then, you have no will," Eliezer said.

"In my changes, no. And without a will I am a nothing."

In God's eyes, yes: no self to save. "How old are you?"

"I am twenty-one."

So young to be so cursed! Eliezer felt sorry for the boy. He himself had poked around in the mysteries at a more advanced age, and so had enjoyed at least some of his life before ruining it. And there remained something of himself, if only to keep him fully aware of what he had lost to his foolish studies.

"What do you want me to do?"

"Kill me, Eliezer ben-Avraham."

"How dare you? You of all people should know I can't do that." The Kabbalah gave him power over the *shape* of life, but the power to give or take life remained the sole prerogative of God. Even the Kabbalah did not grant one the eating of that fruit. Yacob nodded. "Listen, if you're so determined to die, why not just walk into that crowd? They'll oblige you."

"And turn them into murderers? Besides, I would rather they think me dead or vanished than know what I have done and become." His eyes began to widen, as if he felt another change coming on. "Please! I'm not a crackpot." Eliezer caught the reference to the Lurianic creation myth. "Help me cease to be. To cease to be this." Haman raised his hands. "I want to be as stone, wizard, and change no more. Help me, wizard!" With that, he turned and faded into the shadow; a mouse emerged from the other side and raced down the street.

Eliezer returned to the Town Circle. He had never felt such despair. To be asked to kill a young man! and for violating the very laws Eliezer himself had broken. The people were still dancing into the wee hours, and in all their joy denouncing him who had frightened their children and broken their celebration. "This is a very happy and very sad city," he said. They had been assaulted by true and false evil, and had no power to fight it— only to spin their *gragger*s.

Melech expressed doubt about that.

"What power, friend? To tear apart a young man trapped in another's guise?"

Evening services had ended, but people remained in the Circle, celebrating or reviling. Children slept at their dancing parents' feet. The "Queen" — the "real" "Queen" (*oy*, his head hurt at the paradox!) — stepped forth from the crowd and stood before Eliezer, who dismounted and landed a bit hard on his even-worse leg. Now, he bowed low, showing respect for a monarch as real as anyone and anything in this city. For when it came to phony this and ersatz that, who was he to judge?

"What can you tell us, great wizard?"

"You have an academy for the study of Kabbalah."

"Yes, of course; we told you so earlier." So she had. "Our city is a great center of such learning. That is why we have never needed your assistance before. We are One."

"Have your students all been so devout?"

She thought for a moment, then said, "No. One lost his way, and disappeared."

"A shame. Tell me: what would you like for such a one?"

"Peace."

"Then help me find it for him."

Now her eyes widened, as realization (and, coincidentally, the sun) dawned. Golden light brightened the upper part of her face, and spread shining beams over the crowd. The "Queen" asked, "Is that who—?" And the way her eyes began to shine, he wondered if there was more going on here than the concern of a false monarch for one of "her" people. Perhaps he had said too much, or to the wrong person.

She looked up at him. "What must we do?"

4

And the king said unto Esther at the banquet of wine, What is thy petition? and it shall be granted thee: and what is thy request? even to the half of the kingdom it shall be performed.

Then answered Esther, and said, My petition and my request is;

If I have found favour in the sight of the king, and if it please the king to grant my petition, and to perform my request, let the king and Haman come to the banquet that I shall prepare for them, and I will do to morrow as the king hath said...

Then Esther the queen answered and said, If I have found favour in thy sight, O king, and if it please the king, let my life be given me at my petition, and my people at my request:

For we are sold, I and my people, to be destroyed, to be slain, and to perish...

And Esther said, The adversary and enemy is this wicked Haman. Then Haman was afraid before the king and the queen...

So they hanged Haman on the gallows that he had prepared for Mordecai. Then was the king's wrath pacified.

The people of the city, already gathered in the Circle, now formed a single ring around Eliezer and the town's rabbi. Behind him, Eliezer could feel the rabbi's impatience; it was soon time for morning services, and the second reading of the *Megillah*. But the Book of Esther would have to wait a few more minutes; and what were a few minutes for so long a tale? From his pouch Eliezer pulled the book that contained the secrets of the Kabbalah's magic, and from his mind he pulled the words that would link him into the One.

Both the cries against the demon and the noisemakers were silenced; now, the people would call as one for a more beneficial purpose. And so, they entered the Great Circle, with Eliezer as their conduit; through his magic they became a city of wizards. Melech stood apart, but that was only a formality. Like all the rest, in a sense both real and not, he wore a crown.

"We wish an end to suffering and to evil," Eliezer said. "We do not want evil among us."

Summoned by their repudiation, Haman walked from between the walls of the westernmost buildings. Even in the bright light of early dawn, he seemed as shadowed as he had last night.

"Come not among us!"

"Begone!"

The curses flew, but no one spoke his evil name. Eliezer silently pronounced his true name: Yacob. His ancient namesake also had a true, but different, name: Israel. He was the people and the heart of the people and the center of Adam Cadmon, the Primordial Man.

"Vile creature!"

"The would-be killer of men and women and children!"

And the more they cursed him, the more they condemned his evil, the closer he came to the center. He stood before Eliezer, closer now than ever, and Eliezer felt a chill shoot through him, like cold lightning.

"Stand still." Eliezer recited the letters: "*Aleph, raish, yud. Aleph, raish, yud.*" A-R-I. Then he turned to the crowd. "Bow your heads, and say the *brochah* on the beginning of Purim."

"Excuse me!" the rabbi said, obviously upset at being supplanted in his rightful duties.

"Forgive my presumption."

The rabbi led the blessing. And as all their heads were lowered — the "Queen"s, too, as she stood on "her" balcony — he transformed the Evil One. Eliezer could and would not kill him, but he could slow time for him. From a life of constant, unwilled, unwilling change, the young man would enjoy a comforting and refreshing stability; years would be as seconds, decades as minutes. Thus, when the people lifted their heads, they saw that in the midst of their city stood not a demon but what they would take to be a statue. From now on, their Town Circle would be graced with a supposedly artificial lion, roaring and reaching out a paw: honor the king, honor the crown, honor the father. And poor Yacob, in his slow movement and slow thinking, would seem to spend only a few moments in blissful solidity until whatever fate God had decreed for him, just as He threw the lots for all foolish mortals.

Eliezer gazed up into the "statue"s eye, and thought he saw a grateful twinkle.

Finally, and Eliezer considered it his greatest feat, the crowd was silent. Even the rabbi merely stared, forgetting for a moment to move on to the Purim hymn. The "Queen" broke the silence with a proclamation, probably the one and only of her reign: "On behalf of our people, we thank you and wish great blessings on you, great wizard."

"Thank you, Your 'Majesty.' Keep your statue protected; and by attending to it, you will keep its spirit alive forever." She seemed to understand. "*Oy, I need some sleep.*"

Melech, in a rare spirit of consensus, agreed wholeheartedly with the idea. *But first something to eat,* he insisted, as the soft-handed groom led him away.

Eliezer found his own way to his room. On his bedside table he found dishes: a ton of freshly cooked food, including some *hamantaschen* for dessert! and a dusty bottle of wine. Well, what was good for the horse was good for the rider.

Later, stuffed and perhaps a little dizzy, Eliezer undressed and slipped into bed, secure in the knowledge that no mouse, bidden or unbidden, would disturb him. He drifted off to sleep just as the first lines of the Story of Esther began to resound from the room's walls.

5

The Jews ordained, and took upon them, and upon their seed, and upon all such as joined themselves unto them, so as it should not fail, that they would keep these two days according to their writing, and according to their appointed time every year;

And that these days should be remembered and kept throughout every generation, every family, every province, and every city; and that these days of Purim should not fail from among the Jews, nor the memorial of them perish from their seed.

He awoke in the late afternoon. To be precise, he awoke for good in the late afternoon; he'd had to get up a few times to relieve himself, and have a little of the food from the platters that kept being replenished on his bedside table. He avoided the wine, however, fearing what he might see and hear.

Melech? Are you well?

He received an enthusiastic affirmative. Apparently the horse had not slept as long, and had had time to enjoy some of the day's festivities, although he wouldn't elaborate. *Nu?* Even a horse had some right to privacy.

Eliezer dressed, ate a bit more of those marvellous *hamantaschen* (divine!), and proceeded toward the throne room.

The round chamber was filled with royal hangers-on, but these were fatter and cleaner than the ones he'd seen before. As he moved to the front of the ivory throne, he saw that it was no longer occupied by the woman; instead, a man sat upon it, sporting a golden crown and a very familiar paunch....

The King smiled at Eliezer's appearance. "You are awake! We are King Isaac." *And father of Yacob, maybe?* "We thank and honor you for your service to our city," he said.

Eliezer bowed — good and *low* — and said, "My pleasure." Actually, his *duty*, but he might as well be generous in his sentiments. And he couldn't complain about the hospitality.

"Will you stay with us a few days?"

"No. Other people may get to enjoy their static condition; I'm afraid I do not have that luxury."

"Your horse will be brought forth, then." He made some signs, and one of his lackeys sped away. Meanwhile, a young woman came in delivering a bulging cloth sack and a plateful of delicacies for the king's enjoyment. He recognized her immediately: a suitably deferential and attractive maiden with slightly soiled fingernails. "We have prepared a parcel of nourishments to ease your journey, great wizard."

"Thank you, Your Majesty." The maiden handed him the sack, and Eliezer took his leave with another, even lower, bow.

Outside the palace, under the (truly) watchful eye of a far more fit-looking guard, he tied the sack to Melech's saddle, and hung his small embroidered pouch on its pommel. He waited for the horse to lower himself. Melech, engaging in a joke of his own, hesitated to do so, acting up even here at the palace gates. "Come on, Your 'Majesty'!" Eliezer said. At last Melech let him mount, and Eliezer said, "Well, you seem to be in a good mood this afternoon."

Melech said nothing. A few people followed them to the city doors and then out, and waved goodbye. Eliezer saluted them and headed into the desert. And where would he sleep tonight? He reached into the sack; it was filled with *hamantaschen*! He extracted the topmost and bit into one of its three corners; the prune filling squirted gloriously into his mouth.

"So? You're not going to tell me what you did all day?"

Well, Melech began, *to make a long story short* —

"If only," Eliezer said, "if only."

A Little Leavening

IT WAS ALL ABOUT POSITIONS.

When he lay on his back he'd choke, and be yanked from sleep as if he were having a heart attack. On his stomach, and he had no way to draw air into his lungs. If he lay on his side, it had to be on the right side, meaning his left side, and his arm had to be just so....

Melech put in a gentle but firm request for silence.

"So, who tells you to listen in on my thoughts?" Eliezer asked. He adopted his preferred position, tried to turn off his mind (a bit late for that now) and consciously drift into unconsciousness. But all those paradoxes defeated him. Surrendering to the power of his insomnia, he sat up on the woven straw mattress his hosts had provided and stared at the shed door. A shed — well, who was he to complain? Shelter was shelter. Soft pattering and swishing signalled the weather conditions. Melech was in the stable with his fellow equines, though they were incapable of being conversationalists at all, never mind good ones. Melech must have had a boring day.

At least both of them were out of the wind and rain.

"I can't afford this nonsense," Eliezer said. "We have to be on our way early tomorrow."

Melech again beseeched him for silence.

"Please! I wish I could be silent. We have to be in Barshalom by nightfall." For the next evening was the first *seder*, and while a bit of a *shmegeggi* the Prince was at least a good Jew. Eliezer had an open invitation to participate in the royal *Pesach* rites whenever he was in the neighborhood at that time. A chair was always saved for him. To be more precise, *another* chair.

"*Ach!*" Eliezer lay back down, shifted again, tried on his right side (the wrong side). Melech nearly shouted something on the order of "Shut up!" but restrained himself. With a final "*Gevalt*" Eliezer turned back to his left, concentrated on bitter herbs and shank bones, then finally cast a spell on himself as a last resort, hoping he wouldn't thereby cause himself to overs—

"Wizard?"

"*What?*" he shouted, and opened one eye. The farmer's boy stood over him, trembling as the little ones so often did in his presence. Eliezer wanted to throttle him, but then realized that the boy was partially silhouetted against the shed door. The sun was up, if veiled by clouds, meaning some hours had passed. "What is the time?" Eliezer asked in the boy's language, a quasi-Semitic tongue.

"I'm sorry?"

"The time, boy. How long has the sun been up?" Eliezer drew himself to a folded sitting position. Meanwhile, his bladder awoke, too.

"I don't know, sir."

"Never mind." He was sure that he still had plenty of time. But he didn't want to cut it too close… the shed door faced east, and the sun was nice and low. Melech grunted a confirmation; he had an equine sense about these things. "What do you want?"

"Wizard, the chickens, sir."

"*Oy*, what now?" He gathered his robes around him and prepared to stand. "Give me a moment, boy." When the child didn't budge, Eliezer added, but with a little, insincere smile, "Leave!" The boy smiled back, nodded, and exited the shed, giving Eliezer enough time to arrange himself properly, say a morning *brochah*, and make a quick dash to the outhouse next door.

No sooner did he emerge from the odorous stone structure than the farmer himself, a humble but relentless soul, approached him from the main house. "Wizard!" he called across the yard, as if Eliezer were on the other side of the country.

"Yes? Is breakfast ready?"

"Oh." The farmer — Gamel or Chamel or some such name — shook off the hint. "Not yet, not yet. The chickens are behaving badly."

"In other words, they're behaving like chickens." Despite being followed step-by-step, Eliezer went to the well and drew up a bucketful of water to splash on his face. "What is it?" he asked. A glance up told him the clouds were unthreatening; he'd have no problem riding to Barshalom.

"They aren't eating."

Neither am I, Eliezer thought, and Melech, eavesdropping as always, snorted.

"Please."

Eliezer sighed expressively ("Haven't I done enough for you people already?") and said, "Fine." Of course, for the sake of amusement he could metamorphose into a chicken, then infiltrate the brood and ask them face-to-face what was bothering them. But the only one who would get a laugh from the scene would be the horse. With as little visible urgency as he could exhibit, he went over to where the chickens milled about, staring at, cocking their heads at, scraping at, but not touching their feed.

The farmer was right behind him, watching intently, head cocked forward, boots scraping at the dirt... Eliezer fought down the choking urge to release impolite sounds through his nose, and adopted a serious pose.

"Is this the same grain you always use?"

"Yes."

"Distributed by the same family member?"

"Yes."

"At the same time of day?"

"Maybe a little later." He wouldn't say why someone had lolled in bed a tad later than usual.

"Chickens are stupid creatures. Creatures of habit perturbed by disruptions to their routine." Eliezer thought up a spell that would rob the chickens of a few moments of their lives— not exactly forgetfulness, since chicken brains lacked a sizeable capacity for memory, but a slight adjustment of their bodily clocks. He tapped into the Timeless One, the Governor of the hours, and reversed the damage done to the chickens' delicate psychology. Within seconds, they began pecking at the ground, sucking up the tiny pellets.

"A miracle!" the farmer cried. "You are a wondrous wizard!"

"Of course. Now—"

"The goat."

And so it went. A milking problem here, a smell problem there (how else should a pig smell? A disgusting, *trafe* pig?), and all over the farm the aches and pains that were the inevitable legacy of such labor (what did these people expect? unstrained muscles?). The sun rose higher in the sky, and seemed to burn deeper into the back of his neck with every inch it ascended.

Finally the breakfast came, served in the farmhouse's main room once the area had been made clear for the old door now enlisted as a table. The round hole where the knob had been now acted as a well for the jug of recently harvested milk. Fresh biscuits, a small tin tub of scrambled eggs, some bacon he passed on with a flourish of disgust, and a bowl of some kind of meal complete with bran that he very much appreciated. He ate well, but quickly, because he needed to leave soon, very soon.

Once filled to capacity, he sat back and remained so, smiling, as long as he thought was suitably polite: about twenty seconds. "Wonderful, wonderful," he said. "A breakfast fit for a wizard. And now—"

"My roof," the farmer said, his face contorted into an apologetic yet triumphant smile.

But—*!* He'd be late for the *seder*; he'd be late for the *service*; he'd be late for *Pesach*! "I—" It was a theological conundrum: he was obliged by his curse to help all who sought his assistance, yet he was obliged as a Jew to observe *Pesach*. Especially First *Seder*; Second *Seder* was important, yes, but still only Second. After all, wasn't this *yom tov* all about escaping slavery? "Sorry, but I—"

"It's beginning to leak again."

Eliezer sent an appeal to Melech, who of course had no answers for him. Sometimes an equine perspective offered an angle Eliezer hadn't thought of. Not this time. "And can you not repair it yourself? The Lord helps those who help themselves."

"If only I could."

"Our neighbors made it," the farmer's plain, quiet wife added; how did she suddenly find her voice? "They used bad material."

"I fix it," the farmer explained, "it starts to leak again. No use." At Eliezer's look, he continued, "I'll replace it all one day. But, well, you know."

"As long as I'm here, eh?" Such *chutzpah*. It would serve him right if Eliezer converted the entire roof into salt. One good rain, and... instead, he cast a spell on the upper half of the farmhouse that would repel water entirely. For a month.

At last, it appeared that the farmer's catalogue of tasks was completed. Before he could say another word, Eliezer summoned Melech, who marched in stately fashion from his stall in the barn and prepared to accept his saddle and human burden. Eliezer began his usual speech to the farmer: *it has been my duty to use my powers to assist you, and a* mitzvah *besides, and you have repaid me in room and board as required, so I bid adieu in the name of God,* etc.

"Great wizard!" resounded behind him. Eliezer was about to turn around to see the source of the gruff address, when he saw the farmer curl his face in the same half-smile, then add a shrug to his expression. "My neighbor...."

· ✡ ·

As the sun rose, his hopes sank; and when the lamp of day stood at its zenith, Eliezer's spirit reached its nadir. For now there would be no time to travel to Barshalom in time for the *seder* unless, perhaps, Melech suddenly sprouted wings... the horse, listening in as always, immediately rejected the idea. Such a coward— but it was true that Melech was no Pegasus. Then, the tasks begged of him by the many villagers took him into the middle of the afternoon, so that even a magic carpet, even a speedy metamorphosis into a bird (and leave Melech behind?), would not have helped.

He was doomed.

He felt waves of sympathy, and apparently sincere sympathy, not mocking pity, flow from Melech's mind to his own. Melech could well understand Eliezer's plight, for the horse felt the same about every assignment, every visit to a distant village, every offer of work-for-board. Eliezer now understood better than ever before how fully Melech was an entirely unwilling participant in these journeys and tasks. No one had ever asked him if he *wanted* to join Eliezer in his circuits; no one had given him any choice at all. A true beast of burden, with no hope of an exodus....

Well, at least the villagers fed Eliezer a substantial and delectable lunch. Meats spiced to arouse, not burn, the tongue; soft bread-rolls he could not get enough of, especially today when they might be his last such leavened treats for a long time; a tangy paste of sesame and olive oil; all clearly, if not truly kosher, at least non-*trafe*.

That afternoon, while he was in the middle of his depressing ruminations about missing First Seder, Melech asked Eliezer if these people could cook food.

"What?" Eliezer said aloud. Had the horse *not* been eavesdropping for a change? "Of course they can." He was in the process of repairing the damage done to a villager's soil by some subterranean pests. Holes everywhere. The villager looked at him as if the sun had addled what was left of his old brains.

Melech then asked Eliezer if these people could bake.

"Such a question! Wondrously well. Why? Are you hungry? Suddenly you want your hay in pastry form?"

"Wizard?" the villager asked, his face pale, eyes wide open; he'd been in the middle of pointing out another hole in his precious dirt, and the index finger froze in position. The churl was probably thinking he'd have to run for help.

"Mind your own business," Eliezer said to him. "Am I talking to you?"

The reply was an open mouth. The index finger budged not.

Ah! So that was what was on Melech's scheming mind. Such a smart horse! "Of course, my friend. The Lord wants nothing more than to see His holy day, His blessed *yom tov*, celebrated by a bunch of *goyim*!" What was the matter with the four-legged fool? "Are you crazy?"

The villager's mouth smacked shut. The index finger remained in its original position.

Melech reminded him where the original Passover was celebrated, and Eliezer realized he had no more arguments to offer. Was a village of Gentiles really a worse site for this important Jewish holy feast than a desert?

Eliezer finished applying his mole-repellent spell, then turned to the motionless villager and said, "I must speak with your head-man." No reply. "What, are you deaf? I'm talking to you! Chief, Lord, King, whatever he is who rules you!" The villager blinked when he finally caught on that he was the one being addressed, then nodded, then ran village-ward.

"You aren't being serious, are you?" Eliezer asked Melech. Although they communicated mind to mind, this was one time when Eliezer could not hold his tongue. "Hold a *seder* here?"

Melech said nothing, imitating the villager's muteness at the least opportune time; Eliezer was beginning to suspect that Melech had made the outrageous suggestion solely to derive some amusement from what was bound to happen next. For Melech, humans were of no value except as a limitless source of entertainment.

· ✡ ·

To his dismay, Eliezer was brought before Gamel or Chamel. Perhaps his command of these people's language was weak, and they thought he wanted to return to the first man he'd worked for. The peasant was still smiling his foolish smile as Eliezer asked to see the village's mayor, beadle, suzerain, master....

"We decide," Hamel replied. "What do you wish?" he added with a difficult-to-read expression. Suspicion? A shrewd hope he'd get more magic out of Eliezer?

"I was to attend an important meal today," Eliezer explained slowly, trying to find the right words to convey the importance of the ritual. "For my faith. We must all eat such a meal. It is God's will. But it has to be done correctly."

"Yes." By now a crowd had gathered; maybe the others had finally realized that they had enjoyed the benefits of his services essentially for free, and felt they owed him. "What do you need, wizard?" the farmer asked, actual concern on his face. Maybe he, maybe they all, really wanted to help.

"Well." How to explain? "Certain foods. A fresh set of dishes, preferably unused. Wine." Chemal's son hovered nearby, watching the scene with fascination and perhaps trepidation. "Oh, and the boy."

Now it was Camal's turn to gape at him.

Before the poor fool could say a word, Eliezer said, "He must sing." That did not seem to reassure the father. "I will teach him what to sing." To paraphrase: why is this *Pesach* different from all other *Pesachs*? "Introduce me to your cooks and bakers. This is going to be very complicated."

And so he met the village's tradesmen; the men seemed eager to face, even to relish, the challenges he presented. And he met wives, all put forward as the best chefs in the village. But how to explain?

He spoke to the baker and his assistant, two men as fat as their profession would lead one to expect. "I need you to make bread without leavening agents."

"What?" the flour-dusted men asked in near-unison.

"Flour and water. Flatten the dough and bake it. It doesn't matter what shape." Occasionally, Eliezer could summon visuals, air pictures, and he tried to raise a portrait of a *matzoh* in the shimmering desert air before them. They looked highly skeptical, as if he'd failed to get the image right. "Unleavened bread. Very important."

"When does the yeast go in?" the baker asked, and his assistant nodded. "We won't have time—"

"It doesn't!" Eliezer sighed deeply, summoning all his patience. *Goyische kopf!* "Flour. Water. Maybe an egg to soften it, at least a few of those." He remembered as a child eating egg *matzoth*, which he slathered with cherry preserves... his mother let him waste so much on the golden brown squares, those *matzoth* that looked so large back then.

"You," he said to the butcher, "a shank bone." More puzzlement, till he specified and outlined.

"I need bitter herbs," he told one of the wives, a short round woman suffering her own infestation of moles. He remembered his first encounter with horseradish as a boy, his incredulity that anyone would want to eat something so profoundly awful. And now it brought delightful tingles to his tongue. "Something that will bring tears to the eyes."

"Ask Beliya," the woman replied, pointing to a female opposite her. "Her cooking always makes men weep."

Eliezer beat a hasty retreat just as the altercation began. He went up to the farmer's son, put his hand on the lad's shoulder, and said, "Come with me. We don't have much time."

The boy looked back at the crowd, seeking out his father for rescue, but none would come. They would have to work fast, for the sun was already halfway down the western quadrant of the sky, threatening to drop like a flaming boulder. Eliezer looked straight up and engaged in another paraphrase, this time of the heretics' great line of scripture:

"Forgive me, Lord, for I know not what I am doing."

· ✡ ·

"Now, child," Eliezer said, "what is your name?"

"Shimo," the trembling young thing replied.

"Shimo!" Eliezer tried to adopt a comforting smile. Suddenly he was a rabbi, and he recalled the gaunt rabbi who had taught him, many years ago. "My father's name was Shimon," he lied, but did not get the response he'd hoped for. "You must ask me questions." Shimo looked very puzzled, then seemed to be trying to think of something to ask. "No, no, I will tell you what to ask." That only confused the lad more. "I will teach you the questions you must ask. Now, listen:

"*Mah nishtanah halailah hazeh, mikol halaylot?*" Shimo's eyes merely widened— such an unattractive facial reaction! "Hm?" Nothing. "It means, 'Why is this night different from all other nights?' It is the first question that the youngest boy must ask at the *seder*. Then follow four more specific questions. All right, repeat after me. *Mah nishtanah ha—*"

"I don't understand this, wizard," came a high-pitched voice from behind him. Was the boy a ventriloquist? Eliezer turned and saw the farmer's wife, the boy's mother, holding out an earthenware bowl with some supposedly edible material inside. "Is this what you want?"

"Is this the *charoset*?" She had blended unidentifiable fruit slices and what looked like peach pits together into something colorful but nowhere near what was called for in the recipe. "*Oy!* Madam, the dish is supposed to represent the mortar and clay with which our people constructed Pharaoh's temple, in our time of oppression and bondage. This looks more like the bricks." He had told her the recipe earlier, but repeated it: "Apples. Nuts. Maybe pomegranate. Cinnamon. Wine." Unfortunately, he did not know the words in their language for pomegranate and cinnamon. Another exhibition of the whites of the eye as the Hebrew words washed over her.

"We have no apples. We have figs."

"Pears? A nice peach?"

"Figs."

"Do the best you can." He turned back to the child. "Nah. Repeat after me: *Ma nishtanah halailah hazeh, mikol halaylot?*" Silence. "*Mah nishtanah*: why doth differ; *halailah hazeh*: this night; *mikol halaylot*: from all other nights. So, repeat after me: *Mah nishtanah*."

"*Mah shintanah.*"

"*Mah nishtanah.*"

"*Mah nishtashnah.*"

Gevalt! "*Mah.*"

"*Mah.*"

"*Nishtanah.*"

"*Nishtanah.*"

"*Mah nishtanah.*"

"*Mah shintanah.*"

Eliezer looked down upon him with pity. How sad: the boy was clearly a moron.

They went over the words — never mind the tune! — again and again. Shimo could recite the individual parts, but put them into any combination and the result was disastrous. During the eighth or ninth try at the final two words, their lesson was interrupted when a black disk was thrust before his eyes. At first he thought it was a part from some machine, an iron gear, but then he turned to see that it was the baker whose hand held the thing. *Oy, Gott!* Behind him, the assistant awaited with something bordering on terror.

"*How much* flour?" the baker asked. His tone suggested this was not the first of his experimental efforts. "*How much* water?"

The charred catastrophe beneath his nose was too much to bear. "How should I know? I'm a wizard, not a baker!" Eliezer spun around toward the boy once more, dismissing the two fools with a display of his back. Beside his face, the disk hovered for a few seconds more, then withdrew. "You're the baker; you figure it out." Melech, still ensconced in his stall, said, *Temper, temper.* "And who are you to talk?" Eliezer shouted in the barn's direction. "This was *your* idea!"

The boy seemed about to get up and leave, but Eliezer intercepted him with a sharp, "Again!" This time he repeated the whole line in song form, hoping maybe the tune would attract Shimo on a less purely intellectual level. But as Eliezer sang, the boy began to cringe as if he'd seen, or maybe heard, a monster. So much for that.

Was it too much to ask? For the child to learn one question, just one introductory line (he didn't even want to think about the other four questions!); for a proper *charoset*; for a shank-bone, maybe from one of those now-well-fed chickens; for proper *matzoth*!

"*Chometz!*" The lightning bolt hit him, and he moaned in pain. The house was full of bread, whether as rolls or crumbs. "Listen, boy. Boy!" Shimo stared up at him. "Do you have friends? Sisters?" He remembered there being a young woman in the household, maybe a sibling or a servant. "Anything?" A nod. "Summon the other children, servants. I'm not going to try to teach anyone else the questions, because there's no time; you're as close to knowing it as anyone. But I need you to get a team together. Do you know what I mean?"

"No," came through trembling lips.

"I need your house to be utterly devoid of leavened bread. Find every scrap, every crumb, gather it together and throw it into the fire. Do. You. Understand?"

"No."

"Go get your mother."

And he knew what would happen. The farmer and his wife would express outrage that he was planning to root out and destroy all the bread they owned. He would offer to pay them, maybe with some free magic another time, or a few coins if they preferred. But the sun was nearly down, and there was practically no time left to purify the house, rid it of every vestige of leavened baked goods. God would have to understand: he was doing his best. And if it wasn't enough? He was a wizard, not a miracle worker.

Not a baker. Not a (God forbid!) woman. Not a cook, or a farmer, or a rabbi.

The boy returned with his mother, and Eliezer explained what needed to be done, and every time she tried to interrupt he spoke over her, telling her his God would be angry with him if there was a speck of leavened material, a tiny crumb, a shadow of such material, in the house during the *seder*. She left, uncertainly, to assemble her army of cleaners, and Eliezer made the boy sit down again.

"*Mah nishtanah halailah hazeh.*"

"*Mah shintanah halayza....*"

Oy gevalt.

To his amazement, at sundown, something like a seder setting appeared on the tablecloth covering the door/dining-room table. A new set of dishes had been borrowed from one of the villagers, and, in the center of the table, was a large round plate that had been divided into sections with strips of unglazed, unfired, still-wet clay. No matter! In each section was the right consumable, or something like it: a chicken's drumstick; a hard-boiled, roasted egg; a small bowl of horseradish (or at least the local equivalent— he could smell it from here); the *charoset*, still adulterated with figs but at least there were real nuts, almonds, in it; some edible stalks for dipping in the salt-water; and some edible leaves to be the *chazeret*. A tin cup held the salt-water, and others stood at the various places around the table to hold the wine. In the distance stood pots of the feast itself, the mounds of food to be served after the ritual itself was done.

"Oh," he said to the wife, who was sweating profusely from her efforts. "Another setting, please."

"But—"

"One more. For the prophet." She obtained a stool from one of her neighbors, and squeezed it into one corner of the table; Eliezer secured a precious glass goblet, one of the few in the village, for the place setting. Then those who had been invited to participate, all who had helped make the *seder* possible, were summoned, and they arrived in ones and twos, gradually filling up the farmer's house. Meanwhile, servant girls from various homes stood by the walls holding the hand-washing pails. Eliezer glanced over at the small fire the farmer's wife had made in the hearth, and hoped every morsel of unholy bread was being vaporized even as he watched.

For the twentieth time, Eliezer studied the table; everything was in place so far, except for the *matzoh*. Eliezer pulled his *Haggadah* from the pouch that ever flapped at his side, and turned to the pages beyond the color illustration of the proper *seder* plate, to where the beginning of the *seder* ceremony was outlined. As the family members and guests arrived, he read in a subdued voice the first blessing, so as not to waste time.

Just as he was preparing to recite the last of the preliminary *brochah*s, to thank God for keeping him alive long enough to reach another *Pesach*, the baker entered bearing the *matzoh*, which he'd wrapped in linen. What would it look like? Metal? Wood? With the blank expression of the exhausted in his eyes, the hefty baker laid the bundle on the table and with some ceremony, unveiled the fruits — well, breads — of his labor:

A stack of partly burned, barely matzoh-like ridged wheels. Eliezer felt like grieving, but merely sighed. They would do; they would have to. Eliezer re-covered them, biting his lower lip instead of shaking his head, because he didn't want to give the baker too clear a sign of his unhappiness. At least the men had tried. Although God punished those who tried to do the impossible....

"Come, be seated," he said to the baker and his assistant. "Come, everyone! Be seated." His calculations had been exact as to the number of people attending; there were proper chairs for everyone. But the assistant planted himself firmly on the stool, apparently imagining he had earned a special place near Eliezer. "Not there!" At the assistant's wounded expression, Eliezer said, "No one must sit there."

The farmer's family and the villagers hustled and bustled, bumped into each other and argued as they took up places around

the table. Every time Eliezer's back was turned, trying to organize the unorganizable, someone would plunk himself down
on Elijah's stool. "No!" Shimo sat at the other end of the table,
blinking rapidly. Exhausted himself, Eliezer dropped on to the
chair at the head of the table, as much to guard the stool beside
him as to lead the service. He slapped his hands against his face,
and gently rubbed his eyelids with his palms.

He had the participants wash their hands, then took a piece
of the celery, or whatever local vegetable was standing in for the
karpas, and dipped it in the salt-water.

"*Baruch atoh adonai elohaynu melech ha'olam....*" Melech: the
celery looked like the sort of thing the horse would love. Too
bad, my friend, Eliezer thought; stay in your barn! Melech would
be able to watch the ritual unfold from a distance, by looking
through Eliezer's eyes; it would serve him right to be able to
see but not taste the only thing on the plate he might actually
want to eat. Serve him right for coming up with this crazy plan.

He re-uncovered the *matzoh* and spoke aloud, following the
text in the *Haggadah*. With fear and trepidation, he pulled a
matzoh from the middle of the stack, and broke it in half. So
far so good. Would he bother with hiding the *afikoman*? Or was
that a game for Jewish children only? Maybe he should leave
that part out— for now, he would be lucky to get through the
basics. As he read the passage, declaring in a language no one
else understood (except Melech) that now they were slaves but
soon would be free, he surreptitiously crushed one corner the
matzoh between his fingers. The right texture, at least.

Then it was time. "Shimo? You have something to ask?"

With a shivering voice, the boy intoned, "*Mah shintanah halaizah
hameh, michol halaykol?*"

"*Oy vey iz mir!*" Eliezer shouted, then lowered his head and
slapped his forehead again and again with both hands. "Do I
have to ask it myself? I'm a wizard, not some little *putz*!" When
he looked up again, he saw that the boy was on the verge of tears,
and his father, sitting beside him, looked slightly homicidal.
Out of the corner of his eye, Eliezer could see that yet again the
stool was occupied. He turned to face the intruder. "And how
often do I have to t—!"

Eliezer knew immediately that the man seated to his right
was no farmer, no villager. The white hair, the full white beard,

the ancient-looking robes that gleamed as if they'd been dyed in sunlight… the visitor reached for the glass of wine, raised it to his lips, and took a sip, making a little moue in the process. "Not as sweet as I'm used to," he pronounced, "but not bad." Then he turned toward Eliezer. His eyes shone like those of the being — angel or prophet, archangel or other messenger — who had come to Eliezer so long ago to tell him of God's punishment for his sin of poking around in mysteries that were none of his business. Eliezer would henceforth have to serve any who asked, using the powers he had gained to help them. No choice.

"Are you… *him*?" A quick glance around the table made it clear that Eliezer was the only one who could see the visitor. No one else looked at the being seated on the stool. In fact, no one seemed to move at all.

The visitor did not even so much as blink as he stared at — *into* — Eliezer. "Suddenly you can ask questions?"

"Well."

"And sometimes you ask too many, or you wouldn't be here. I have a question for you: *Who do you think you are?*" Elijah scanned the table. "'Great wizard'!" he snorted. "Maybe with your magic you could have fashioned perfect *matzoth*. Perfect *charoset*. But you're no cook." In a mocking imitation of Eliezer, he said, "I'm a wizard, not a baker!"

"I."

"It's all a matter of positions, eh? What's your position? 'Great Wizard'? Maybe I should lend you something for your bed-time reading. The Book of Job." Elijah waved his hand to dismiss the idea. "Nah, too obvious." He took another sip. "Perhaps you've forgotten why we came up with this holiday." Elijah leaned toward him and shot him a sharp look. "Hm? And don't give me any of that 'old head' nonsense of yours." The prophet smiled. "I'm a bit older even than you. Well? Don't you have something to ask?"

"Ask?"

Eliezer lowered his eyes for just a second. (Dare he ask what he really wanted to ask? *Have you come to tell me it's all over, that I'm free?*) That was all the time needed for the stool to become empty. Eliezer swallowed his shame and gazed at the boy across from him. "*Mah nishtanah halailah hazeh,*" Eliezer sang, a boy again, "*mikol halaylot?*" Why indeed? Before asking the Four Questions that arose from the first, before answering his own questions — the brief version of the answer; they were all hungry — he said,

"Perhaps one of you could release my horse from his prison. He might like a little of what you have prepared here, too."

Melech thanked him.

"This is the greatest *seder* I have ever attended," Eliezer said to the gathered congregation. The baker, his assistant, and a few women broke into self-satisfied grins— even the boy, to whom Eliezer transmitted a special nod, managed a little smile. "Now I will ask the other questions in your own tongue. And then I will tell you a story of slavery and liberation, and explain why this night is different from all other nights."

· ✡ ·

The next morning, Eliezer awoke at dawn. Or at least, he awoke for good at dawn, after a typical number of nocturnal interruptions. He still couldn't manage to find the best way to lie on his straw mattress, and to stay that way for an entire night.

This day, there would be no mistakes, no delays; he would travel to Barshalom immediately, arrive in plenty of time for Second *Seder*, and if anyone tried to detain him he would promise to return after Passover to fulfill all requests. He felt too drowsy to work much magic, anyway.

But most of the village was asleep. Only the farmer and his family, who had once more accommodated him and Melech, were also awake. The boy stood beside his mother, still wearing his nightshirt and barely able to keep his eyes open. Eliezer held out his hand, and the boy took it. "You are a fine questioner," Eliezer said. "But let me give you some advice: be careful what questions you ask; you might not really want to know the answers."

The farmer brought Melech around; the horse looked to be in fine condition, even recently brushed. "You're well?" Eliezer asked, and Melech nodded.

Eliezer climbed up into the saddle as quickly as he could, given the usual morning aches and pains. The farmer held Melech's bridle, as if that were needed.

"And you?" the farmer asked him. "Did you have a good night's sleep?"

"*Mah nishtanah halailah hazeh, mikol halaylot?*" Eliezer asked. Only Melech and the boy laughed.

So be it.

OF THE LAW

ELIEZER KNEW THERE was something wrong when Melech fell utterly silent. On the dusty verge of the ancient town of Ashobah, Eliezer's mount, friend, and adviser ceased to be his usual chatty self, even to *kvetch* at another mysterious summons.

"So," he said out loud, "nothing on your mind?"

Melech did not reply for quite some time. Finally, he said, *There's something here*, his tone as ominous as his words. Then, nothing.

Eliezer was well aware of Melech's ability to sense spiritual wrong, and readied himself to face trouble; on the other hand, he couldn't help being annoyed at the lack of specifics. He steered the horse (as best he could, given the ache in his wrist today) toward the town, where a delegation of five old men in vari-colored robes awaited him before the perfectly round temple. Each High Priest wore a garment of a distinct hue: a nice bright blue one at the far left end, a shimmering red one at the right, a gleaming white one in the middle, while the others wore green and butter-yellow. The robes hung loosely on their withered human shapes. Something had inspired dour expressions, fur-rowed brows, and narrowed eyes above their long, narrow silver beards; something had provoked a compulsive shifting of weight from foot to foot. Instead of exuding confidence, as officials should, these beings were human embodiments of pure fear. "So these are the great leaders who summoned us?" Eliezer asked as he approached the colorful greeting party, but even that instigating query drew no response from Melech. "*Ach*!" he said. "Fine. Don't talk."

"Greetings to you," said the Priest in white, the tallest, best-bearded fellow: Huyag the Chief Priest. Eliezer remembered him from his last visit here many years ago, when he'd been asked to repair some city equipment. Sewer pipes, of all things. "Please help us, O Wizard of the People of the Law!"

"Greetings to you," Eliezer replied. Melech trotted to within a few feet of the ancient Chief Priest, and Eliezer looked down from his perch into the man's gray eyes. Last time, only Huyag had greeted him; such a turnout of silverbeards meant something was up. "So, your boy came to summon me." Interrupting Eliezer's precious sleep in the process, and on a day he was so greatly looking forward to rest. "You have a problem, then?"

The Chief Priest raised his arm, and the sleeve as it fell away exposed a bony hand. "Come with us, and I will tell you all." The multi-colored greeters separated themselves into two ranks, flanking Eliezer and Melech as they followed the Chief Priest up the sloping street toward the House of the Priests, which overlooked the town. Once they were past, the High Priests formed their single rank behind them and followed. The sandstone houses were just as Eliezer remembered them: of largely uniform shape, but painted in many different hues. Huyag's residence and headquarters stood on a slight but, given the area's general flatness, definite rise.

And as far as Eliezer could remember, the people, if they rode at all, rode camels and the occasional ass. He asked, "Have you a stable suitable for my steed?"

"Of course," the Chief Priest said over his shoulder.

Eliezer dismounted, and the same boy who had delivered Huyag's message to him — a starved-looking lad in a multi-hued striped robe (a novice, presumably) — took Melech's bridle and led him away behind the House. After a few moments, Melech said, *I'm not alone.* Were there other horses here? That raised an interesting question, one that Eliezer had never considered before: how did Melech communicate with his fellow equines?

"Good," Eliezer subvocalized. "So you won't be lonely." To Huyag he said, "And he will be well provisioned?"

"As well as we can manage. We know our duty to you and yours." Eliezer did not have to go through the routine, then, about the expected payment of room and board for his assistance. "But," Huyag continued, "we cannot give what we do not have." Eliezer asked Melech silently how he was doing, and the horse confirmed the sparseness of his lunch. Eliezer rolled his eyes; they'd had a good breakfast! Well, could one really describe a horse as a pig (*feh!*)? He realized that Huyag was still speaking: "We remember your earlier visit, and how your meals are to be prepared." Good— the rules of kosher were often difficult to explain to the *goyim*. "I just hope they will be enough to earn your assistance, wizard!"

"You know that I must help you in any way that I can."

"But can you?" Huyag stopped just before the House. "We know little of the extent of your powers." The boy returned and rushed into the House.

Eliezer shrugged. "I do what the Lord requires and permits. I have power over the shape of nature, although of course to create or destroy life is the prerogative of God alone. I can cast spells, but only to achieve virtuous ends." He pointed a warning finger at the Chief Priest, just to drive home the point. "No funny business!"

"Please!" Huyag replied without rancor. "What do you take me for?"

"Also, I must work fast. Tonight is *shabbos*." A time of enforced rest— he would have to perform his task before sundown.

Inside the House, the High Priests took up positions on either side of the door while Huyag assumed his throne: a wood-and-stone structure shimmering with streaks of jasper, onyx, and carnelian. Such consciousness of and devotion to color! The boy fetched a chair from against the whitewashed wall. Huyag motioned Eliezer to take a seat, and the *goyische* Joseph held the chair for him as he lowered himself to its soft cushion. It felt good to sit on something more accommodating than a saddle!

"Wizard," Huyag began, "how much do you know of our religion?" Last time, they'd discussed drainage, not theology. At Eliezer's head-shake, Huyag continued, "We are the people of the Gods of the Colors." *No kidding!* "In the days of the Grandfathers, all the Gods were one and shone with a glorious emanation throughout the universe." Huyag paused, as if waiting for signs of recognition from Eliezer. As if everyone should know such myths! And yet…. "Then at the Creation they divided into the Gods of the Light and the Gods of the Darkness; the Gods of the Colors of light shine from the sky above, while the Gods of the Colors of darkness have opposed them from below. When the Gods of the Colors of light manifest themselves after bringing nourishment to the soil, we praise them and give thanks. You have no knowledge of this?"

Eliezer nodded this time. "We have a different idea, but not so different." He then told Huyag the Torah story about Noah and the Ark, about the conquest of evil and the triumph of good in the working out of God's wrath, and the covenant painted in the sky. "The rainbow tells us there shall never be another Flood," Eliezer said, "although how the Lord will deal with our current wickedness is anyone's guess."

"So. Sometimes, one of the Gods of the Colors of darkness rises from below the ground and haunts our world, killing our beasts, poisoning our crops, trying to bring the darkness to the land. Strange things have been happening, Wizard. Crops die in the fields; beasts die in the pastures; even our food rots in the pan. Drought, starvation. We think one of the Gods has come to us from the dark, and has taken up residence somewhere, or in something— perhaps one of our animals."

A demon: something from Shekhina's realm, from the *sitra ahra*, the "other side": a spirit from the place from which God had withdrawn while limiting his light in the days of creation.... He asked Melech a vague question, mind-to-mind, to confirm what Huyag had said. Melech, exercising his very strong sensitivity to the presence of dark spirits, confirmed again that something nasty was indeed present. Mainly, though, the horse seemed to be obsessed with his empty belly.

"And you want me to do what?" Eliezer asked Huyag. "Exorcise it?"

"Yes. Find it and send it back to its home beneath the Earth."

"A simple task," Eliezer said, carefully keeping his tone from crossing the line from irony to sarcasm. How do you find and expel a demon, all in the space of a few hours at most? He'd need a guide, someone with a sensitivity to the presence of evil.

Melech, he thought, *I'll need your nose.*

· ✡ ·

The Priests lodged Eliezer in a comfortable room in the House, to the rear and not far from some neighboring homes of the lesser classes; the room featured a good bed, a small dining alcove decorated with splotches of various tints in a dizzying collage, and private personal facilities that were important to a man of his age. Stained glass filled the broad window frames, dyeing the plentiful sunlight as it streamed into the chamber. Melech reported equally pleasant accommodations in a camel stable just down the "hill."

Not long after he settled in, "Joseph" entered with a lunch of bread and cheese; meanwhile, Melech said he'd been fed out of the camels' bin, some odd mixture of dates and wheat, and found it nearly inedible. It wasn't like him to complain — at least, about food; he was perfectly capable of complaining about everything else — and Eliezer was truly sorry that fate (and his own curse) had dragged them here, in the midst of a famine. "I'll make it up to you, my friend," he said. Hay: that was what Melech craved, but where could one obtain it if not in a stable? Still, the horse was ready for duty, and when Eliezer summoned him Melech appeared forthwith in front of the House. Huyag was away, perhaps tending to his false-believing flock, so Eliezer climbed upon Melech's back (with a little help from the novice) and let the horse's sixth sense guide them.

It was a town of strange yet beautiful sights. Eliezer remembered from his earlier visits that the streets were kept well cleaned despite the hosts of animals populating them. Goats, camels, asses, chickens, a few sheep, and of course the pigs that seemed to be unavoidable in *goyische* villages, all roamed about or remained uncomplainingly in their pens. Townspeople led their dogs or goats or humped mounts through the streets; those who were doing their marketing or trading or selling had piled half-empty bags of goods on their beasts, and Eliezer knew that Melech envied his fellow animals' relatively lighter, and more importantly silent, burdens. It couldn't have been pleasant even for such a complainer to carry around an old *kvetch* like himself.

"So, my friend, what do you smell?"

Something is very wrong here, Melech replied.

"I know that. But where?"

Melech stopped before a large wooden structure squeezed between an apothecary shop and a smith's, and stared inside. Through the open door Eliezer could see mostly empty bins of diverse cereals, including one of oats. The horse turned his head as far as he could to look up at Eliezer— and his expression could only be described as begging.

"What? Are you serious?" Well, Eliezer had a few coins, of course. Perhaps he could negotiate with the owner for a little snack…. "Hello!" No answer. With a profound "*Oy!*" Eliezer dragged his aching bones off the steed and entered the feed store, if that was what it was. "Excuse me! Hello?" Nothing. Nobody. "Maybe later, Melech, eh?" But there was no hint of patience or forbearance in Melech's eyes. "Now? Seriously?" When Eliezer tried to mount him again, Melech shied. "Come on, don't be ridiculous."

Just a little. You can pay for it later.

"*Gevalt!*" It was true, though; in fact, it was the owner's own fault for not being around when customers called. "All right, but just this once." No feed bags to be found, and nothing quite right among Eliezer's current equipment. Perhaps a little magic— he scooped some dust from the road, and with a few words he fashioned a kind of bowl held together only by his spell, but strong enough to hold some kernels. He trickled a handful of oats into it and held it out for the horse to lip it up. "There you go."

Very nice! Waves of satisfaction flowed from Melech's mind to Eliezer's.

"It had better be. What, *more?*" As he sprinkled a few more grains into the bowl he approximated in his mind how much he had taken. At so many shekels per pound, yet considering that he'd had to serve himself, plus an additional few pennies for the sake of earning and maintaining some goodwill.... "All right! I'm made of clay, like these houses, not money!" And considering the people might have to pay a tithe, as so many *goyim* did, and more importantly had little enough for themselves, it wasn't right to deplete their meagre supply.

Enough, Melech finally said. His head jerked up. *There!*

"Where?" With a valiant effort, Eliezer remounted the horse, distintegrated the bowl (ashes to ashes, dust to dust, the pot cracked again!), and let Melech aim himself where he needed to go. At the northern edge of the town was the daily market — not to be confused with the much bigger weekly market held in the center — where a person could obtain basic everyday needs. Melech trotted directly for it. "There? Really?" And thinking about days and weeks reminded him of a salient fact. Sunset loomed, and if he didn't accomplish his task before sunset, he and the Priests would have to wait a full day before he could work again. And if it was true that a demon was loose in town, better to get rid of it sooner rather than later.

It's here! Melech nearly mind-screamed, so agitated was he by the presence of evil.

"All right. So show me." Melech took him into and through the north market square. A few merchants stood at their booths, hawking fruits and vegetables, animals for slaughter, lengths of cloth and sewing supplies, even some scrolls. A literate people, then, although of course nothing like the People of the Book! Melech wandered up and down the rows, sniffing here and there, stopping at some of the animals to gaze and ponder. *Nu?*

One of them..., Melech said, his voice uncertain, hesitant, *but I don't know which one.*

"You're sure at the market?"

Yes. But not this one.

Then at the weekly market— but that was held, if memory served, on just the one wrong day: tomorrow.

Shabbos.

"If you're right, and I'm sure you are, we're going to have to have a talk with Huyag." What a mess. Such bad timing this demon had!

· ✡ ·

When he returned to the House, Huyag was just on his way back, too, his beard shiny and his robe now gleaming with more brilliant colors than could seem to exist, all running up and down in even rows. At seeing him, Huyag raised his eyebrows in a silent query.

"No luck. Your demon is here, to be sure, but exactly where is unknown. Can you provide any more information?"

"Forgive me, Wizard," the Chief Priest replied, "but I have been busy preparing tonight's rite. We gather for our Farewell to the Light." Huyag led him inside. "What would you like to know?"

"This demon you speak of."

"God," Huyag said, correcting him as he would a schoolchild at religious lessons.

"Whatever we call him." They were both seated as before. "What manner of being is it?"

"A creature of the darkness, of course." At Eliezer's evident lack of understanding (which Eliezer expressed through a carefully assumed perfectly blank expression), Huyag continued, "One that thrives on evil. Feeds on it as we do our dwindling supply of food. Without evil, it is nothing."

"And evil is...?"

Huyag looked a bit puzzled at the question. "Why, what man does, obviously." Huyag gestured with open hands as if to say, *Why are you asking such an obvious question?* "The evil that men do feeds the darkness."

"So I suppose the question is, what have you been doing?"

"I beg your pardon?" Eliezer couldn't tell if the question was an expression of true incomprehension or defensiveness. "Wizard, we are an obedient people, like yours." God forbid! If all people were as obedient to God's Law as the People of Israel, the world was doomed. "We perform our duties, as do you; we perform our rites, as do you. You are a People of the Law, and know of these things. We obey the laws. Our laws."

Maybe that was it: they obeyed a set of laws, but not the Law. Something was drawing the demon here. "Obedience is one thing," Eliezer said; "there has to be more than that." The Law was the Law, yes— but the Law was more than the Law. How could he explain all of that to a *goy*? "There is the letter, and then there is the spirit."

"Yes. And for us, there are two sets of spirits. One of them is invading the world of the other. Tonight, we ask the sun to return tomorrow morning, and shine a proper light on us again."

Melech, listening in as always, nearly shouted, *Join them!*

"What?" Eliezer shouted back. Huyag nearly jumped out of his skin. "Forgive me, Chief Priest. My horse is advising me."

"Your... horse..."

"A fine companion, and a creature of surprising wisdom."

"Your horse." Huyag smiled. Eliezer had no intention of explaining further. Huyag continued, "Part of your magic. What is your companion's name?"

"In my language, Melech. In yours, King."

"We have no King to lead us." Only priests, in a theocracy Eliezer believed was fairly benign. Still, not a town he would have enjoyed living in.

"We have only one true King," Eliezer said. "And He lives on high. On the other hand, if another King leads me to wisdom and truth, who am I to say no?"

"What does your King advise?"

"That I attend your rite. To learn."

"And will you attend? You would be most welcome, Eliezer ben-Avraham."

"This would not be according to my Law."

"But it would be according to the spirit." Now it was Eliezer's turn to raise his eyebrows. "For you are here to help, is that not so?"

"Yes. And the performance of a *mitzvah* transcends all laws, and all Law." Or so he thought, and he hoped for the sake of his soul that he was right. "I will be there."

"You have faith in your King, then."

"He has never steered me wrong."

Eliezer then told him about the oats; Huyag said he himself had been speaking to the owner of the granary, to try to arrange for better distribution of the town's remaining resources, although such were the effects of starvation that neither of them could remember who had summoned whom for the discussion. Huyag told him not to be concerned with payment. "But please be patient with us," he said, "for while we would like to show great hospitality, we are short on supplies for our own animals."

Thus it came about that, at dusk, Eliezer found himself in the *goyische* temple, standing with the townspeople like a true believer. Huyag and the High Priests officiated in the center, the Priests looking outward toward the circle of worshippers while Huyag faced west, toward the setting sun. Eliezer, in his own secret rebellion against this very unJewish activity, chose to face in the opposite direction. *God forgive me for what I am doing!* But of course an act was only part of what constituted the sin or the *mitzvah*. To stand here and pay homage to a false polytheon (to any polytheon, for that matter!) was less significant than why he did so.

"Bless us, Gods of the Colors of light!" Huyag intoned.

"Bless us all!" the congregation replied.

"We bow before you!"

"And so we bow!" And so they did: all bowed before their rainbow gods, the colors that decorated their lives even if no real spirits inhabited them. And with yet another plea for divine forgiveness, Eliezer bowed, too, and knelt, and simply, reluctantly, meaninglessly followed the crowd.

"The Light must leave us, and give way to the Darkness, but in that Darkness is the promise of Light."

Later he would hold his own, proper *shabbos* service, without a rabbi and without a cantor and without a *minyan* but with all the faith he could muster. He would break some of the laws of worship of the Sabbath, but God would understand if another rite preceded the correct one.

"Come again, O Light! Shine thy brilliance upon our heads, and wash away the Darkness with thy divine Colors!"

What they didn't realize, Eliezer thought (but wanted to tell them all), was that they were more correct than they knew. The Light was real, and so were its beneficent effects; indeed, the ten *sefirot* that, according to the kabbalistic masters, were the principles and components of reality all had their own unique colors. He could conceivably sit these deluded ones down and explain the colors to them: you want green? try *Binah*; you want red? try *Gevurah*. And through them all, the great blinding invisible white of the absolute...

Melech? he whispered in his mind.

You're doing fine, the horse replied. *But*, Melech told him from his camel stable full of roots and spiny plants and dried dates, *I'm hungry.*

Eliezer nearly laughed, but held himself in check, and continued to pretend to be a devout believer in the holiness of God's rainbow.

So typical— of himself, and these people, of humanity in general: to mistake the sign for what it signifies. This was not the first time he'd seen the delusion, and even participated in it, much to his everlasting regret.

· ✡ ·

That evening, "Joseph" brought him a diverse but sparse tray of food: thin slices of bread and fruit, and in an enameled bowl a few dollops of stew; what it lacked in quantity it made up for in aroma. Cubes of assorted meats, light and dark, some reddish, floated in pink sauce. Even their food was in multiple shades! Eliezer spooned up some of the dark pieces and chewed with delight. Very nicely done. He started to fish up one of the pink chunks, curious as to its source.

No! Melech shouted in his head; Eliezer nearly bit his tongue.

"What is it, my friend?"

Don't eat that!

A thrill of horror shot through him. *Trafe?* Was the bowl filled with forbidden foods? Melech confirmed that it was. Apparently, these people had forgotten after all, despite Huyag's reassurances. A shame— everything had looked so good....

"Thank you, my friend! Once again, you have saved me."

You're welcome. And Melech told him a story. While being led to his stable, the horse had smelled some delectable scents wafting from the house next door. Knowing his oats from his barley, Melech could tell the meal was entirely vegetarian: no danger whatsoever loomed in its ingredients.

What to do? Tell Huyag, of course, who needed to be informed of the problem. But Melech feared that that would be an insult to Huyag's power of memory and to the cooks who had made the meal, and to what end? For the people of this town would never suddenly become kosher butchers, and there was little enough meat to go around anyway. How true!

Melech guided him in eating only a little chicken, which seemed untainted by whatever horrors shared the bowl. Then, when the novice appeared again, Eliezer said to him, "Thank you so much for this delightful food. But my digestion is acting up again." A virtuous lie to obtain a virtuous meal. "I have a request. Can you please ask our lovely neighbors for some of their vegetable stew?"

"Joseph" looked very puzzled, but shrugged and withdrew, staring into the offending bowl as he carried it away (perhaps to partake of some of the leftovers himself— let him enjoy!). He returned in triumph a few moments later, bearing another bowl half-filled with a delightfully fragrant mixture of perfectly safe foodstuffs. Grains, root vegetables, onions, perhaps prunes... it smelled wonderful. "Great Wizard," the boy asked, "how did you know?"

Eliezer smiled with what he hoped was an imposing degree of the enigmatic and the wise. "I am a wizard, son."

Suitably impressed, the youth nodded, and prepared to leave him to his meal.

"No word of this to your masters," Eliezer said.

"No, no, Great Wizard!"

"Then you may go." And go the boy did, his face beaming as if he'd seen one of his Gods. The blue one? Orange? Eliezer chuckled and settled down to a slight but marvelous — and perfectly kosher — supper. If only there were more....

"Thank you, Melech," Eliezer said, before realizing he'd forgotten to thank the Lord for His boon! He put the spoon down, said the appropriate *brochah*, then scraped the last of the stew from the bottom of the bowl.

· ✡ ·

Eliezer dreamed that night: he dreamed of the neighbor woman and her cooking skills. He had never seen her, but he pictured what she was like: fleshy but not fat, well endowed but not grotesque, above all an expert with the knife and sauce, the ladle and the fire. Strangely, Eliezer knew that he was dreaming, knew that it was all a fantasy he had himself created out of the gentle but insistent pangs of hunger, a picture he had drawn deliberately in his mind. He had had such dreams before, where he had become aware that he was asleep and only imagining the strange places and people and events, but his awareness had always come partway through the fantasy, and that conscious-ness had always killed the dream immediately. For how can one accept the reality of an illusion and know it to be an illusion at the same time? It was a paradox the sleeping mind could not reconcile, and so the dream would explode and he'd awaken. But now he knew from the beginning that this was a dream, yet kept dreaming. He was seated at a rough-hewn table in the fine lady's house, a small but more than adequate house, with plain furniture and a few woven hangings (like flax rainbows!) on the walls to add a bit of color to their clay tones.

"Good lady," he said to the created cook, "another bowl?"

"Yes," she said. Her long hair was tied behind her in a long, fat queue, a black counterpart to the High Priests' silver beards. She served up another bowl, this time nearly overflowing, of her delicious vegetable stew. And as she did so, he knew she was married, that her husband would be home from the fields soon. It did not matter, since this was nothing but a dream. For now, he would be her husband; he sat at her table as she placed the brimming bowl before him, and he ate like a pig — worse, like Melech — and every morsel tasted as good as the last. He was ravenous, a bottomless pit whose appetite no amount of food could sate. And in the dream the woman smiled as she watched him eat. A little ashamed of his gluttony, as soon as he reached the bottom of the second bowl he stood up, said, "Thank you so much for your generosity," bowed, and left the humble abode. He ended the dream entirely there, so that he could savor the meal in his sleep and not dilute it with further nocturnal wanderings.

If he dreamed again, he did not remember the dream, let alone control it. But even in his sleep he knew that his belly was full, his taste-buds happy, and his mind content.

The next morning Eliezer awoke early to say his *shabbos* prayers. After dawn, a different boy brought him his breakfast, two slices of bread and some weak tea, and rushed out. As Eliezer sipped his tea slowly, to make it last, Huyag himself came to his room, dragging a distressed-looking "Joseph" behind him.

"And so, Wizard," the Chief Priest said, releasing the very sombre boy. "I caught this young man bringing you breakfast not from our refectory, but from the lady next door! What schemes have they been concocting, do you think?"

"What, today?" Had the lad taken it upon himself to seek food in unauthorized places?

"Yes, it seems that she insulted us with her offers."

Melech suddenly piped up, calling into Eliezer's mind, *Protect her!*

Oy, the poor woman, caught in the act of violating the rules of hospitality, acting as if she believed the Priests were incapable of feeding him. "It was my doing, Chief Priest," Eliezer lied as his poor heart pounded with shame and fear for her. "I asked her to supply me with breakfast."

"You?" "Joseph" cringed behind his master, brows creased in confusion. Let him see the terrible behavior of his supposed "betters." "This was your doing?"

"Forgive me, Huyag. My stomach has been upset— for quite some time. Your foods are too... too rich for it. The excellence of your food is, paradoxically, its flaw as far as my delicate constitution is concerned. I said nothing because I did not wish to insult you. But as it turns out I have done so after all. Forgive an old fool, please."

Huyag relented. "You should have said something. It is nothing." He turned to face the novice, who slunk out of the room. "The boy must be more careful in his reports in future. He said it was her idea."

Eliezer nodded, and came up with more nonsense. "Well, clearly they were trying to protect me from my own foolish efforts to avoid being a bad guest."

"Strange. Such strange doings." With a smile to cut the potential harshness of the words, Huyag said, "Perhaps you are the demon, scheming away, eh?"

Eliezer grinned. "A scamp. That's me. Listen, please ask the boy to return, for I must seek his forgiveness, too. In private."

"As you wish." Huyag rubbed his beard. "And today, Wizard?"

"It is my Sabbath, my day of rest. I must think about what to do."

"Help us, Wizard, as far as you can." But his dissatisfaction was plain; he clearly needed his demon exorcised. Obviously, his color gods were no match for their dark foes, and had none of the powers that a lowly wizard like Eliezer possessed. Perhaps Huyag had bigger things to worry about here than who supplied his breakfasts.

We have to go! Even as Huyag withdrew, Melech betrayed his sheer distress. Eliezer had seen him encounter evil before, and lose his reason, but never like this. The horse had become a nervous wreck. Before he could say anything reassuring to Melech, the trembling novice arrived for what he must have expected was a severe dressing-down.

"Boy, what has been going on?"

"Mrs. Gliy wanted to help you out, sir. She knew you needed and wanted her cooking. She prepared something for you because she knew you wanted it."

"But," Eliezer said in as gentle a voice as he could, "I didn't ask for it. Your efforts on my behalf — both of you — were so nice, but unnecessary. She should never have dreamed this up for me, so to speak."

"Oh, but she did."

"What do you mean?"

"She dreamed that you wanted more from her."

"What?" Now this was too strange. "What do you mean?"

"That's what she said, sir. Great Wizard. That she had a dream, that you sought food from her."

"Of course she did." Of course she did: the demon's doing, to wreck Eliezer's plans somehow. Curious. *Reassure him!* "Perhaps I did send that dream to her," he said.

"If so, you are truly a great wizard! She said you are not like us. Where do you come from?"

Be careful what you say! "Melech, please! What's gotten into you?" To the lad, he said, "From the world out there," and waved vaguely at the land beyond their town. Somewhere beneath the arc of their blessed and divine rainbow. A land far away from their comfortable beliefs. But he would not violate those beliefs, and he would not challenge the novice's faith, even if it meant pretending he was not born of human parents, just like the boy himself. It was not his place to deny their color gods, or to suggest his powers came from the true and only Lord— gained through unlawful means, and leading to his curse, his obligation to use those powers to help even such unbelievers and firm believers as these. "I come from another realm"— and he pointed vaguely outward, as if indicating their realm of Light. "I am here to carry the Light and fight the Darkness."

"Joseph" beamed; if Eliezer had to deny his heritage to bring such happiness into the boy's life, then so be it.

As soon as the novice left to attend to his more spiritual duties, Eliezer readied himself. Yes, it was the Sabbath, but Melech was becoming more and more insistent, even if that urgency was communicated through waves of raw emotion rather than words. Eliezer passed from his chamber through the House and beyond; Huyag bowed slightly on seeing him, and Eliezer returned the bow. Melech was already outside, and Eliezer — since the distance to travel was so short, and his joints discouraged him from the effort — chose not to climb on to his back but to walk beside him instead. The market square lay a short walk from the entrance of the temple, and most of the town had gathered, both sellers and buyers, to crowd into its confines. Melech did not hesitate an instant; he walked straight toward one of the booths at the far end, silently but almost disdainfully ignoring the vendors of birds and fruit, of nuts and metal goods, of banners and thimbles. This was the world of Man; Melech was solely focused on the world of gods, or those claiming to be gods, beings aspiring to godhead but emerging out of darkness like so many of the ignorant and the evil. Melech stopped just before a seller of goats; the vendor, an old man with virtually nothing on his bones — much like the Priests, in this world beyond the world — gaped at the single-minded horse.

It is here! Melech said.

"Here?" But of course: how perfect. All of evil concentrated in the body of a goat. Sacrifice the goat and release the world of its sins. "And you're sure."

Of course, Melech said, clearly exasperated at Eliezer's skepticism.

Yet it seemed *too* perfect. "A goat." A crowd gathered around them, and whispers of "wizard!" skittered through it.

Don't listen to me.

"Well, you don't have to be that way about it." Such an attitude for a horse! Melech said to the seller, "Let me have that beast."

The seller was speechless, too stunned by what was happening to respond. Eliezer would have bought it if he needed to, but he didn't want to break the Sabbath laws any further. "Sir?" finally came from the vendor's trembling lips.

By now, Huyag had arrived in Melech's wake, his High Priests trailing behind. The Chief Priest said to the old man, "Give the wizard what he asks for." The goat, seemingly unaware of the turmoil it had caused, but only putting on a fine act, shook its head at Eliezer as he grabbed the rope tied about its neck. "Come; it's time for an exorcism."

The Kabbalah had much to say about demons and demonology, but few consistent beliefs. Yet there were rules and procedures for their removal, and Eliezer relied on what he knew from the *Ha-Malakh ha-Meshiv*. Evil spirits normally infested people, but they could also ride beasts, the way that Eliezer rode Melech. This was a struggle between knights, in a way, and as much a battle between the forces of Light and Darkness as any in these people's mythology. Whatever this spirit was, however evil or Godless, even if it were the direct offspring of Lilith and Samael, King of the Demons, it could not withstand the power of the Light. The true Light.

"Eliezer," Huyag said, breaking his concentration, "have you truly found the god?" The crowd watched the action like spectators at a play.

With an impatient sigh, Eliezer replied, "Long ago, my friend."

He put his hands on the flesh of the animal and closed his eyes. Then he spoke the words of the exorcism rite, calling upon the light beaming from the eyes of Adam Cadmon, the primordial Man and the One, to cast out the darkness and bring God's light into the animal and the world. Only by shining God's ineffable Being into this beast could the Nothing, the Dark, be driven away. "God be in you," Eliezer said, and then recalled the fact that such creatures had no soul. To say such a thing to a soulless creature, one without a spirit, was to waste God's name. But to do so here and now was to honor the name of the Lord by using it against God's enemies.

It's still here! Melech cried, and suddenly the horse's legs seemed to be trying to move in four directions at once, as if he, too, were seeking the Beyond and the Unity that brought the four corners of the universe together.

Eliezer tried again, restoring his concentration and his will and calling once more upon the power of the One to drive out the Other. The goat, for its part, seemed unperturbed. Nothing was happening.

Kill it!

What? "What? What did you say?" Eliezer turned to face Melech.

Kill it!

"An old, stupid fool." He shook his head and thought back to what Melech had been saying ever since they came to this place. "You have been trying to tell me for some time, haven't you, my friend?" He put his hand on Melech's flesh, and spoke the words again. Melech tried to shy away, but could not break the bond of flesh to flesh, spirit to spirit. Now Eliezer felt the thing, too: a Blank, a Nothing from beyond God's light, riding in Eliezer's place. "Kill it"?

So hungry, it said.

He began to channel the Prophets and the *Zaddik*s, the authors of the *Zohar* and the other Kabbalistic books. "Thou evil being who feedeth on evil! And so much greater a fool even than I! For evil lies not in the deed alone, but in the intent: what is in the heart as well as what is in the hand. The Law is the letter, *and* the spirit, demon!" *It is even permissible to work on the Sabbath, foolish demon, if the work is to save a life, or soul, or world.* "Of course thou hast remained hungry, demon! Where is thine evil sustenance? In the just action that only seems unjust? In the breaking of the Law in the name of the Law?"

"*Hungry!*"

"Then starve, demon!" And with that the demon fled, to whatever darkness it had come from— the darkness and the ignorance that had made it think it could challenge the Good by using Good for evil ends. "Go back to thy lightless realm, thou foolish manipulator, thou pathetic usurper!"

And take my sin with you, Eliezer said within himself, and reddened with shame. *My terrible blindness. Please.*

· ✡ ·

Eliezer, Melech, and the Priests returned to the House, all perfectly silent. Eliezer could not think of what to say; he was too embarrassed, and frightened for his friend, worried about possible long-term effects. Finally, as they neared the House's front door, he subvocalized, "How are you? Is it gone?"

Yes, I'm here. Thank you for getting rid of that thing.

"Sorry I didn't catch on earlier." "Kill it"! As if Melech did not know better.

Melech made his forgiveness clear, if in a shaky mental "voice."

It was truly remarkable what the demon had gotten Eliezer to do, supposedly in violation of his most fundamental Laws: to steal, to covet, to dishonor, to bear false witness, put other gods "before" Him, even to take the Name in vain... yet, in its moral darkness, it had never understood some very important truths about right and wrong.

At the door, Huyag asked, "Did you know all along?" The High Priests stood beside them, arrayed like the bands in a rainbow, awaiting Eliezer's answer.

He could have lied then, to impress them and awe them with his wisdom and insight and power. But that lie would save nobody, would save nothing except his damnable pride. And even if he had indeed committed no true sins during the past twenty-four hours, despite "breaking" nine — nine! — of the Commandments, he was not ready to violate another moral law.

"No, Chief Priest. I was a stupid old man, blinded by my own ignorance and arrogance." In the dark, so to speak.

"Blinded by your faith, perhaps?" Before Eliezer could come up with a reply, Huyag continued, "That is hardly a sin, I would think."

Later, Eliezer visited the camel stable in which Melech was housed. As it was still *shabbos*, they could go nowhere, and would rest from this most frightening of all their experiences. For one day, Eliezer had lost his companion, friend, and adviser, and had groped in the darkness as a result. Not something he wanted endure ever again.

"How are you?"

All right, Melech told him; *but a little stuffed.* In spite of the demon's claims, the stable had enough suitable nourishment to satisfy a horse. Melech's digestion had paid a heavy price for the demon's determination to maintain the lie about physical hunger.

"I'm very sorry that I didn't listen to you more carefully."

Melech gave the equine equivalent of a shrug; for a second, he seemed more like a Jew than ever. Eliezer suppressed a chuckle.

"When I think of all that I did, and what it tried to have me do!"

Eliezer shook his head, then prepared to return to the House for a bowl of perfectly fine stew, served by the lad in the many-colored robes, who now enjoyed once more the favour of the High Priests and the Chief Priest. As Eliezer was leaving the stable, Melech said something truly unforgiveable about possession and the Law, something that did not bear paying attention to, let alone repeating.

TOWERING PRIDE

ELIEZER KNEW THERE was trouble as soon as he saw the five-winged silver penguin rolling across the sky. The monstrosity flapped its flippers in a vain attempt to gain control over its trajectory as it whirled toward the western horizon.

"Well," Eliezer said, "you don't see that every day." But he knew Melech could see through his wry comment, that it was a flimsy veil over a troubled soul. Eliezer didn't have Melech's nose for sniffing out black magic, of course, but it wasn't hard to see something very dark was going on.

Melech nodded in a perfectly equine way, silently, and Eliezer knew what he was thinking: more humans behaving badly.

"We'd better investigate," Eliezer said.

Melech didn't respond at first to Eliezer's kneed command to turn right, toward the east from where the bizarre creature had flown.

"I know, my friend," Eliezer said, "but I can't let such a thing go, can I?" It was true that he wasn't responding to some desperate summons, that there had been no formal call from a family or community for assistance from the wandering wizard. Instead, this was a matter of Eliezer seeking out problems on his own, something he'd never done before. Understandably, the horse resented such a voluntary pursuit of headaches. So be it! Magic of the sort that had produced a creature like that spinning, soaring *thing* was a serious matter. Metamorphosis was perhaps the most benign of the Powers, but even there one had to exercise both caution and virtue. One could play with God's creation only so far. "We must not ignore such an exercise of irresponsible power."

Melech snorted as if to say, "And why not?" But he pointed his hooves in the correct direction at last.

For quite some time, as they plodded across the packed beige soil, all that greeted their eyes was more barren land, hardy but isolated patches of scrub, and the occasional lone tree. Low hills promised new vistas but failed to deliver; topping a shallow rise merely meant encountering more nothing. Eliezer wondered if he was going the right way after all, or if he would instead find himself in the middle of a wasteland.

"*Oy!*"

He reacted even before he fully saw the human-faced sand-rat that gazed up at him from atop a stony knoll. Horrific! And a fascinating product of the art of change... Eliezer shook his head and urged Melech on.

Finally, they came upon a village: a few brick houses, their walls composed of hardened blocks of the soil and therefore the same dun color, lined up along a winding road as if waiting for a parade. No one was in sight except two young children in loose robes that were the same dull color as everything else. They saw Eliezer, shrieked, and ran for safety into one of the houses through a "door" made of canvas strips. Melech said something about the parade having arrived but Eliezer ignored him. A tall, white-bearded man, fully swathed in brown robes, emerged from one of the brick houses further down the road and walked up to him, eyes wide. Eliezer nodded a greeting.

"Who are you, stranger?" the man asked in one of the local dialects Eliezer knew passably well.

"I am Eliezer ben-Avraham."

Before he could identify himself further, the man said, "You are the wizard we have heard so much about!"

"I am, indeed. I saw some very strange things. Are you in need of assistance?"

"Come." The man led them to the far end of the village. "I am Egudar, the village Elder," he proclaimed, as if that were supposed to mean something to Eliezer. It did not; he had been hosted by Kings and Princes and Chiefs, and in any case by now he was not impressed by titles. Eliezer simply nodded in apparent acknowledgement of Egudar's vast importance. Walking with a stiff gait, the Elder led him to a cube of about ten feet to a side that stood at the very end of the village and some yards apart from the nearest houses. Its walls were iron or steel bars between which clay had been inexpertly stuffed. Noises — grunts, shrieks, poundings — resounded from within, as if a hellish orchestra had been let loose upon the world. Eliezer recognized the honk of a goose. Egudar said, "The goose is eight feet tall."

"What are these abominations?" Eliezer asked.

"Blasphemous creations," Egudar said. "They come from the monastery." He pointed further east. "There— they make these things." He slapped at the cage wall, and a shower of brown dust sprinkled the ground. "We catch what we can and toss them in here, where they can do no damage except to each other. We hope. Other *unauthorized* things appear in the east," he said with an offended tone: "once, a pillar of flame shot up to the sky, and, many years ago, an orange ring of cloud."

"What are they doing at this monastery?"

"We don't know. But they are the Speakers of the Tongue."

"Ah, I see." Whoever they were...

"They have been there for as long as we can remember, and have grown in recent years. The Fathers tell us that something bizarre has happened or come our way at least once every year for many years." He waved his arm toward the village, perhaps to call further attention to its deserted street. The gesture involved a curious element of the possessive. "Can you help us? We fear what will come upon us next."

Eliezer nodded. "For a bed and sustenance, I will do what I can. It is my duty to assist you." Bed and board: a small fee for what might prove to be a very large task.

Eliezer was accommodated in the home of an ancient villager who had recently lost his wife and had plenty of room to offer. Gashen seemed to be genuinely thrilled to play host, whether out of a sense of the honor of the role or for the companionship it was hard to tell. He prepared a fine bed out of straw and vari-sized boards he scavenged from around his property and beyond. Women from the village came by to fill the larder with fresh bread and jugs of chilled fruit juices that were only lightly fermented. Melech, meanwhile, was given space behind Gashen's house, where he could lip up some of the softer, if sparse, vegetation growing there. Melech transmitted to Eliezer a sense that these were unique plants, but not bad at all.

"Monsters!" Gashen told him between rotted teeth, as they sat at a table that rocked upon mismatched legs. "They come down from the monastery, and we capture the ones we can and lock them up. Weird beasts, like the end of time!" He ladeled some thin soup into a coarse stoneware bowl that stood, though a bit tilted, before Eliezer.

"So you people believe in an End?" That might be important.

"Yes, of course! You are a Hebrew, yes?" Eliezer gave a single nod at the truth of his statement. "We, too, believe in the beginning and the end, and one proper God of all gods."

"We believe in only one God," Eliezer asserted with the confidence born of the certainty of millennia. In the face of the Egyptians and the Greeks and the Romans with their pantheons, the Hebrews had kept their faith in the Lord, the *only* God.

"Do you, then?" Gashen asked, and a few drops of spittle (*feh!*) punctuated the question. *Please, not in the soup...* "We believe in many, but worship only one."

"No, my friend, we believe..." And suddenly Eliezer wasn't sure *what* he believed. For instance, what was Ba'al? A god, but a false one? But then, if a false one, not a god at all, because there could not be other gods, for as the Commandment said... no, it said something very different. His head spun. "We worship the one, true God," Eliezer said flatly. He desperately sought to escape this disturbing conversation— above all, by spooning up some of the soup, blowing on it, and opening his mouth to accept the bland broth.

"And we believe we should have no other gods in place of our own."

Eliezer froze, mouth open. He would have to look this up when he had a chance... He put the spoon in his mouth, drank, and tried to calm his fiery brain.

"Well," Gashen said, "what are you going to do?"

"Go to this monastery of yours and find out what they're up to."

"They won't let you in. They don't let anybody in."

"A fine policy," Eliezer said. "Good for keeping secrets." And as for secrets: he did not tell Gashen that he had no intention of limiting his arriving outward form to the human— metamorphosis had its good side, too.

After the soup came a disk of flat bread and a flavourless, meatless pottage delivered by fussing village housewives and their unseductive daughters. Was there no color or spark of liveliness anywhere in the village? Eliezer thanked those who came with food, but despite all his questions directed at Gashen and the female servers, he failed to obtain specific information about the monastery's location.

"Perhaps, Gashen, you could ask Egudar to come and help me find this monastery of yours."

"Ha!" Gashen said. "He doesn't know any more than the rest of us. We only just elected him Elder. He's an ignorant old herder, like the rest of us." He stretched his neck until he looked as stiff as Egudar, and assumed a mock-dour expression. "He is now a very important man, you know." Gashen laughed, and Eliezer sheltered his dish with his arms.

"So he knows nothing? A shame," Eliezer said. The man had seemed so authoritative— but then, a good politician was also an actor. "Does no one know where this infamous monastery is?"

"East." Gashen ripped a flatbread in half and offered Eliezer the other half; Eliezer politely declined. "Every time somebody gets too close, some monk runs at him and turns him away. *Shoo! Shoo!*" More spit. Eliezer was grateful his beard was thick enough to protect his cheeks from the shower. "Twice, some poor soul tried to get in, and never returned."

Obviously, a direct approach would be impossible as well as inadvisable. "So I'll fly," he said to himself, and Melech, listening in, expressed the opinion that since he'd gotten himself into this mess, it was entirely up to him how he handled it. No help at all— such a horse!

"When will you go?" Gashen asked toward their meal's end. The ugly soul fed himself an unidentifiable but decidedly juicy fruit for dessert. Eliezer held a napkin to his face as if threatened with a sneeze, and managed to keep his nose, eyes, and brow dry during the ensuing deluge. But the back of his hand got disgustingly moist.

"Tomorrow morning," Eliezer said.

"Good!" Gashen cried with his mouth nearly full, and Eliezer turned away just in time. "You'll have a very comfortable night. Very comfortable."

I will, Eliezer thought, *when I have cleaned up a bit*. Melech, unable to mind his own business, snorted.

He went to bed, but tossed and turned for what seemed like, and might well have been, many hours, trying to reconcile what he knew of his religion and what the Torah seemed actually to say. Ba'al: a god? Not a god? A god but not the right god? No, it wasn't possible— there couldn't have been such a belief, such a heresy (or was it a heresy then?). To be a Hebrew was to believe in only *one*! And yet—

He recited the *shema* to himself: "*Shema Yisroel, Adonai elohaynu, Adonai echod.*"

Hear, O Israel: the Lord is our God, the Lord is one.

· ✡ ·

His night's sleep was interrupted by dreams of monsters, hordes of normal creatures in ghastly combinations. He awoke in a shivering sweat, rubbed his face, and struggled to wipe the grotesque images from his mind. When he finally managed to calm himself down, he joined his host for a breakfast of gruel made palatable only by a coating of sugar and some wizardly protection from Gashen's damp diatribe against Egudar's self-importance. The shield-spell with which Eliezer surrounded his table setting successfully deflected his host's unpleasant volleys.

"I gather, then," he said drily (*mazel tov!*) to Gashen, "that you do not like Egudar."

"A fool!" Gashen literally spat. "Pride is the worst of all sins. And he's a sinner of the first rank!"

"Yes, a deadly sin." Gashen showed no sign of recognition; perhaps he did not know of the famous Seven. "You honor humility? Is that why everyone dresses so, well, plainly?" *And eats so insipidly?* he wanted to add. Oh, for a *little* spice!

"We are of the earth, wizard, and have to show that we know it."

"True." Still, a *little* color... but he wasn't about to get into another philosophical discussion with the man. "For my own pride, Gashen, I paid a heavy price. And now to the work I condemned myself to perform because of it."

"Wonderful!" Gashen declared, and Eliezer's magical shield proved its value once again.

As he was preparing for his excursion, Egudar came by Gashen's house, and Eliezer made sure to display proper obeisance to him. "Greetings, O Elder," he said, his tone dripping with feigned delight at the honor of Egudar's visit.

"Greetings, Wizard. Is your stay proving comfortable?"

"Indeed, yes." Eliezer bowed. "I feel as refreshed as if I had immersed myself in a vast, cool, drenching lake. And now, I go to perform my task."

"And yet, Wizard," Egudar said, shifting weight from one foot to the other, "all that is done on behalf of the village must be cleared through its Elder."

"I see." Eliezer noticed that Gashen never offered Egudar a seat, and thanked him silently for keeping the self-satisfied fool uncomfortable. "Well, I travel now to the monastery to see what is going on, and perhaps resolve matters to your satisfaction."

"So." Eliezer waited to learn what that meant. After a few moments, Egudar asked, "And how will you do so?"

"Magically." He bowed as low as his aching spine would permit. "At your service, Elder; I must depart immediately." He walked by Egudar, out the door, and into the alley between Gashen's house and his neighbor's. Before Egudar could recover from the shock of being so suddenly forsaken, Eliezer transformed into a sparrow, a bird small and plain enough to elude notice— and one whose wings were spare enough to suit his aching shoulder. He flitted above the village and scanned the eastern horizon. He saw almost immediately one hill that surpassed all others, although that was not saying much in this nearly featureless landscape. Eliezer flew to the likely candidate; he soon made out on its summit a complex of buildings, a set of spare, geometrical constructions, the central one dominating the rest in all three of its dimensions. The entire complex was enclosed in a circular wall, against whose eastern extremity was a pen housing a sizeable herd of goats and a few chickens, while a garden curled along the northern rim. As for the buildings, every structure seemed to be composed of the sort of bricks that made up the village's houses: local clay roughly pressed into shape. Except that on closer inspection, he realized they were not bricks at all, but slices of bricks, thin clay wafers. A few men in brown robes and cowls crossed from one building to another along paths laid with dark stones, but the place appeared otherwise unpeopled.

All looked typically *dull* and bleak and rationally designed, except for the giant toe rising above the southern gates. "*Gevalt!*"

The main building — presumably the hub of their perhaps nefarious activities — was a truly massive pile, with severe straight lines and absolutely no embellishment. All that kept it from looking like a box or prison was the fact it was made up of those thin sheets of clay, which gave the walls a pin-striped look. Thousands upon thousands of the paper-thin brick-sheets mounted to the sky, broken by rows of horizontally narrow windows, while the roof was made of a local wood every bit as *earthy* in color and design as the rest of the structure.

Before he knew what was happening, he lost both his wings and sprouted twigs instead; his beak flattened into something mole-like, an elongated snout that led his body in a plummet toward the stones. It took quick thinking and nearly as quick recitation to transform himself into a beetle just before he suffered a deadly impact. He bumped his forehead against the stone, while the rest of his carapace absorbed most of the blow.

Oy— what was that? He took a few deep insectoid breaths, calmed his nerves as best he could — he was too old for this! — and finally released his wings so he could rise somewhat and observe his surroundings. He was just outside the main hall (for that's what he decided to label the building), and he was able to inspect what he took to be the front doors, which were made up of the same type of thin sheets, only these were face-on rather than lying flat and were heavily marked up: the surfaces were practically black with symbols of some sort.

Symbols: he knew writing when he saw it.

The door opened, and Eliezer slipped inside just as a hooded monk stepped out. The interior was vast, a single undivided, undecorated, hollow shell of immense size echoing with a constant hiss, and an occasional cough or quickly-shushed whisper. Now he could see them: dozens, maybe even hundreds of monks, all seated at rows of desks and all etching symbols into clay tablets.

At the risk of panicking the crowd, Eliezer found the key to resuming a human appearance right in their midst. It wasn't easy, because he couldn't reverse whatever spell had robbed him of his earlier form, but he could go around it via his own transformations. One of the monks, startled by his manifestation, cast a stunned look at him from under his cowl, then the expression became one of profound irritation, and he returned to his work. The rest completely ignored him.

"Hello?" Eliezer said in a normal voice; then he repeated the word but somewhat louder; then he practically shouted the greeting. So he tried a variety of languages, beginning with Hebrew and moving through many others with which he was familiar. Couldn't they at least tell him to shut up? But all he received in return for his efforts was complete indifference. Until...

"Stop that!" someone yelled at him, a monk like all the rest except for the fact he paid Eliezer some attention and was headed right for him. The monk let loose with a string of unfamiliar sounds, some harsh, some loud, some in Aramaic... Eliezer could make out such a remarkable variety of languages— the man was a linguist whose skills left Eliezer's own in the dust. "Stop doing that!" the man said in the local vernacular as he stood face-to-face with Eliezer. Another stream of alien tongues followed, with Greek (both ancient and modern), Italian, and Russian in the mix. And some that did not sound as if they were even of this world.

"All right!" Eliezer shouted back. "*Nu*, I'll keep my mouth shut."

"Who are you? What are you doing here? Are you a fool?"

"Three very different questions. One: Eliezer ben-Avraham, a wizard foolish enough to explore mysteries that were none of his business. Two: trying to find out what terrible things you're doing, because I have a duty to use my powers to help others, even when they don't ask me to, I suppose. Three: yes."

"Idiot." The monk looked around the hall, as if to ensure everybody was doing his duty, too, and then said, "Come with me." He marched Eliezer toward the door. Eliezer thought he was about to be thrown out bodily, but the monk accompanied him out to the landing beyond the doors. "How did you get in there?"

"Not so hard when you know how. I have some questions for you: who are you, what are you doing here, and are you crazy?"

"I am Bellar. Beyond that, it is none of your business. You are in great danger."

"So is everyone, I believe."

"That is not my concern." Bellar crossed his arms, and Eliezer found it easy to resist the apparent effort at intimidation. Another self-satisfied fool— for a people who believed in humility, there was precious little here. But then, rarity bestowed value. Bellar said, "I believe you understand holy tasks, wizard. We have heard of you, and we know your power. And your Powers. You are, in some ways, an inspiration for us, although a relatively recent one."

"Me? An inspiration? I have no spirit to give you."

Bellar shook his head. "Trust me: we have been doing this far longer than you have been around. Our task is an ancient one. Out of the many, great wizard, the One." Bellar turned to go back inside, but Eliezer was not about to let him get away. As quickly as he could, he metamorphosed into a hummingbird, zipped around to place himself between Bellar and the doors, and hovered close enough to the monk's face to be extremely annoying. Bellar tried to bat him away, but Eliezer eluded his flat hand. He put on a human face, and with tiny vocal chords squeaked, "Talk to me!"

"You fool!" Bellar glared at him. "You are in very great danger here! The walls are there to protect us and you, too; you are within them, and in contact with the One!"

The hummingbird would not be denied. Eliezer flapped tickling wings at his nose. "You must stop whatever you are doing and speak to me."

"For our God's sake, wizard!" Bellar waited. "Fine, but only for a time! Let me enter." Eliezer flew aside and let Bellar back into his precious hall. Eliezer hung motionless in the doorway as Bellar shouted at the others, "Stop! Stop, do you hear?" He followed that with what seemed to be the same word in a dozen, dozens, hundreds of other languages, some old, some young, some dead, some alive, some arising naturally in the course of human speech, some created artificially by those who dreamed of uniting humanity in a common tongue....

That was when Melech, always listening in but so stubbornly quiet until now, finally broke his silence and sent his thoughts to Eliezer. And what he told Eliezer seemed utterly absurd, yet utterly plausible. One of the languages in which Bellar had spoken the word "Stop" was horse.

The truth about Bellar's skills broke upon Eliezer's mind at last. For here it was: the blessed dream of the ancient language spoken by Adam himself.

The monks stopped their scratching of stylus on tablet, and the hiss faded. The hall became as quiet as a mausoleum. The language or languages they were using faded to nothing, like the very spirits of the dead in Sheol according to the ancient teachings. For there is nothing until and unless God speaks... Bellar, evidently the abbot of this place, a man with authority, shot Eliezer-the-hummingbird a look of combined fury and exasperation before returning to the landing outside.

"There," he said, "you have halted the work of centuries."

Eliezer became a man again, speaking the magical words he should never have learned, and, in half-mocking imitation of Bellar, crossed his arms. "You spoke of danger; all I can guess is that I halted the dangerous work of centuries." Before Bellar could fully voice any objection, Eliezer continued, "You called me a fool, and I admit that I am one, but I wonder if you have earned the name more fully than myself."

"We do our duty, as you do yours."

"Then explain your duty."

Bellar sighed. "Let us retire to my office, then, wizard. We can both use refreshments." He led the way to a small cube of a building that proved to be somewhat more partitioned than the hall. Bellar's headquarters were composed of a set of living quarters and an office with a desk, a high-backed chair, and a couch. Every furniture part that was not upholstered was made up of those sheets — those tablets — which, he now understood, became building material once fully covered with writing. The walls were lined with the things, so that there was no visible difference between book and bookshelf. A servant-monk brought them steaming cups of a type of tea Eliezer had never tasted before. He sat on the sofa while Bellar took up his place behind the clay desk. "We once used vellum," Bellar said as Eliezer examined every inch of the desk's front. A staggering number of tablets! "But there are not enough sheep in the world to supply us with our needs."

"Forgive me if I think this is madness."

"Spoken by the man who turns into birds."

"I do so when I need to." He sipped the tea with some emotion and nearly burned his lips in the process. Such a strange, yet fine, flavour! "But this…"

"You speak the local language well, wizard Eliezer. You are to be commended. So many languages."

"Too many languages," Eliezer said.

"Too many, indeed. Among them all is the One Tongue." A fully capitalized phrase, it was easy to hear. Eliezer nodded in recognition of the old story, but in a twisted form. The pre-Babel language was supposedly long gone. "In all the sounds, in all the symbols, the One Tongue must exist. Speak a million million sounds, write a million million combinations of letters, and among them is bound to be the One Tongue of our God."

"I see. So you speak as well as write?"

"In the morning we write, in the afternoon we speak. Unceasingly. Every language, every sound of which a human is capable. Only we have the skill and dedication to pursue this work." Bellar adopted a pose that made him resemble Egudar — maybe they were brothers. "What greater calling can we have than to become God's living tongue and library?"

"And yet." The implications were clear: verbalize and write enough random syllables and words, and these people would inevitably stumble on the right ones to perform magic. They might be accidental incantations, but they would be incantations nevertheless, for the power of magic, the power of the Divine, was in language. These fools, however unwittingly, were tapping into the Power. "You create monsters and affect the weather," Eliezer said. "You turn people into animals, animals into hybrids, God knows what else you make with your voices and pens."

"We know many gods, wizard, but we worship only one as the Right God."

"Monolatrists."

"And we know many languages, but there is only One true Tongue."

And so they would strive for centuries, if need be, to speak that language and become one with their God, even at a rate of one word per century. An admirable dedication. "And an admirable goal," Eliezer said, choosing to complete his thought verbally. "But at a heavy cost."

"We do not seek to affect the world, yet at times things stray into the range of our voices and books, by flying like yourself, or crawling, or, in the case of those fools, trying to get into our monastery. We seek to harm no one, wizard— thus, our walls."

"A fortress of books." Yet while the walls might keep out intruders — although not those that crawled upon the ground or flew through the air — magic did not respect physical boundaries. "How long has this gone on? How long will it go on?"

"To answer your first question, the Speakers of the Tongue have been seeking the One for many centuries, although we have attracted many novices to our monastery in recent years. Fearful people hear of us," Bellar said, and the undiluted pride in his monastery's work filled his voice, "and join our community of seekers of Truth."

"A bastion of certainty in a contingent world." But ironically also a veritable cauldron of constant transformation, as the magical words, however accidentally recited, mutated the very stuff of existence. Such thoughtless playing with the world!

"As for your second question: till our God silences us."

"How large will your library get, then, Bellar? How high will your building rise? How many millions of slices of clay will rise from their soil, aspiring to be one with the divine?"

"Only time will tell."

These people had learned no important lessons from all their unholy creations, blinded as they were by their self-righteousness. Virtuous aspirations could easily become presumptions. These people frightened Eliezer as no one ever had before. He met Bellar's eyes, and detected no doubt within: only pure faith, not in another but in himself. Eliezer saw the hall growing like the ancient Tower, reaching to the heavens, till God and its own height and the Earth itself pulled it back down to the soil out of which it grew.

"In our teaching," Eliezer said, "God is a jealous God."

"Really?" Bellar tapped his chin. "Jealous of whom?"

· ✡ ·

Eliezer was granted the privilege of staying in some hastily assembled guest quarters — the monastery never entertained guests, or at least not invited guests, for obvious reasons — until he could decide what to do about this. He had much to puzzle over as he sat drinking that tasty exotic tea in his narrow room. He dreaded to think about the number of monks who, over the years, had been turned into other living things, or possibly killed, because of a magical incantation recited purely by chance. He could not imagine what might happen if the monks stumbled upon the formulae for summoning demons who would pay little attention to the book-walls surrounding the complex. He could hear one now: "What? I'm not allowed to leave the premises and bring evil unto the world at large? All right, then, I'll just sit here." These people were playing with fire, in many ways, and it might not be just the monastery that would burn.

Melech offered no solutions, and that was truly unusual; even when the horse's suggestions were crazy, at least they came. But Melech seemed to feel he was far out of his depth here— and Eliezer felt the same way. People doing what they thought was their God's duty were not to be dissuaded easily from a potentially apocalyptic path.

Bellar agreed to a pause in the monastery's pursuits until the two men could reach an agreement. Bellar knew that he and his followers had all the time in the world. So Eliezer decided he would sleep on the problem, and rather than return to Gashen's home spent the night at the monastery, hoping none of the monks would talk in his sleep and turn him into a spider.

As he lay on the hard cot they had provided, his mind couldn't resist returning to his earlier conversations. He'd always taken monotheism for granted, and now he was faced with some very, very upsetting thoughts. He would go down one theological path, find himself trapped in a logical corner, say, "*Oy!*" and go back where he started from. "But of course there's only one God!" he cried aloud; all others were delusions. And now there were many languages, not one! It was too much for his old head to take.

"Melech?" The horse responded that he was listening. "What was it like hearing a human speaking horse?"

Melech told him in a combination of concepts and images how upsetting it had been. For if a human could understand horse, so many equine secrets would be divulged. Melech refused to elaborate, of course. More secrets, more forbidden knowledge?

"Not even a little hint? *Ach!* What am I saying?" Eliezer had had enough of such deliciously tempting conundrums in his life! *Be careful what you ask,* he told himself; *have you not yet learned the dangers?*

He had a difficult night, tossing, turning, and rising often to relieve himself. He finally fell into some hard slumber but was yanked out of it by a crescendo of voices: a chorus of syllables rising in volume by the second. He looked out the window of the closet in which he'd been housed, and was able to determine that the sound came from the hall. "*Oy,* no!"

He raced out of the storage building and opened the unfastened door of the hall, only to be met by a blast of sound like the trumpets at the final call. The monks, however many hundreds of them, were all vocalizing in a horrifying cacophony, louder and louder— what were the idiots doing? No one would be able to hear him if he tried to silence them. Where was Bellar? The answer to his question came as the abbot tapped him on the shoulder from behind; at Eliezer's distressed look, Bellar leaned in and shouted in his ear, "Morning prayers!"

"Make them stop!" Eliezer shouted back. "What are they saying?"

"Who knows?" Bellar replied; Eliezer had to read his lips to get the full answer. "It will not take long!"

"It might take too long!" Eliezer yelled. He felt himself losing his voice already. "What if they say something effective? This is crazy!"

Two things happened: first, one of the monks blurred, shifted, shimmered, and became a tiger-faced, eight-legged pink bat, which proceeded to ascend and attach itself to a ceiling beam and hang upside-down for an indefinite time; second, the prayer abruptly ceased, and as was almost entirely predictable, Eliezer's shouted "crazy!" was the only sound left in the hall. Monks looked up at their transmogrified brother, in pity and amazement, and some tried to wave him back down. The bat ignored them.

Eliezer said, "I could try to help him, as I helped myself."

"No," Bellar replied. "It is his willing sacrifice. He must be as our God has willed him to be."

Poor fool! The bat flew to another beam, and resumed its pose on its new support, emitting a subdued growl from its little striped mouth. Eliezer looked at Bellar, whose expression was perfectly placid. He would never think of himself as either arrogant or cruel. Just devout.

"*Nu*?" Eliezer said, gesturing with his whole hand at the ill-fated creature. "Is this what you want? And how much more will you cause to happen? How many more will you condemn to such a fate?"

"This is our way, Eliezer. What would you have us do? Cease to worship our God?" This sort of obscene transformation was just a price he and his monks were prepared to pay. And it was true that many in other lands had suffered worse fates in defense of their faiths. Bellar watched the bat gnaw at its fur. "I believe that is Caduat. A fine scribe, he was."

"Can't you just be more careful, then?" Eliezer asked. "Surely you can find a way to avoid such stupid, risky behavior! What if your next chant takes away a life as well as a form?"

"As our God wills."

Such sophistry! "Not God's will, Bellar; your own!" Like his wandering, which had been provoked by his poking into forbidden knowledge: not God's will, but his own. "I learned things I shouldn't and now I pay the price for my folly. You need to learn the same lesson!"

Then teach him, Melech practically commanded, in a voice that filled Eliezer's cranium.

"Teach him?" Eliezer said aloud, much to Bellar's surprise. "Teach him what? To be less stupid? And please don't shout." Bellar watched Eliezer address an invisible audience, obviously unsure how to react.

Teach him what you were taught.

Ah. Eliezer finally understood. "Would it make a difference, you think?"

Ask him.

"Bellar," Eliezer said, "I have a proposition for you."

·   ✡   ·

Ironic, it most definitely was. Under normal circumstances, Eliezer was asked by others to perform certain tasks, and he fulfilled his obligations in a short time and was able to leave fairly quickly. This time, however, he had thrown himself into the task, without summons or invitation, and volunteered his time and efforts to solve a problem that came his way solely by chance. A chance problem involving chance words... yet this would be the longest job of all, taking him away from his wanderings for weeks, if not months. And all to prevent the world from being destroyed: well, it was a small price to pay, in the long run.

He returned to the village and met with Egudar, who greeted him with all the self-importance such a man could muster. "So you will become a temporary resident of our fair village, wizard?" Egudar said after all was explained.

"Yes." And so would Melech, who was developing a taste for some of the odd plants growing in the region. Eliezer began to wonder about the weird tea, the scattered sprouts of weird foliage on the ground, and whether they, too, might be products of the monastery's unwitting sorcery. "I will have to strain your hospitality, I'm afraid."

"Not a problem, great wizard! But I will ask that you report to me regularly." Egudar made a dismissive gesture, as if having been obliged to cite a burdensome formality he wished they could dispense with. "It is my duty." And he adopted an erect posture, stretching his head toward the sky, as if trying to tower over Eliezer....

"So be it, your Elderness."

Melech snickered, but Eliezer managed to keep his expression neutral.

Thus, he settled himself into Gashen's home on a slightly more permanent basis, much to Gashen's delight. Gashen could now regale him with damp tales both true and unlikely about his life, travels, adventures, and wife; Eliezer, in return, could listen and try vainly to get a word in edgewise. Both Eliezer and Melech benefited from the substantial edible contributions of the village: largely flavour-free stews and sauces, bread, and water for one; unfamiliar but delectable grasses and grains for the other. Little round balls of packed sugar-and-honey treats for both. In an odd way, Gashen's house became the closest thing to a home Eliezer had had for many years, and the stability, the knowing he would have a roof over his head, food in his belly, and human companionship — however soggy — for a substantial length of time, comforted him. He even had one or two good nights' sleep.

In exchange, each day he rode up to the monastery, leaving Melech safely outside its walls, and taught Bellar what he knew about the Power. He told the abbot what syllables cause what transformations, what words produce what strange effects in the natural world, what strings of words and incantations caused people and animals to obey or become frozen in time or grow horns or visit the Great Circle. He explained Adam Cadmon, the One, the teachings of the prophets and wise men, and the wisdom of the *Zohar*, book of the Kabbalah. He lectured only on the most dangerous combinations of sounds; the last thing he wanted was to give to another the keys to the entire realm of forbidden knowledge. He left it up to Bellar to decide how to enforce the restrictions among his people— naturally, as Eliezer understood very well, Bellar would jealously guard his own authority and accept no guidance from Eliezer or anybody else. And because Bellar believed in many gods, he was able to absorb all that Eliezer taught in a way Eliezer himself, as a monotheist, might not have been able to.

Assuming, of course, he really was a monotheist...

And then there was one other thing he could do. For many nights he pondered how to limit the scope of the monks' power, so that it would not threaten the world at large. He would enter the monastery through those thick walls made of tablets, thinking he could perhaps construct a dome of binding magic around the place. As he crossed through the gates one morning, he wondered, how long would his spell last? For he and his sorcery would not be here forever.

Unless the books themselves, the language-laden stones from which the walls were made, could exercise their own magic. It would not be the first time holy books exhibited such power.

And so, with a few of his own magic words here and there, he turned them into the generators of a self-renewing binding spell. As the walls rose over the centuries, so would the zone of protection.

"You are a good teacher, wizard Eliezer," Bellar said once, as they were going through a list of syllables whose sequence must be understood and avoided at all cost, lest demons appear and eat the speaker. "Aren't you afraid to give me such power?"

Eliezer rubbed his beard. "Yes, of course. You are becoming a Kabbalist magician, Bellar, and are now in my position. But you were already there in a way; I am merely giving you the power to control your Power."

"And what if the words you teach me are the words I need anyway? What if your sounds are the language of my God?"

"Then you must decide what to do with it, in full knowledge." To teach him what not to say, how to maintain silence instead of exercise speech— an odd sort of education. In fact, a reverse version of his own... and there could well be systems of magic Eliezer did not know about, and perhaps at some point the monks would stumble upon the words and phrases that, in this other system, would bring the whole world crashing down around them all. If so, that would be God's will.

Melech, eavesdropping as always, questioned that.

"One can only do so much," Eliezer said at last, to both the abbot and the horse. "As long as you know what you're doing. Now," he said, returning to the lesson, "here's something you should never, ever say, because it will make it possible for you to communicate with your horse, and you will pay for such knowledge for the rest of your lives..."

THE EIGHTH DAY

Day 1

"OY," **ELIEZER SAID** to Melech. "What are *they*?"

Eliezer thought at first that a passing group of villagers or Bedouin had been attracted out of curiosity to his blowing of the *shofar*: the *Tekiah* and the *Shevarim*, long and short blasts of noise. Then it became abundantly clear that these were not your typical desert people— or people at all! The faces were vaguely snout-like and almost scaly, as if they had excessively dry skin. The beings wore loose-fitting linen shirts and trousers, and the behinds of the latter had been sliced open to accommodate their abbreviated but still protruberant tails. Their feet were bare and elongated, ending in gnarled toes or claws.

Melech merely swung his head, silenced by having no curses he could pronounce on human folly, since these were obviously not human.

"Wizard," one of the leading beings hissed, "thank the gods you have come!" The voice was scratchy and of undefined gender. Whatever the thing was, it could not be easily or comfortably labelled in any way: by species, sex, any God-given category.

"So you know me?" Eliezer was well aware he had a reputation among people, but it had never occurred to him he was gaining a name for himself among God's other creatures. If these were God's.... "What do you want of me?"

"Animals!" it replied, in a fervent non-sequitur. He could see emptiness in the creature's eyes, and indeed in those of all the freaks of non-nature bunched together in the desert and blocking Eliezer's path. "There is an evil book!"

"An evil book," Eliezer repeated. Evidently, someone somewhere was engaged in necromancy and experimenting with the forces of metamorphosis. Yet to create such horrid quasi-humans! The spokesthing for the group nodded, flicked (there was no other word for the action) its eyes, and gestured with its head for Eliezer to follow. The creatures accompanying it slithered more than walked into a ring around it; the leader led, and Eliezer, remaining astride Melech, followed across the packed sand toward a rugged hillock in the near distance. Each of the beings possessed its own odd coloring: splotches of pink, green, and brown, even some bright red here and there, suggesting a variety of original species. Some wore hoods, while others were bare-headed and seemed to have not so much hair as bristles. It was very disconcerting to see them try to walk, when it was obvious they were unaccustomed to being bipedal; the pain evident on their faces was excruciating to watch— he could not imagine how bad it must have been for them. One small being (a child?) even tried to walk on all fours, but gave up that effort very swiftly when its arms and legs proved to be of quite the wrong lengths and configurations for such a position.

"How did you get this way?" Eliezer asked, seeking a clearer path. It was his duty to help these monsters, but without more specifics he could not see how.

"The wonderful terrible book!" his guide informed him, uninformatively. "See!" It held up a five-fingered paw; the ridges and whorls on its palm were limned in black. "*Shalom!*"

Eliezer started at the Hebrew. "*Shalom* to you, too," he responded slowly. "You are educated creatures, then."

"No! We yearn, wizard! And we hurt! Forgive, master!"

Now it was Melech's turn to start, which he paradoxically exhibited by stopping; only after a moment did his gait resume. No other animal had ever considered Eliezer its master, in all these years, and the horse was obviously not at all sure what to think of such an address. Eliezer asked, "Am I truly your master?"

"Oh, yes!" The "s" was eerily elongated. By now they had reached the top of the slight rise.

"Nice to know."

The leader stopped and began scraping at the ground with one of its angular toes; the rest dove at whatever it was trying to uncover, like a pack of insane squirrels attempting to unearth a long-buried nut. Melech shied from the swarm of half-humans in instinctual dread. "Now, now, my friend," Eliezer counselled, "don't be so prejudiced."

"Ah!" the leader cried, as he pulled a roll of parchment from out of the ground to the ambiguous cries of the swarm. Melech made an uncomplimentary comparison to a bird yanking a worm from its hole. A curious parchment it was, of a sort he'd never seen before, with bizarre striations that suggested a most unusual animal skin for such a purpose; there was no way to tell what kind of back it had come off of. "Ssseee!"

"Where did you get that from?" Eliezer asked.

"There!" the leader cried, pointing vaguely westward. "Shiny village! Shiny mountain!" Then it proceeded to unroll the parchment, and in the process rubbed its feet all over the ink-covered surface. "Listen!" And it began to recite something in an alien tongue, one that even Eliezer, with all his travels, could not recognize. But it swayed — it *daven*ed! — it was mimicking the intonations Eliezer had used during his lone recitations of the *Rosh Hashanah* services these past two days, in what was a mock-rite, a parody, an appalling travesty of a holy ceremony! They had watched Eliezer, emulated him, and perhaps had done the same with other religious leaders; lying unseen in houses of worship, they had witnessed priests performing their rituals, learned the words and gestures— animals pretending to holy devotions! Disgusting!

"No sorcerer did this to you!" Eliezer shouted, in fury and horror. "You did this to yourselves!"

"Evil wonderful book!" the leader declared. The others sibilated in response, like a grotesque congregation in an inverted temple. "See!" The leader ran its hand-paws over and over the surface of the scroll, showed off its stains, then read some more. "More! And *no more!*"

"Stop!" Eliezer's fury grew by the second. "In the name of all that is holy, cease this blasphemous farce!" The creatures looked up at him, staring as if waiting for some sign, some token on his part. From humans these animals had educated themselves, raising themselves from the dirty ground to become horrific shams of pious humanity. And had turned themselves into monsters in the process, with the help of this strange scroll and its potent magic. "You have stolen this book from a guide of men's souls," Eliezer said, "while you have none of your own."

Temper, Melech said; he was right, for these were animals without will, or soul to lose, or moral understanding. At least, they *had* been.... and now they aspired to be what they were not and should not be, and despised what they had become.

The leader gazed at him in what might have been pleading or defiance: with no soul behind the eyes, it was impossible to read their expression. Eliezer, now much calmer, knew what he had to do.

"This is *Rosh Hashanah*," he said, "the New Year. As I celebrate the new, you shall revert to the old." For as he knew full well, never should a lowly being *yearn* to be something it was not meant to be. Whatever power the words in their book possessed, he would fight it, overcome and reverse it, and remake them into what they were supposed to be, into what the Lord had intended them to be. He used his own power, drawn from the wisdom of the Kabbalists and the strength of his virtuous purpose, to reshape these abominations, and as he recited the words of the spells he knew, he also prayed to God to forgive his labors during this holy day. There was, after all, no sin in working on the High Holidays if the purpose was to restore what was right and natural and proper.

"No! *Yes!*" the leader exclaimed as it saw its limbs shorten, its snout lengthen, its skin calcify. Whatever these things had once been, they were becoming again, restored to their true selves and returning to the ground from which they had been perversely raised, from which they had perversely raised themselves. The monsters crowded together as they shrank and dropped to all fours, then scurried away into the desert, the smallest, the youngest one, trailing behind. What had been the leader glanced briefly over its shoulder at Eliezer, and it was impossible to tell if its face showed gratitude, or distress, or more likely much of one and some of the other. Eliezer picked up the scroll, opened it slightly and glanced at its smudged, utterly foreign script with dismay. He re-rolled it tightly, or thought he did, but if he didn't know better he could swear it reassumed its original cylindrical shape of its own accord, as if concealing its surface from his eyes. So there *was* strong magic in the thing.... he vowed to return it to its owners, whoever they might be. A solemn and maybe futile quest.

As he watched the creatures disappear, maybe burrowing into the very ground beneath their feet, Eliezer raised his *shofar* once more and completed the sequence of *Teru'ah*, and the long, plaintive *Tiki'ah Gedolah*, and then finally the *Shevarim Teru'ah*. All the sounds, long and short, wailing and staccato, filled the dry air about him until his lungs ached. For it was a special call this year: a call to renew and rejuvenate and purify a world that had seen such perversions arise in it. *May order return.*

"*Oy*," Eliezer said again. "Normally, I don't mind sharing the High Holidays with converts, but...."

Day 2

As the sun went down, and after Eliezer finished reciting the *brochah*s (sadly, without a *minyan*) on the end of the first High Holiday, he proceeded west to seek out the strange glowing village on the "shiny" mountain the quasi-animals had referred to. He let his eyes rove, and finally spotted a glimmer emanating from the side of a hill. He steered Melech toward it, and as they neared they came upon a small collection of huts rising up a slope that seemed to sparkle with a thousand tiny diamonds. The display vaguely reminded him of something. The main street wound its way up the hill in leisurely switchbacks, so that Melech was not sorely tested as he climbed into the midst of the white-brick homes. On either side of the street the little points of glitter made it seem as if someone had gathered the light of the sun and all the stars and concentrated them on this village.

A few people, mostly the very young and very old, wandered the alleys between the houses, although it appeared most were away in the nearby field, walking in circles as they worked upon the rough grass or grain, whatever it was that they were cultivating. Eliezer bent to see what might be creating the sparkle, but could not identify the stones. One of the boys stared at Eliezer, then came boldly up to him and bowed. Such a polite *putzele*! The boy began to speak, and Eliezer adjusted his mind to accommodate the language, a variation of Aramaic it seemed. "Hello, sir! What can I do for you, sir?"

Eliezer held up a hand in greeting and to signal that the boy could relax. "Better that I should ask, what can I do for you?" He looked around. "Do you have a chief or leader of some kind?"

"Oh, yes, sir, but he's in the field. He's our Lord."

"Ah." So, a feudal society.

"He's the most important man here, always leads us in our work. And he's the teacher, too! He—"

"May I speak with the gentleman?"

The boy shrugged.

"What is your name?"

"Banach, son of Galiel. There are some things I have to do for my mother. She asked me to bring some wine from Strion, over there. His wife makes it and it's excellent, she says. I'm not allowed to try it but I'm looking forward to drinking it. They say—"

"If you could run along and fetch this Lord of yours, I would appreciate it."

"Oh, I'll do that, sir. I'll get him as soon as I fetch the wine. I'm not supposed to tarry." Then he smiled in a way that was charming and vaguely disturbing. "I will be your servant."

Eliezer pointed his thumb at Melech. "I already have a servant."

"The *horse*? Don't make fun of me. I am just a boy. Do you like our village? I helped decorate it. Well, we all do, but that's because—"

"My son—"

"—it's our duty, the Lord says, to keep Khalem (that's the name of our village now) shining and raise our light to the sky. It's how we become one with the Great Circle and—"

"I am an old man and don't have time to hear the whole story. Please!"

"Yes, sir." Banach took hold of Melech's reins and began leading horse and rider down the street. Melech was not keen on the idea, suggesting they run now, but Eliezer thwarted their escape with some basic common sense: where would they go? Maybe the child would run out of fuel soon. "My mother told me not to talk to strangers" if only, if only "but you're not a stranger, you're a visitor, and I guess that's different. I'll bring you to our house and you can stable the horse. Well, we don't have a stable—"

"Just run your errand. We'll be fine."

"—but I'll let you tie up the horse and then go to fetch the wine. I have to bring three bottles, because the last time I only brought two and my father was upset because he ran out of..."

And so the child regaled Eliezer with virtually his life story, all while directing them to a clean and brilliantly white house not far from the center of town. Then the boy (*danke Gott!*) ran off to get his wine, and Eliezer dismounted slowly, as exhausted in ear as in back and leg. As he straightened himself and prepared to knock on the doorframe — since the door itself was a mere canvas hanging, although the windows to either side boasted glass panes — a woman emerged from within and bowed to him.

"Hello, stranger," she said, her eyes humbly trained on his chest.

"Greetings, good woman." Melech waggled his head at the formality. "Your delightful son brought me here. I am Eliezer ben-Avraham, a travelling wizard, and—"

She began to laugh. In fact, her amusement persisted long after the point of reason, and entered the realm of the very rude. "Wizard?" she gasped at last.

"Yes, wizard. Now, what I do is perform—"

She just laughed again. So Eliezer conjured a ring of tiny flying elephants and had them perform a complicated dance for her; her laughter turned instantly to shocked (and blissfully silent) amazement.

"Now, as I was saying, if there is any task I can perform for you, I shall be happy to use my powers for your benefit, and all I ask in return is room and board."

"Wizard!" she screeched, pointing at him as if she had just identified Satan himself. "*Wizard!*" She fled inside, and all Eliezer could do was stand there, utterly perplexed, till villagers came running in response to her scream. Before he knew it, he was surrounded by trembling peasants, some aiming hoes and other farm implements at him. He adopted a dignified pose, or as close to one as he could manage given the ache in his back, and waited to see what they would do. One somewhat less soiled figure walked boldly up to him through the crowd and stood with his arms crossed, eyes narrowed. Out of his thick black beard came, "Who are you?"

Eliezer went through the whole spiel again, and then said, "I am not used to being treated as Evil Incarnate."

"Wizards are evil. What do you expect?" With all that facial hair, it was difficult to tell what expression he had on his face, but it was certainly not a friendly one.

"Not all wizards choose to be evil," Eliezer informed him, "and some don't even choose to be wizards." Well— it was a harmless half-truth, or maybe benign lie. "I ask only to serve. Are you the lord of this place?"

"I am the Lord and the Light, yes." A humble man! Eliezer only barely managed to resist rolling his eyes. "What are you doing here?"

"Following my servant," Eliezer replied as he saw the boy return. The whole scene apparently left the child speechless, thanks to God's mercy. Like the lord, Banach passed through the circle of villagers and looked up at Eliezer.

"You can really perform magic?" Banach asked, and was prepared to elaborate on his question when Eliezer held up a finger and *shush*ed him.

"If the people of this village want to make use of my magical services, they may do so; if not, I shall depart forthwith." He turned to the lord. "Now, I have introduced myself; may I ask *your* name, sir?"

"Khalem." The lord reached up and rubbed his chin or his beard— it was hard to tell which. "We can use your services, Eliezer ben-Avraham. I want you to make stars."

Now it was Eliezer's turn to gape. "Eh? Forgive an old man his deafness. You said—"

"Make us stars. We have many and must always have more." He gestured toward the ground.

"I see." Of course he didn't, but no doubt an explanation would come; meanwhile, Eliezer couldn't help pondering whether his powers could actually extend so far as the cosmic.... "Now, where shall I find my humble reimbursement for such labors?"

"By our laws of hospitality, and they are strict, you will stay with the first of us you encountered." Now he motioned toward Banach's house.

Eliezer's heart drooped. With the little *patp'tan*? The walking *gragger*? "If you please, I'm an old man, and I need my sleep."

"Do not insult Galiel," Khalem warned. Galiel's wife, now mollified by her lord's acceptance of this *wizard*, smiled at Eliezer, but he detected no real warmth in her expression. Meanwhile, the mob dispersed, their excitement for the day now having reached its anticlimax.

"So these people consider all wizards evil?" he asked the lord.

"Certainly. Any magic other than my own is *wrong*."

Eliezer raised his eyebrows. "You have powers?"

"Of course! I am the Lord!"

Something inside Eliezer's head snapped shut, much like the scroll's common mannerism; he instinctively recoiled at such divine pretensions. The *shema* came to mind just then: *"the Lord is One"*!

"I see. Then why did the lady laugh when I told her I was a wizard, as if such a thing was so ridiculous?"

Khalem spread his palms out in a gesture indicating, "Why are you so surprised?" Then he said, "Well, look at you!"

Eliezer pressed his lips together to avoid replying to that. When he'd swallowed his fury, he said. "So I shall be looked after. And my horse?"

"You may secure him anywhere in the village," Khalem said, "you need have no fear for him. My people will treat him well."

So Eliezer let Melech go find his own shelter. The wife led him inside, and showed him to a hidden bed that seemed to have been waiting for him. It was tightly stashed in a cozy recess at the back of the house, and a set of privacy curtains hung from rings embedded in the ceiling. She brought him a basin full of heated water and said, "To wash." Which he did.

Then, not long after, Banach returned home from wherever he had gone and proceeded to talk about his day. And talk. And talk. The child was the very definition of empty palaver. "My shoes got untied then, so I had to stop and…" It was as if a greater power than any that either he or Khalem or the very Ancients in the Torah ever wielded had entered the boy's vocal chords. Didn't the lad have to *breathe* like a normal human being?

The father of the family came home shortly thereafter: a husky young man with dust all over his face, bare arms, and clothes. He washed at a well outside, then saw, with some surprise, Eliezer watching him through the window. He raised the cloth that covered the doorway, and stared at his visitor as he entered.

"Hello," Eliezer said. "I am your guest."

Banach then told the whole story, in excruciating detail, until Galiel's eyes became as glassy as his windows. "That's enough, boy," Galiel said. "Wizard, eh?"

"Yes. But a virtuous one, I assure you."

Galiel's eyes now expressed skepticism. "And you will help us with our work?"

"Your work?" So members of the community could make stars? Was there such power here? "Yes, if I can. But I'm an old man, and so—"

"He always says that!" Banach declared.

"Hush!" his father said, and Eliezer silently thanked him. Galiel turned to Eliezer and said, "Then you'll come with us tomorrow, and we'll see what you can do."

For the family supper, the couple allowed him to sit on a low stool — the only legged seat in the room — while the wife hustled and bustled and gathered some nourishment for them. Eliezer watched the amassing of edibles with some pleasure; she seemed to have many baked and preserved delicacies, and he was able to avoid the meat without *insulting* her. The rules of hospitality governed guests as well as hosts.... she tried to serve him some of the wine, but he very politely declined, citing a delicate stomach.

That night, as the family retired early and Eliezer crawled into his bed in the curtained alcove, he had even more trouble getting to sleep than usual. The anticipation became obsessive: how could they do such inconceivable deeds? He might now learn some magical arts he'd never dreamed of — and he had to stop himself by force of sheer will from becoming thoroughly obsessed by the prospect. Waves of something like reprimand flowed from Melech's brain into his own, and to be fair what Melech was "saying" was fair: what had curiosity of that sort done for him, except lead him down some very unfortunate paths?

So he pushed himself into sleep, and awoke almost refreshed to the sound of Galiel calling him in a harsh half-whisper. "Wizard! Come!"

He gathered himself together and exited the alcove to find the low table set once more, this time with flatbreads and cheeses; the wife was busily preparing a hot drink, a tea of some sort that smelled tantalizing. In the opposite corner, the boy still slept (thank God once more!), and the only sound coming from him, mercifully, was a steady if wheezy snore. Galiel motioned for Eliezer to eat, and they shared a silent breakfast under the wife's attentive ministrations. Such was an honorable woman!

They exited the house into what seemed like the blaze of two suns' light. Yet what he was seeing was God's one lantern and its reflection from the houses and those curious sparkles all over. Galiel led him along a well-trodden footpath, climbing up the hill past the field where the peasants worked to a shimmering stretch of bare rock. There, a number of workers — women as well as older men — were chipping pieces of stone into iron pots, and muscled men of Galiel's age carried the full pots away and pounded on their contents with massive black pestles. Khalem stood with arms crossed supervising the operation.

"Wizard!" Khalem came up to him with a smug grin on his face. "Here, see our work!" He scooped up the contents of one of the pots and brought his hand up to Eliezer's face. When he opened his fist, he revealed a palm covered with tiny sparklers. Glass. They had decorated their village with thousands of glass particles.

"And this is how you spend your time?"

Khamel laughed. "No, this is how *they* spend *their* time!" He scattered the glass like seeds on to the rough ground, and opened his arms to indicate the entire village. "And the more stars we spread and shine up to Heaven, the more blessed we are! So, please, use your magic to increase our blessedness."

Eliezer was ready to leave at that moment, forego certain meals and a comfortable bed and a roof over his head. Such madness! And, as he expected, Melech made his usual comment about humanity's inherent insanity. "You're no help," Eliezer whispered. "Stand aside, grinders of stone!" All around him, the people stopped working and stared at him. Fine, let them stare. He closed his eyes and touched the Rock, the foundation of physical existence, and became a conduit for the Power. But this was a dangerous Power, for it was the power of disintegration and, if not carefully directed, even chaos. He of course did not have the power to uncreate the world, but he could rip some terrible gashes in its fabric. He pictured the contents of the nearest iron bowl, pulled the shards apart again and again till nothing remained but grains of pure glass. "Nah!" Eliezer said. "Look in there."

Khamel peered into the bowl, and his expression burst into a wondrous glow. "Magnificent!" He turned to one of the boys. "Here, have the honor." And the boy, happy to be a slave to superstition, carried the bowl away and commenced spreading its contents all over the spiky grass on either side of the footpath as he walked down to the village.

Eliezer now scratched at the hillside, and with the Power raked a little sand-slide off its gleaming face. A thin line of diamond mites streamed through the air and into the bowl. The peasants stood and watched in amazement, and didn't seem to mind that he was doing their work for them. But the Power and his constant need to restrain it drained him quickly, and he had to rest after only a few minutes' work.

"You are a mighty wizard," Khamel said, when Eliezer finally dropped to a seated position in the grass. "Your power is great, nearly as great as mine."

"Then why don't you do this?"

"I don't have that power, wizard. Mine is transcendent." Eliezer looked up at him, and now recognized the fraud for what he was. "I am the conduit between my people and Heaven. I lead them and carry their spirits up to the skies," Khalem said. "To be their lord and guide: *that* is my power."

"They are lucky souls indeed," Eliezer said. "You are indeed their saviour." *Shmegeggi!* He pronounced a silent curse on the man. "Give me a few minutes."

"Of course. We are already ahead of schedule thanks to you."

"Heh," he said, and gave a half-nod. Such a compliment! "I should advise you, however, that I must not work past sundown."

Khamel seemed briefly concerned, then waved dismissively. "No matter. Your health is important, of course."

"I am no weakling!" Eliezer said, ready to defend himself against what was in fact a just insinuation. "This evening begins my required period of rest. I have my own beliefs, you understand." He tried to explain: "It is my Sabbath."

"Ah! We have such a rite, too. The weekly Day of Thanks."

Close enough— every religion had something similar. But he pictured the peasants being convened to address their thanks not to their god or gods, but to their lord.

And so that day, while he was able, he poured his energy into facilitating their mining of glass. His efforts, of course, did not relieve the peasants of their own; Khamel made it clear his work was intended to supplement, not replace, their labors. So even more tiny stars found their way all over the village. It was a wonder the place wasn't completely buried in the stuff by now. And as that image flickered in his mind, he was once again vaguely reminded of something.

Banach arrived to contribute to the work an hour or so after Eliezer, and the boy found the periodic rest breaks a wonderful opportunity to pour statements and questions into his exhausted ears. Eliezer, in a moment of burning exasperation, toyed with the idea of eliminating the child's mouth for just a brief time— he'd seal it up, pretend he did so by accident and was trying desperately but in vain to remember the counter-spell… too cruel a trick to play, but all too tempting. Finally, Banach asked something that Eliezer actually wanted to discuss. "When you were a boy, did you collect stars?"

"No. Not in this way, that is. I had my own way of collecting Heaven's light. I studied, boy. I read and I studied. And I looked up into the night sky and wondered what the stars were. I had to know." Such times he'd had as a boy! Learning was like eating: too full of offered delicacies to resist. He looked at Banach and smiled. "Everything was a wonder then, my boy, because I knew nothing." He shrugged. "Now, I know too much."

The boy commenced a story, something about a dog, and when its tedium became all too clear Eliezer gleefully ignored him as his thoughts returned to his childhood. It hadn't been an easy one, but it hadn't been horrible, either. So much he'd forgotten, or thought he'd forgotten. A lifetime of gathering stars— so many, he couldn't remember them any longer. Such a waste!

"Banach," he said, and then repeated the name with greater and greater volume until he succeeded in interrupting the latest narrative. "How many stars are enough?"

"Enough?" A creased brow: was it only the boy, or had the thought never occurred to these people at all?

"Yes. Are you all supposed to cover the ground with them?"

"Well, I guess so. Anyway, the wind was so strong..."

As the prattler prattled, Eliezer thought about Khalem and his people, about the futility of processing such natural glass just to add endlessly to the village's glitter.

"Melech," he said aloud, even as the boy continued to speak. "How does one satisfy these people?"

Remember, Melech said, and dredged up from Eliezer's mind a picture: it was himself, although of course seen from the inside. Those days of play and fear, when there were moments of delirious childish fun and others of alarm, worry, danger, since a child is a vulnerable creature subject to constant threat. But the fun! The silly behavior, and even Eliezer himself, like Banach (although not nearly to the same degree!), wanting to speak to the adults and make them listen. Pay attention to me! he would insist as his parents concentrated on more pressing matters; listen to the wonders I have seen! he wanted to demand, not understanding that they had already seen such things and no longer saw any wonder in them. But he would refuse to keep his peace even in the face of their impatience.

To be a child again— he yearned for such a thing, and wouldn't wish it on his worst enemy.

The wonders: the breathing of leaves, the music of birds, the tender promises of first buds on trees, the blue of the dusk sky, the first time one held a girl's hand, the first—

"Melech!" So wise a horse.

Eliezer, with a mighty effort, lifted himself from the ground and sought out the lord. He would have to use several spells: binding, protection, even tap into the *En Sof* for a touch of Heat Paradox… it was insane and glorious, yet such spells, and in such variety, were much easier to apply to the nonorganic than to beasts. And perhaps he could free himself and maybe others. "Great lord Khalem!"

"Wizard! Are you ready to return to work?"

"I am afraid it is getting late, and I must leave, for that is my curse. But I offer you a blessing drawn from my memories, of one of my greatest wonders."

"Yes?" Khalem looked eagerly at him, an expectant grin on his face.

"Hot and cold, mixed and in mutual denial: it can be done, and you can have a blanket of stars upon your land, more stars than you can ever extract from the Earth, and they would lie there defying the forces that seek to destroy them." And if he succeeded, he could escape the lord who thought he was a Lord, as well as the boy and his stunning inability to control his linguistic powers. Indeed, Banach was more like the Lord than Khalem was, for the boy could fill a universe with his words. "Banach!" The boy answered his summons, and stood waiting for Eliezer's commands. "Have your mother prepare some of her wonderful baking and other delights for me to carry as I depart."

Banach looked crushed. "You're leaving?"

"As I must." Already, the sun was beginning to fall toward the western horizon, and Eliezer had a scroll to deliver to somebody somewhere. "Don't worry; you'll find another audience soon, I'm sure." At Banach's quizzical expression Eliezer smiled and patted the boy's head. "I come from far away, north of here, and I will give to you the gift of my own story, which contains its own wonders. Now go!"

As Banach ran off, Eliezer turned back to Khalem, who was apparently awaiting an explanation for what Eliezer was planning. "You will have your field of stars, Khalem, and your people will be blessed as I was when I first saw such a sight under God's heaven."

"What do you mean?" Khalem's voice was suspicious, as if Eliezer had cheated him somehow. Little did he know what treasures he would soon find showering upon him. The lord was fully erect, head pointing directly to Heaven but without a *yarmulke* to ensure and proclaim the gap between God and man. Khalem would soon watch the stars fall, and maybe, just maybe, wonder again.

"I must be on my way, lord. Duty calls, and I have others to serve. I am on a quest, you see. My exact destination is unknown, but I'm sure I'll find it."

"Then seek out the town of Balai Cherot; they will certainly provide you with a resting spot and any information — or anything else — they can offer you."

"Thank you, Great One." He turned and walked down the hill toward the home of Banach and Galiel and the unnamed woman; the latter had prepared a linen sack for him, and inside were enough tasty-looking items for much hearty *fressing*. "Thank you, good woman," he said, then regretted he had never asked her name. But he would remember her in his prayers.

Banach followed him down to where Melech stood. Eliezer tied his pouch with its precious contents, including the scroll, to Melech's saddle. It immediately rose from the horse's side and stood out horizontally, aiming at the west. "Patience, patience," Eliezer said to it.

"What!" Banach said, pointing, his mouth agape. He watched in silent awe: at last! "Look at the magic! I—"

"Yes, that is indeed magic, but I will show you much greater magic." At the edge of the village, Eliezer raised his arms, spoke his incantations, and, just to look and sound impressive, clapped his hands. "When I signal to you," he said, "turn around." *And see a sight, boy, that you have never seen before, and that you will remember till you are a very old man.* When they reached the last house of the village, he stopped Banach and made a twirling gesture with his forefinger. The boy turned to face his home, and Eliezer continued, leading Melech by the bridle to where the desert began again. He did not have to look back to verify the success of his efforts, for he heard the boy gasp, and exclaim, "*Oh!*" Eliezer smiled and walked on as the snow that would never melt began to fall behind him.

Day 3

If Balai Cherot was indeed such a nice, accommodating place, he hoped to avail himself of its hospitality. His desire came from more than just the wish to find a comfortable bed and a roof for the night. It was during the High Holidays, the whole period from *Rosh Hashanah* to *Yom Kippur*, that he most felt his solitude; to be alone, and to have to honor the holy days with his one, sole voice, tore at his heart every year during the first week of *Tishrei*. He would look up at the sky, and ask the clouds if his punishment was not perhaps a little too harsh, but then he'd have to shrug and accept the answer that never came. Not a punishment at all: that was the logical reply to such futile pleading— not a punishment but a self-inflicted fate. At these difficult times, Melech was his only salvation, his companion, the one he never had to leave behind. Eliezer could complain, gossip, practice logical arguments and try out some proposed exegesis of a Biblical text, and the horse would be obliged to listen. Obligations, sought or unsought, all around.... in any case, a visit to a village promised human companionship.

"What do you think?" he asked Melech as they neared a collection of low houses. "Will we get room and board? Will we be welcomed as needy travellers?"

Melech offered no opinion; he simply signalled his impatience by increasing his gait.

The village was a sleepy place, its people unhurried as they wandered its streets. He got the sense that even when they were working, they did not strain themselves; nobody rushed, nobody appeared to be suffering from strain or stress. He stopped a passing gentleman leading a donkey on a short stretch of rope. "Excuse me," Eliezer called in what he understood to be the region's local language, "may I ask you something."

The man — aged, stooped, with a gentle voice — smiled and said, "Of course, old gentleman. Anything!"

"Is this Balai Cherot?"

"Yes, good sir!"

"And is there anyone who needs assistance? Someone who can provide me with a bed for the night in exchange for a little magical work? For, you see, my name is Eliezer ben—"

"Ben-Avraham!" The smile turned into a veritable beam of light. "The great wizard we have heard so much about! Come, come!" He motioned for Eliezer to follow, and the four of them formed a single-file line, alternating man and beast, as they walked down the village's main thoroughfare. "You can help us if you wish, but we take no payment for doing Akhtat's bidding."

"And this Akhtat is—?" A Prince? Chieftain?

"Why, the Principle!"

"So many names I have heard for leaders," Eliezer said, "but this is the first I have heard of such an official outside a school." So be it. He'd had enough of kings, "queens", and especially mayors....

"Oh, we are all well educated," the man boasted. "The Principle directs us."

"As he must."

"Eh?" The apparently deaf old man said nothing further, but just continued toward some unknown destination. Light flickered now from many corners as the villagers greeted the deepening night with their fires. One particularly bright flame blazed outside a two-storey building in the very center of the village, into and out of which passed men and women through a thick, rough-hewn door. "Here! Come! This is the home of the Principle!"

"He is a popular man!" Eliezer shouted in his ear, and the old man reared back.

"No need to raise your voice to me! I am a mere Minion."

"You have been very kind, Ameer!" Melech chuckled, and Eliezer realized his mistake too late; the old man was gone, although the mule remained unattended. Eliezer left Melech standing before the hitch, remembering to throw the rein over it to provide the semblance of securing his horse; such a precaution prevented misunderstandings. He pulled the heavy door open, and revealed a room — no, a veritable hall — overflowing with villagers stuffing their faces from silver trays carried by boys and girls, and swinging clay mugs around. He must have stumbled upon a party of some sort!

As soon as he entered, he was beset by greeters: everyone in the room rushed up to him and noisily (and irresistibly) offered him food and drink. Of the former, he accepted as much as he dared, provided it looked reasonably kosher (or non-*trafe*); of the latter, he was careful to avoid anything harder than wine, for it was not Purim and he dared not indulge too strenuously today. He didn't get a chance to speak, or introduce himself; the treats came at him without pause, without hesitation. Eliezer looked around and saw the old man, the Minion, talking to villager after villager and gesturing in Eliezer's direction.

Finally, someone came up to Eliezer — a middle-aged and very fat woman with a shorter man following in her wake — and spoke to him without offering refreshments. "Great Wizard!" she yelled over the noise. "Welcome, welcome! Fill your stomach!"

"Thank you, um…" With his rising inflection and eyebrows he invited the woman to identify herself, but the effort failed miserably.

"There are rooms upstairs for travellers; feel free to choose any one you like." She glanced left and right as if she were about to let him in on a state secret. "I would recommend one at the rear, as they're quieter!"

"May I speak to the Principal?"

She cast him a puzzled look. "What have you to say of it?"

"I'm sorry?" He gave her a similar look.

"You have an opinion?" Now, in the back of his mind, he heard Melech chuckle again, but other than laughter the horse offered nothing.

"Your ruler!" Eliezer said to the woman. "Akhtat!"

"Yes, the main force, the First of all that rules." When Eliezer just stared, she smiled, then spun and lifted from a passing tray a tasty round roll slathered with butter. "Here. Eat!"

"But what must I do?" he asked her. "I must earn my bread."

Now, her expression turned to shock, as if he'd blasphemed. Maybe he had— it was so hard to tell with these *goyim*. She turned away, though not with any malice or desire to abandon him— she just seemed baffled, and out of her depth, and wishing only to find a more comfortable conversation. *First of all*, Melech whispered to him in mind-speech. Eliezer awaited the rest of the sentence, but it never came, and now he stood utterly confused in the maelstrom of noise and movement (and eating!) until he had to surrender. He reached for another pastry, a honey-and-cream confection that delighted tongue and tummy, and hunted for the stairs.

Toward the back of the crowded room he found a set of solid stone steps leading up to the guest rooms above. Eliezer began to climb, the arthritis in his legs berating him for his presumption; then, suddenly, he found himself lifted up bodily in the air and planted aboard a palanquin of sorts carried by four bulky young villagers. Meanwhile, a squadron of boys and young women preceded him up the stairs, and hung about his "carriage" while he looked down the dim corridor at the various open doors inviting him. He calculated which might be the quietest room and pointed to it; the attendants raced ahead to prepare it, while his porters hurried him in its direction. Such indulgence! And yet he felt ashamed that they would think him so frail... "You may put me down," he said to the nearest carrier, who replied with a vigorous shake of his head.

"The Principle guides me and tells me what to do."

Eliezer nodded. "I understand, but—"

By then his room was ready, and the carriers brought him inside and lowered the palanquin sufficiently for him to disembark. The bed was practically buried with accretions of sheets and blankets; curtains both practical and decorative coated the walls; an entire meal awaited him on a short but wide stand next to the bed. The preparers stood in a circle around the bed, leaving just enough space near him to pass through. Were they going to stand here all night?

Then it became clear that, yes, they would!

"I am fine now," he said. "You may go."

"No, we will help," one of the young women said, and began to pluck at his clothes.

"No!" *Gevalt!* "Please, let me be!"

The distress on their faces — women, boys, men — was just as distressing to see. The stalemate lasted seemingly for hours, but in reality endured only a few moments. Then one of the young women came up to him, smiled, and proceeded to pull at her own garments!

"*NO!*" He stood beside the bed, fists on hips, and said in a voice that, despite all his efforts at self-control, trembled, "Please be good enough to get out!"

"But we are commanded by the First One, the Principle—"

"I understand!" No movement. "He is a powerful leader, but as your guest I beseech you for some privacy!"

Within seconds, the room cleared. His heart pounding from his near-death-by-embarrassment, his head pounding, Eliezer finally managed to take a proper breath. He took a moment to look at the door: no lock. So, with a few chants, he fashioned one: he watched the doorknob sprout a keyhole beneath, and a key float before it, insert itself, and twirl the bolt home. Eliezer collapsed on to the bed, nearly crying as the relief at his escape flowed through him, and without even taking time to undress or slip under the many blankets he drifted off into a deep sleep to the sound of merriment and generosity rising from below.

He was awakened the next morning by pounding on his door, by frantic efforts to turn the doorknob and break into his room, and cries of "What do you need? What do you require, Great Wizard?" It was chilling. He called to Melech, who transmitted grunts instead of words, or perhaps snores — certainly nothing coherent or even approaching language. It was obvious what he must do. The room had a window, one he managed to open with some effort, and he looked out over the village, which was now in full daytime slow-moving activity. People walked, aimlessly it seemed, and when two met at a corner they couldn't seem to agree on who should proceed through the intersection first. Villagers carried jugs and bags and platters of food around, stopping at houses to deliver what had been ordered or, more likely, had simply been needed.

Generosity to a fault.

These people surrendered themselves to each other, all at the behest of some quasi-divine ruler who commanded them to do more than accommodate each other. It was a tyranny of kindness, a dictatorship of altruism, and he would seek out this Principal and try to reason with him, if that were possible. For it was one thing to be kind; it was another to be obliged to be so.

The horse laughed.

"Melech, you're awake! Help me here." Eliezer began the process of transforming into a butterfly so that he could flutter to the ground and search for his ultimate host, the one who had an entire village show him an unsustainable amount of raw hospitality. He would insist — demand, if need be — that he be allowed to pay for his accommodation, his appallingly kind treatment.

But before he could complete the metamorphosis, another voice sounded at the door: the Minion. They had evidently summoned him, thinking he could coax Eliezer into further self-abasement. "Great Wizard!" came the old man's cry, blurred by the thick wood.

"Leave me be, Minion!"

"But it's time for breakfast!"

"No! Enough!"

"I will leave it at the door; take what you want."

Despite all his efforts at fortitude, Eliezer's belly betrayed him, grumbling in the midst of his defiance. "You can't conquer me!" Eliezer said, whether to his stomach or the Minion he did not know. Well, just a peek— he heard nothing more outside his door, and opened it a crack. At his feet was a tray laden with foods: a bowl of meal drenched in cream, breads that had been dipped in honey before being baked (he recognized the golden brown crust, the delectable aroma!), cheese so fresh it perspired.... well, maybe a taste....

"Melech," he said with his mouth full, "what shall I do?"

Follow the Principle, the horse said. And of course he was right; for although he should not take kindness without offering his services in return, it was a kindness to accept. And thus he exercised a different sort of magic. Obedience to these people's master was their highest virtue, and so should it be his own. Melech said something mysterious about reflections, but Eliezer couldn't make it out.

After eating as much of the proffered breakfast as he felt he should — and once he began he found it difficult to stop — he cautiously left the room and went downstairs. The place was now deserted except for one bundle of clothes curled up by the fireplace; it wasn't hard to recognize it as his old friend. Eliezer tried to exit without awakening him, but he couldn't take a step on the creaking floor without the Minion jerking into consciousness. Eliezer steeled himself against a potential onslaught as the Minion rose to life.

"Great Wizard," the Minion said on seeing him. "You are well?"

"Wonderfully well, thank you."

The Minion got to his feet. "I am sorry if we were a little too, well, enthusiastic."

"That's all right."

"It's just that it was my duty according to the Principle to be your host, and, well, I did what I was required to do."

"As do we all, my friend." Eliezer moved slowly toward to door, glancing in various directions to ensure no mob would assault him from his blind side. "I must go on, but I must first thank you for everything you did."

"Nonsense. We obey our Principle."

"And so do I."

"Is there nothing more we can do for you?"

"Well—" He pulled the scroll from his pouch and showed it to the Minion. "Have you ever seen anything like this?" He tried to unroll the parchment but, oddly, could not find its edge. *A powerful book it is!*

"Such a strange hide," the Minion said, eyeing its streaks. "We have heard of bizarre beasts raised in the west. May I take you th—"

"No!" Eliezer strained and managed to produce a smile. "Thank you. But your greatest kindness would be to let me find this thing's home myself."

The Minion bowed. "The light will always shine for you, Great Wizard, in your travels." He then gestured to the front door, inviting Eliezer to depart if he wished. And he did so wish.

"I'm sorry that I did not have the opportunity to greet and thank the one who commands such delightful treatment of guests. Where may I find this Principal of yours?"

The Minion pointed to his chest, and Eliezer smiled. "I should have known. I am very pleased to meet you."

The Minion stared at him in what seemed like utter confusion. A little stupid, then, but as well-meaning as they come.

Melech waited outside as always. The horse was nibbling at a pile of barley and hay that lay at his feet; there was no telling how high that pile had originally been. Apparently, the two had both been very well accommodated. Melech lowered himself, and Eliezer climbed aboard, so to speak. Before turning Melech toward the street leading out of town, he found the corner of his eye caught by the bright light of the torch that continued to burn above the front door.

"Theirs is a powerful Principal," Eliezer said.

Melech nodded, then emitted an enigmatic snicker before obeying the reins.

Day 4

The feast continued all that day and into the evening, for Eliezer discovered not long after leaving Balai Cherot that his hosts or host had added a canvas sack filled with treats to his usual arrangement of saddlebags. Their hospitality, it seemed, stretched far beyond the borders of their village, and for that he was truly thankful. He munched on a roll filled with prune jam as he approached a sizeable city, its own boundaries clearly delineated by a high wall of massive stone blocks. The masons had done a masterful job of cutting and joining the blocks; no mortar or remaining daylight appeared in the seams between them. Eliezer wondered if he should ask for admission from whoever might be guarding the gate, but his request was forestalled by a sonorous voice.

"Who goes there?"

"Eliezer ben-Avraham, itinerant wizard." He looked around for the source of the question but was unable to make it out. Meanwhile, dusk was falling, and he hoped he could earn a bed soon.

"You are one of *them*," the voice declared. Eliezer feared that he knew what that meant.

"Then I will not bother you," he said. The back of his neck tingled.

"You are not welcome here."

Without bothering to reply, Eliezer turned Melech away from the gate and proceeded toward the desert. Better a stone for a pillow than hate for a blanket. Yet the gates opened, and the city beyond — despite the fires illuminating its streets and houses — exuded darkness. Back home, in his own village where he had pursued his forbidden studies, he had seen such darkness and known such fear. Or was he inventing a crisis? Was he measuring the present unjustly by the past?

"You are not welcome here," the voice repeated. "But if you must be among us, so be it."

"I decline your reluctant invitation, faceless one."

"Seek your own kind; you will find them within."

"You expect me to come where I am not wanted?" The city itself seemed to be trying to swallow him, and if it weren't for the powers he possessed, he would have raced away from that maw, with its stone teeth and lightless, invisible tongue. His strength lay in the very skills he wished he'd never gained. He needed to understand these people, or whatever they were.

"You will come where you must. Your people need your help."

Doom: it had gone from an invitation to a requirement. Eliezer patted Melech's neck, apologized mind-to-mind, and steered the horse inside. As if to consciously reinforce his unease, the gates shut behind him with no evident human assistance.

Eliezer rode Melech through the bleak-looking streets. No one was out; no one even patrolled. What now? He found himself going in circles, riding down one street and then another and then returning to the same one he had left, or so it appeared; it was almost impossible to tell street from street. *Edges and perimeters*, he thought, and chose to hug the wall, remaining as close to it as he could while tracing it in a counter-clockwise exploration. Melech's hooves echoed off the bare, blank stone.

In a matter of an hour or two, and in the deepening night, he finally found what he'd sought: a cluster of warped houses huddled against the wall on the far side from the gates. If he didn't know for certain what it was at first, he certainly could not mistake it when he saw the squat brick building with the *Mogen David* upon its front, above a round window of stained glass and, at ground level, a set of doors. In this ghetto, as elsewhere, no one was abroad. Eliezer dismounted with a grunt that also resounded in the silent night, and approached the doors of the tiny *shul*. Not *shabbos*, not *yontif*, but would there be an evening service, a *Maariv*? He took hold of the chilly iron handles and pulled.

In the unlit interior, a single candle glimmered; a few figures were silhouetted in the front row of pews, and heads turned immediately at his entrance. What he saw amazed him: a row of bearded faces, ancient and worn, eyes widening at his appearance. Then, the scratchy whispers rose:

"No!"

"It's impossible!"

"Maybe it's not..."

At that, the faces showed terror, and some of the men half-rose as if to flee.

"Who are you?" one of them demanded.

"I am Eliezer ben-Avraham, the wizard. I—"

"It's a miracle!"

That was when Eliezer counted the heads, and in the dark the truth dawned on him. For there were only nine.

"How long have you been waiting?" he asked them. "How long since you have had a *minyan*?"

"Many years," they said, not in unison but in a chaotic chorus. In such circumstances, they would have done without, by necessity, but he could understand why they would wait and hope, to see if a tenth man appeared to make up the quorum. The *shul* and its services had been on hold for a very long time.

"None to be *Bar Mitzvah*ed," one said.

"None would dare," said another.

"None with the courage."

"None with the ability."

The explanations and complaints came fast and furious, and Eliezer listened with a growing pain inside. For a small community, such losses were death. Lose the *minyan*, and watch the remaining members age, and eventually there would be no one to serve at all. "Let us begin the service," Eliezer said, provoking an instant scrambling as the old fellows took up positions, one at the front to lead the others: their ancient rabbi, performing his duties in a bleary light with no doubt bleary eyes. And for the first time in many, many months, Eliezer was one with another nine.

After the service, Rabbi Hakim invited Eliezer to stay with him overnight. Hakim was as gaunt a man as Eliezer had ever seen, as gaunt as the famine-beset people he had seen in his travels, but Hakim's hunger was not wholly from lack of food. Hakim told him horror stories of the Guards, the ones who ran the city in the name of its King and determined who got what and when. It was the Guards who kept the small Jewish population confined to their ghetto, and ensured that they would have a difficult time performing even the most innocuous rite. A *briss*, maybe; a *Bar Mitzvah*, most unlikely. The Guards would starve the community physically or spiritually, whichever was most effective.

"No children of your own to take over from you?" Eliezer asked, as they sat in Hakim's hovel. His wife, a tight-lipped and dour woman who seemed to have not a single tiny area of unwrinkled skin on her face and hands, served them tea without looking at either man. The house, which barely deserved the name, was draped with drying clothes and packed with books jammed into every corner and against and under every piece of furniture. The place had an inescapable smell of age, decay, and cramp.

"A son."

"And where is he?"

"I cannot say."

"And you can't leave?"

"To go where at our age? If the Guards would let us out in the first place?" Hakim would take a sip of tea, then rise to move some of the books over here, some over there, trying to clear a space for Eliezer to sleep. "The young, the few that there are, do labor, pay taxes, pay obeisance to the King, and offer us nothing for the *shul*."

"And the Guards' plan for the community?"

"Oh, that's where it went!" Hakim said as he lifted one of the volumes. "*Nah*! We are the scapegoats until such time as we disappear and they find another group to justify their power. What else?"

"What else is new?" Eliezer wanted to stop Hakim's perennial fussing, but didn't want to disturb what was becoming a treasure hunt. Hakim broke out in a broad smile over dredging up one particular leather-bound tome. "What can I do?" Eliezer asked. On their way to Hakim's home, he had explained his curse and burden.

"Do? Stay and make up our *minyan* forever?" For a moment, Eliezer feared that that was precisely what Hakim would ask him to do. "And to what end?" the rabbi added. "Tomorrow, the day after, another will pass away. I'm an old man, we're all old men, and what's the point of trying?"

In due course, the dusty, flattened divan on which they had sat became an oasis of fabric in the midst of the vast landscape of books, and the wife found cloths of suitable dimensions to act as sheets and blankets. Melech, meanwhile, had been left outside in the alley beside the house, and reported that he had found some tufts of grass to nibble on. Once again, Eliezer had not bothered to tie him up, and said to him now, silently, "When you're ready, please look around, and tell me what you see."

Melech agreed to the assignment, but for now drifted off into a deep equine snooze. Once they had all gone to bed, Eliezer tried to perform the human equivalent, but had too much on his mind to find sleep so quickly.

The next morning, he awoke from a restless slumber (exacerbated by a divan with no more give left to give) to a hasty breakfast and a rush to *shul*, where the rabbi would be able to perform his first *Shaharit* in many, many years thanks to Eliezer's presence. And it would be Eliezer's first time at a morning service for a shamefully long time. As the two men walked to the *shul*, Eliezer sent an inquiry to Melech, who promptly informed him that being a horse made it difficult for him to snoop around.

"So what do you want me to do?" Eliezer subvocalized sarcastically, not anticipating that Melech would take the question very seriously. What Melech implanted in Eliezer's mind at that moment, the image that the horse called forth, made him stop in the middle of the street. Rabbi Hakim, walking a little ahead of him, also halted, and looked back at Eliezer with a cocked head. "Are you crazy?" Eliezer shouted, and the rabbi reared back, mouth agape. "Not you, blessed rabbi. Are you completely out of your equine mind?" Now the rabbi looked utterly befuddled, and after a hesitant step or two rushed on ahead. "*Gantse meshug-gah? Ferkakte goyische kopf!* What is the matter with you?" The rabbi, in something of a panic, all but ran to the shul.

Melech was insistent. He would need a disguise, yes, but....

"You've suggested some crazy things in your day, Melech, but *this*? No!"

And so, despite the objections of every particle of his better judgment, Eliezer performed the spell of metamorphosis on his own horse, and somewhere out in the streets of this Godforsaken city there suddenly appeared a stranger carrying a pouch with a *Mogen David* on it and wearing a garment that oddly resembled a horse blanket... Eliezer, hoping prayers would keep him from being damned for this madness, raced toward the *shul*.

The prayers began as soon as he stepped through the doors and quorum was achieved; the men *daven*ed and muttered the *brochah*s, the blessings, the prayers and requests to God to sanctify this day and help His people avoid sin. Eliezer failed to remember the prayers after all this time, so he had to read along in the *siddur* that rested in its place in the pew, its ancient binding almost worn through and its pages ready to tumble into Eliezer's lap. The Hebrew script, on the other hand, shone through crisply on the paper, and that reminded him of the scroll he still carried in his saddlebag. Or that another gentleman now carried.

Ridiculous!

Throughout the service, even during the recitation of the *Barku*, one of the old men coughed wetly, wheezed between the coughing fits, and tried to stifle the noise only to cause it to reemerge more loudly.

After the service ended, Rabbi Hakim took Eliezer by the elbow and led him to the door. "Honoured wizard," the rabbi said, "how long can you stay among us?"

"I don't know. Until I figure out a way to help you, I suppose."

"A week? To perform all the services for a full week would be, you'll forgive the expression, divine."

Eliezer shrugged. As if he had anywhere to go. Maybe a week in such an environment would do him some good; after all, he had spent very little time in any one place, and learned to relish any time he could spend not wandering the desert. "A week? I don't know. As you say, however long I stay it would do you no good in the long run." He pointed to the cougher, who was doubled up next to the *shul*, ready to spill his lungs on the ground. "But you'll need to renew your congregation. Your friend is not well."

"None of us are well, Eliezer. The boys are our hope. Even the ones in their forties and fifties, who have never been *Bar Mitzvah*ed." Without a *Bar Mitzvah*, a man was not a man, and could not be counted toward the *minyan*; and yet, the Guards seemed determined to prevent anyone from achieving such manhood. Eliezer looked around the narrow streets of the ghetto, and caught a glimpse of one middle-aged "boy" pulling a cartload of varied cloths, while another in the distance tugged on the rope linking him to a stubborn goat. Somewhere a dog barked, and he watched as a cat atop a barrel licked its paw, then suddenly decided it had to charge across the street immediately. "The Guards are spying everywhere," Hakim said, "and as soon as we start to organize a *Bar Mitzvah*, they come and threaten us with imprisonment or worse."

"On what charge?" As if it mattered.

Rabbi Hakim snorted. "As if it matters?"

Eliezer smiled at the echo. Now that he was conscious of them, he started to notice the other animals: birds falling and rising among the houses, a horse being backed up into a stable … speaking of which … "I must seek out a friend," Eliezer said.

Hakim furrowed his brow, then shrugged. "Who am I to question a wizard?"

Eliezer called out to Melech as soon as the rabbi left, and was directed through mental pictures to a district close to where the ghetto began. Here, small shops — butcher, baker, even a maker of *yahrzeit* and other candles — fronted the narrow street; tiny faded signs hung in front of the doors, suspended from rotting posts, announcing in ghostly Hebrew letters what was on offer inside. If this was advertising, it was in whispers. Eliezer gazed into the window of the bakery, noticing some delectables he might buy for the rabbi and his wife.

"*Shalom!*"

Eliezer turned and stared. A good-looking, if snouty, beard-less young man smiled at him. "*Oy vey iz mir.*" It couldn't be but was, as he knew full well, for he himself was responsible for this walking impossibility— or rather travesty, just like the ones that the scroll had engendered. "Melech? Really?"

The "man" nodded.

"*Gevalt!*" It took a moment for Eliezer to come up with his simple-minded question: "So, what's new?"

"I was almost arrested," this bizarre version of Melech said in an impressive, low-pitched voice. Eliezer scanned his handiwork: nice skin, good bone structure, a little warped in the ears but otherwise not bad. "Excuse me?" Melech emitted an exasperated sigh. "Are you listening?" Eliezer kept expecting a whinny to burst out between the words. The hair looked wrong... "As I was saying, I was almost taken by one of the Guards."

"Does it itch? The hair? What?"

"Eliezer ben-Avraham!"

"Sorry."

"I saw one." And then, because they could still communicate that way, Melech transmitted the scene directly to Eliezer's mind:

Melech walking the street, looking around. Then, suddenly, a voice: "Who are you? Where are you going?"

Melech looked around for the speaker, and finally found, in the harsh morning shadow cast by a house, a tall figure who seemed to be wearing a pointed helmet. "Sir?"

"Who are you? I haven't seen you before."

"A beast of burden," Melech told him. He showed the saddle-bag. "Carrying goods for my master."

"My memory must be failing me, young fool." So this was one of the Guards. They always hid in the shadows, or carried the darkness with them, and cloaked themselves in such lightless nothing. "We are your masters. You need to be taught that lesson." The Guard moved slightly out of the shadow and reached out a hand. But before he could grab Melech's arm, the horse shied and broke away, galloping on two legs faster than any man could run.

"Such danger!" Eliezer said. "And such arrogance."

"They're everywhere," Melech said. "They'll find me."

"Then a horse you shall be once more, my friend."

"Or..."

Of course— there was no need to change him back to what he was; with his power, Eliezer could turn him into another being, or even another person, entirely. Eliezer reshaped his face, aged him, gave him a stoop.

"How can I go from a boy to a man without a *Bar Mitzvah*?" Melech asked in a voice that was half-equine, half-codger. The cat Eliezer had seen before had apparently followed Eliezer and now crouched under a wagon, ready to pounce on some air. "And what about him?" He pointed at a bird pecking at a house. "And him?"

"What do you mean?"

"Listen: the Guards are out, so the people are not. But the animals are everywhere, wandering around." Melech grinned at that— so pleased with himself for his subtle irony! "Because the people are in the shadows," he continued, "the cats, the mice, the birds, the rats—"

"*Feh!*"

"—everything else is out in the open. And even if they wanted to, too many for the guards to chase."

"Ah." Eliezer nodded; he saw what Melech was getting at. "A thousand little *boychuk*s, young and old, hidden in plain sight." He had to hand it to the horse, who frequently showed such good sense. The monsters he had seen on *Rosh Hashanah* could be an inspiration, even if they were never truly inspired.

· ✡ ·

As he knew from much experience, a ghetto had its own system of communications; messages always found a way to pass from house to house, even under the eagle eye and fox ear of Guards or their equivalent. No matter what the land or language, people in such conditions found a way to speak when they needed to. Eliezer's message spread from rabbi to congregation to just about every man, woman, and older child, and the usual network was assisted by Melech; Eliezer kept his transformations constant and random, so that Melech never looked the same for more than a few minutes. Meanwhile, Eliezer confirmed with Rabbi Hakim that the preparations would take no more than a week; the entire congregation would become rabbis, teachers, guides to religious manhood. If only he could stay to watch! But spending day after day observing creatures learning and reciting Hebrew was a waste of his time and talents, and he also didn't relish the prospect of imposing further on Hakim's hospitality, or of sleeping another night on that flattened divan. And he had a prior task to perform.

"Can this work?" Hakim asked him over a glass of tea in the house bulging with books.

"Their arrogance always blinds them," Eliezer said, "and so they can't see what they're looking at. There are always more of us than of them." He sipped the tea a bit too quickly and nearly burned his lip off; that was what came from impatience! "Strange, though, my friend."

"What?"

"Why did they let me in the city in the first place? Surely they couldn't believe I would be no trouble to them."

Hakim shrugged, in a gesture so much like Eliezer's own. But then again, it was a common gesture among his own people. And it felt good to be among his own. "Who's to know? Such mysteries." But there was something behind the statement, something Eliezer couldn't read.

Before starting the process, he pulled out the scroll. "Speaking of mysteries, have you seen anything like this?"

The rabbi held the scroll gingerly in his skeletal hands, and turned it over. He was no more successful than Eliezer had been in pulling the parchment open. "No. Where did you get this?" Eliezer explained how he'd found the thing. "For words to have such power!" The rabbi shook his head. "But then, you know all about that, eh, Wizard?" He handed back the scroll, a bit reluctantly, it seemed, and Eliezer secreted it once more in his pouch.

"I will return it to its rightful owners," he said, "when I can figure out who they are. That alphabet, from what I've seen of it, looks vaguely familiar, but I can't place from where. Such an old head!" He swallowed the rest of the now cool tea, and made his way outside. He stood with the rabbi in the late afternoon sun, while Melech, in his proper form, stamped one hoof on the ground in anticipation. Soon, there would be not one but a hundred strangers for the Guards to question; soon, there would be dozens of *Bar Mitzvahs* all over the ghetto, and there would not be enough Guards to stop them all, true or false, real or sham. Eliezer began the spell, and gave it a time limit: one week. It would be up to Rabbi Hakim and his people to ensure that was enough time.

All around them, the cats, birds, goats, horses, and indeed the very insects — seen and unseen, in light or shadow — blossomed; they grew or shrank, sprouted noses and fingers and tongues, even gained voices: hissing, warbling, huffing, neighing voices. A hundred soulless "people" would walk among and study alongside the true boys of all ages. Somewhere, in all that confusion, some real metamorphoses would occur, real boys would transform into real men. He wished them short *Haftorahs* and long lives.

Eliezer mounted his horse and prepared to ride toward the gates and whatever fate awaited them there. Would they be permitted to leave? Would he have to come up with some ruse— or, more likely, ask Melech to think of something? Before he could even begin his journey, a young boy stood at Melech's nose, gazing up at Eliezer. "May I come?" the boy purred, and Eliezer recognized his little friend. "I can eat your food!"

Eliezer shook his head. "Thank you for the offer, but you'll have to catch your own mice. After you've completed your studies."

"Thank you, Wizard," Rabbi Hakim said.

"Thank you," Eliezer replied. "It was nice to share a tea with a *landsman* again."

He steered Melech through the now-crowded ghetto: people everywhere, and no way to know who was what. Let God Himself sort them out when the time came; this was the time of the High Holidays, after all, the period of Judgment. Whatever Eliezer did, God would ultimately decide.

He got to the gates of the city at last, and looked around for someone, anyone he might have to deal with. Sure enough, the voice came: "You were welcome here after all, Eliezer ben-Avraham." The same voice.

"Yes, I was." And for a moment he felt smug, felt he had conquered the shadow at least for now, and was tempted to lord it over this Guard, this minor Haman. Then the gates parted, so easily he began to wonder. And not to wonder any longer whose voice this was. Yet he had to be careful, because there was no way of knowing who was listening. "And I am just as happy to leave."

"*Shalom*, Eliezer ben-Avraham, the Great Wizard!" the voice said, in what was supposed to be, or supposed to sound like, a tone of stinging mockery. But as it spoke the first word, the accent was unmistakable; for just that split second, it was so like the rabbi's it might well have been an echo.

Day 5

Eliezer was still trying to get over how Melech had looked as a young man and then an *altekacker*; he couldn't be sure if he should laugh or be appalled and say the *brochah* on seeing a freak of nature. He hoped his spell cast on the other animals would be equally effective and disorienting, and he tried to imagine what the Guards would think of seeing dozens upon dozens of new "Jews" in their midst. He hoped it gave them conniptions.

In fact, he felt as if he could hear the confusion even now, although it was nothing more than a ringing in the ears. He suffered such symptoms when he was low on sleep, and thus experienced them frequently. Usually the sound faded over time, but this whine just seemed to get worse, till he was ready to jump off Melech's back and either curl up into a snoring ball right there, or slap the sides of his head till the noise ceased. Things got worse, not better, when he neared an oasis; despite its green and blue, so refreshing to see in the midst of all that sand and rust, it seemed less like a refuge than a Siren's isle inhabited by tone-deaf sprites.

"A headache like you wouldn't believe," Eliezer commented, and Melech, who couldn't help listening in (and never tried to resist in any case), conveyed his agreement. Eliezer jammed a pinky into his right ear and dug away, to no avail.

The oasis was comprised of a central round pool, a swatch of thick vegetation including twin palm trees, and a tent; the latter was square and quite large, with a peaked roof. A flock of strange birds, entirely white except for a red crown, flapped around the tent, alighted on the palms, and generally made a nuisance of themselves to whoever might be resident here. Eliezer endeavored to signal his approach to the tent with some coughs and humming, yet elicited no response from within.

If subtlety didn't work, perhaps the direct approach would prove more effective. "Hello!" He was mistaken— on the other hand, if the tent was not abandoned, perhaps its inhabitant was in need of help. Eliezer left Melech to enjoy some lush green dinner as he dismounted and approached the tent's flap. "Anybody home? Everything all right?" The birds — somewhat pelican-like, except far more elegant-looking — swarmed him as he neared the white structure, and the ringing was magnified. "If you're not there, may I use your shelter?"

"Come in!"

Ah! He pulled aside the flap and saw a remarkable sight: a pudgy, well bearded soul dressed in pyjamas or some such thing, lounging on a hill of cushions, and surrounded by foods of many types hanging from the insides of the tent walls. Fruit, vegetables, long and round loaves of bread, even some fish that somehow did not smell up the place. Grapes hung from the ceiling; bottles of wine sprouted from the floor; a side of beef protruded from the back wall; a line of drumsticks demarcated the intersection between the front and left walls. "I am Eliezer ben-Avraham," he said, "a wandering wizard, and—"

"Come in, come in. Wandering wizard!" One of the birds tried to get past Eliezer into the tent, but he shooed it away. "No, no, it's all right. Leave it be." The bird swept Eliezer aside with a beat of one wing, walked straight up to the man, and opened its long beak. The man reached in and removed the contents of its pouch: another fish. "Excellent! A fine mackerel." He turned it over once or twice, glanced at one of the other fish in his collection, and said, "This one. Fire!" The cry sounded so much like a military command that Eliezer instinctively ducked, but all that the man did was toss the fish back into the bird's beak. The bird marched out to attend to whatever its errand might be. "Forgive me. I am Farod. You'll also forgive me if I do not get up."

So! The man was a gourmand but disabled, poor thing. "Of course."

"A wandering wizard. You do magic tricks?"

"Not exactly. I earn my room and board by helping others."

Farod looked shocked. "Helping others! Such a waste of time." He swung his arm around. "Can I get you something?"

"Can I help you?"

"Certainly." He looked at a chain of sausages above his head. "Those would be nice. Can you cook them?"

"I am a wizard, not a chef, but I can try." With a few commands he was able to levitate the sausages and freeze them in place about five feet off the ground. Tapping into the Source, he called forth fire, and with the Life-Breath formed a cylinder of flame around them. Within seconds, the skins of the sausages were crackling and dripping— dripping right on the pillows, in fact. "Sorry—"

"No! This is wonderful! Clean!" One of the birds walked in and proceeded to clean grease off the stained pillow with its tongue (*feh!*) until the fabric shone. "Lovely birds; they can do anything." He motioned for Eliezer to sit, and Eliezer found a pillow to his liking.

"What are they?"

"Why, mine, of course."

Melech, the foolish thing, let forth a subvocal whinge. As if owning animals was somehow a sin! As if he himself was not possessed, too!

Farod reached under himself and pulled out a plate; the sausages lowered themselves delicately on to it, and Farod raised the frontmost sausage to his mouth. He beamed after a few chews. "Excellent! You are a fine cook." He yanked the rearmost link from the chain and held it out to Eliezer. "Here— some for you!"

Eliezer's gorge rose. "No. I am afraid I have severe dietary restrictions—"

"Poor thing!"

"—and so I must be careful in my dining." *Trafe*, and handled by this fat being, the sausage was everything he wouldn't go near. "But some of these vegetables might make a nice stew, and perhaps I can have some of these greens I see growing from the floor."

"Do take what you want!" He waved his hand. "Select what you'd like, and we'll have it prepared for you."

"'We'?"

Farod laughed. "Well, of course, not *we*! Come, pick, pick." Eliezer pointed out the vegetables he would appreciate having for supper, and when he was done Farod yelled, "Take!" A bird flew in, pecked Eliezer's choices from the walls and ceiling, and carried them in its beak out to some mysterious destination. Eliezer made a face and was about to object to the now-disgusting meal being readied when Farod said, "Oh, stop worrying; don't be so squeamish. Everything will be cleaned and made suitable for you."

"As you say." Eliezer bowed from his seated position.

"Now, a wandering wizard: do tell! What is your story?"

So, Eliezer told him his background, about his studies and his curse. "And so I must do—" Melech hissed in his head, even louder than the ringing that had still not ceased. "Please!" Eliezer said aloud. "As I was saying, I am obligated—" Another hiss, a shouted *No!* and even a demand for silence. Eliezer stopped speaking, and stared into Farod's attentive, anticipatory eyes. As an experiment, he said, "I am required—" and Melech again shut him up. "—as an appreciative guest to ask you if there is anything I can do for you."

"At the moment? No. Except, can you pass me that pickle?"

Eliezer yanked a cucumber out of what should have been the floor of the tent, which seemed to hover between being fabric and soil. He handed it to Farod, who munched away on it. "These birds of yours," Eliezer said; "where did they come from?"

"I summoned them. I have a bit of the magic myself, you see. Not like yours, of course." He shifted in his makeshift bed. "Just enough to get by."

"Did you learn after your injury?"

"What injury?" He reached under himself once more and withdrew a pair of glass goblets. "Wine?"

"No, thank you." *Oy*, could it be? "So you can get up?"

"Well, when I have to. Please?" He held out one glass, and cast a glance at one of the hanging bottles. Eliezer got up with great difficulty, his arthritis punishing him for his presumption, and snapped a bottle from its clutching vine. He handed it to Farod, who called out, "Open!" A bird entered, grabbed the cork in its beak, and with a little help (very little!) from Farod managed to twist it from the bottle's mouth. "Not even a little?"

"No, thank you." He lowered himself once more to the pillow. "My arthritis: my legs, my back. I must not try to strain myself like that again, you see." His brain was in full flight. "For if I do that too often, well, I'll likely cripple myself and have to remain with you." He smiled as if he were trying to make a joke out of a horrible truth. "Forever. Eating you out of house and home."

"More work for the birds!" Farod laughed.

Mein gott! The bird that had assisted with the bottle hadn't left yet, and it seemed to gaze pleadingly at Eliezer. *What?* The ringing came again.

"See my shelter?" Farod asked. "Such delights, and I have trained my little friends to keep it well stocked."

"We have something similar in our religion," Eliezer said, now careful about his every word. "At harvest time, we build a shelter and line it with foodstuffs, just like this." He motioned around him as if happily comparing the *sukkot* to this— well, the word "travesty" came to him again. A week of travesties! "However, the difference is that our shelter is lined with foods we ourselves have harvested."

"No!"

Well, it wasn't entirely true, but Farod did not need to know that. "Yes, it is how we celebrate our hard work in sowing and reaping that which sustains us, and how we thank God — our God, I know nothing of yours — for His bounty. It is a very humble celebration."

"Such a waste! Why harvest your own when my birds can do it for you?"

A good question. Eliezer shook his head; not one word would sink in when it came to this embodiment of sloth. There was nothing more to say.

After a few moments, Farod said, "Here you go!" A bird walked in slowly, carrying in its beak the wire handle of a steaming pot. Inside was a lovely looking and nice-smelling vegetable stew, thoroughly non-threatening in terms of the laws of kosher, but representing something terribly disturbing. But was this really any different from how he treated Melech, who surely had no more choice in how he spent his days and energy than did these fowl? A beast of burden was a beast of burden, whether that burden was a pot or a man. Yet still, this all seemed entirely wrong.

They know you can hear, Melech said.

So it *was* the birds! An animal himself, Melech could interpret their cry far better than he could. He asked Melech what they were saying.

Let us go!

"What?" Eliezer couldn't help himself, and blurted out the word. Silently, he demanded, "Do I look like an avian Moses?"

Farod watched him fail to eat, despite the spoon now being held out to him by a second bird. "Is there something wrong, wandering wizard?"

"No." He had to eat, so he took the spoon carefully to avoid any bird saliva getting on his fingers, wiped the handle with the nearest accessible flap of pillowcase, and raised some of the stew to his lips. It was delicious. And all cooked by birds? Domesticated birds— just like dogs, cats, cattle? If one trained a dog to fetch a stick, or one's scroll, or shoes, was that any different? But Melech wouldn't let him escape: *Set us free!* he translated, and Eliezer shook his head once more. The ringing in his ears — the psychic bird-calls — wouldn't go away, wouldn't even fade. Eliezer stretched his jaws, thinking that might provide some aural relief. It didn't.

"Farod," he said. "May I ask a favour of you?"

"Yes."

"I found this scroll." He hunted for and extracted the scroll. "Does the script look familiar to you?"

Farod managed to open it just a bit before it flicked back into its original cylindrical shape. In fact, it seemed to be rolled tighter than ever. "Odd. I'm afraid not, what I could see of it, Eliezer ben-Avraham. Should it?"

"No. I was just hoping you could direct me to its owners. I must return it, you see; that is my primary duty. I must pursue this quest as soon as possible."

Farod looked disappointed. "Oh, but you must stay the night. There's so much to eat! So much to do!" It was indeed too dark to leave, and find another refuge, or slave-camp...

"Yes, but in the morning I must be on my way." And now he understood Melech's warnings, for had he divulged his obligation to agree to any and all moral requests for help, he might well have found himself one of the flock, subject to demand after demand after... the real Moses had not been prepared to tolerate such bondage. "Tell me, Farod: do your birds ever fly away?"

"Ha! They are beasts, wizard; they have no will."

Whatever he had done — summoned them, created them — they could not control their own limbs or destinies. Farod had seen them as less than human, as indeed they were; and lacking in souls, as indeed they were; and existing solely to serve him, as indeed they were. And yet...

"It is a desert, Eliezer ben-Avraham. I would not survive without them, and they would not get far without me."

"Yes," Eliezer said, keeping his tone as neutral as possible, "it is for their own good."

"And mine!" Farod laughed, then actually moved a little, if only to make himself even more comfortable. "Tell me about this harvest festival of yours!"

Eliezer began to tell him about *Sukkoth*, the time of joy at earned plenty, but then pleaded fatigue and was able to earn a place among the pillows. But before he settled down for the night, he went outside to relieve himself, and as he did so plucked one of the fish from the wall when Farod wasn't looking and threw it to a tightknit group of the birds, who devoured their dinner with fervor.

Another largely sleepless night, in spite of a full belly and very comfortable "furniture." Farod snored on the other side of the tent, and the plaintive wail of the slave-birds rang unceasingly. But what could he do? And what right had he to do anything? The birds were the man's property, just as all of nature was man's to do with as he pleased. For in the Garden had not Man been given dominion over creation? Man had been given the power to name the plants and animals, and thereby control them purely by identifying them. That was the power, the true power: the word, the name.

Just before he fell asleep, Melech asked him, mind to mind, to identify the species. Even if it was a pre-existent genre of bird, Eliezer was no ornithologist, and didn't care to guess, and was too exhausted to care right now, anyway. So he fell into a shallow snooze, shutting out the snoring and wailing and pleading.

For breakfast, Farod allowed him to choose from his hoard of baked goods, and Eliezer selected some fine buns. He had no idea how birds could do such work, but obviously Farod knew how to train them to perform any desired task. Melech was awake, too, and asked repeatedly what the birds were called.

"Forgive *my* curiosity," he said between bites. Farod lay in what appeared to be exactly the same position he'd been in the night before. "But what are your feathered 'friends' called?"

"Called?" Farod adopted a thoughtful expression. "I never bothered to determine. I just call them birds."

"And such they are. But..." The ringing intensified to the point of being truly painful. "Ouch!" It wasn't just the birds, either; Melech was adding his own inarticulate complaints to the chorus.

"Are you all right?"

"Yes, yes. Please!" He waggled his head. "A species, whether brand new or newly discovered, must have a name. I have a name to suggest. A humble recommendation."

Farod laughed with sheer delight. "Yes! It would make summoning them easier, I think. What name shall they have, wandering wizard?"

"*M'shuchrarim.*" Yes, a good name for such creatures.

"*Meshkug...*?"

"*M'shuchrarim.*" He'd considered *B'nai cholin*, but had feared committing blasphemy by taking the phrase from the *Haggadah*. "A fine name. It has such a lovely ring to it."

"What is this name, wizard?" Farod asked.

"It is Hebrew." He held up a finger to forestall conversation. "Wait." It was true! Silence! Blessed, divine silence in his head. Farod, now truly baffled, stared at Eliezer. "So quiet," Eliezer said.

"But what does it mean?"

"'The freed ones.'" Eliezer rose, stuffed the last of a delicious bun in his mouth, and bowed. Once his mouth was free of tasty treat, he said, "It has been a pleasure enjoying your hospitality. You have so much fertile land here, and water; you have every opportunity to learn how to plant and sow." He stepped outside the tent, and sure enough there was not a white bird to be seen. Melech stood in a patch of tender green shoots, and paused just long enough from his own breakfast to flash Eliezer a grateful glance.

Farod did not follow him outside; he was probably having trouble lifting himself off the bed, after lying there for so long, except to reply when Nature called. But Nature had a thousand voices, and some required fuller attention than others.

Melech lowered himself closer to the ground than he normally did, as if bowing or perhaps just wanting to be more than usually accommodating. Eliezer mounted, gathered himself together, and said, "Let us go."

Day 6

He saw the birds once more. In the late afternoon, a V of smaller white Vs that changed their angles in pulsing rhythms arrowed across the sky, swooped low toward Eliezer, glided and dipped their wings in his direction, and then seemed to disappear — except for a line of tiny red dots — against a fluff of brilliant white cloud. After a daylong ride, every bone in Eliezer's body ached, and for a moment he wished he could join them up there, riding air rather than fighting gravity, but it wasn't to be. For now, he was earthbound, and his shoulder wouldn't take a lot of flapping right now.

He cradled the monsters' scroll in his palms. To think that a beast could take on human form just by touching it! The animals had listened in on human speech, witnessed their behavior, and learned more than people would ever imagine possible. He himself was learning something: that animals, God's soulless creations, weren't so stupid after all.

He patted Melech's neck. "There are people everywhere," he said. "Humanity has made the world its own, even though it hasn't made the world." He looked up again, but the birds had gone and taken their aerial geometry with them. "So be it, Melech. We must find some of these people, ones who are not so isolated, and bring this scroll home."

But where to look? The creatures could have found the parchment anywhere, and dragged it along with them across uncountable miles of sand and soil. He almost wished he didn't have to return such power to those who wielded it, but he was in no position to judge. Especially during this week, the week when every Jew's soul faced the Maker and His annual judgment day. "Well, my friend, what do you think? Which way?"

For a moment, silence; then, *This way; west.*

"Then straight west it is."

After a few minutes of silent riding, Melech raised his nose to the air, and sniffed.

"*Nu*? What's up?"

The horse's senses were acute; his nose was as literate as Eliezer's eyes. So Eliezer gave him his lead, rested the reins, and let Melech follow whatever scent he chose. To his dismay, the target proved to be a bush of sweet leaves.

"That's it? You're hungry again?"

If a horse could shrug, Melech did so. While the horse had his snack, Eliezer took the opportunity to look once more at the text of the scroll; before he had a chance to unroll it more than a tiny fraction, and catch only a glimpse of the inky smudges, the inside of his head growled, and he sensed more than heard, *Do not look!*

When Melech issued a warning, Eliezer knew full well it was a good idea to obey. So he gripped it tightly in his fist, and was about to ask Melech what the problem was when he felt a painful resistance in his hand. Melech seemed as puzzled as he was.

"So, that wasn't you, my friend?" Just to be perverse, he held the scroll up to one eye and looked down the center as if it were a telescope.

What he got then was a gentle but firm "poke" in the eye, a kind of invisible finger jabbing his cornea from the inside.

"A good idea, O truculent Document. No point in starting up with you!"

He slid it back into the saddlebag and watched the landscape glide by as Melech kept up a steady pace, his gait deliberate and relentless. The horse suddenly stopped and raised his head.

"And now?"

Melech had sniffed out an underground stream, and pawed away the cracked soil above it. He spent ten solid minutes at the task, scraping at the ground, till some clear water trickled through the sand. As Melech lipped at it, Eliezer once more extracted the scroll, his curiosity burning like the sun. Just a peek?

No! Again, it wasn't quite a mental word, but more like an intellectual command.

"For a thick parchment you are remarkably thin-skinned. *Nah!* See? I'm putting you away again. You'll be fine." And he did have the scroll halfway back in the pouch before raising it out again. What was so special, so taboo? He pulled at the edge. A corner, a mere triangle of letters: he saw some alien characters grimy with dirt and animal sweat, smeared and faded. The letters were angular, but only vaguely Semitic; they looked more like streaks of ink, as if written with a brush and not a stylus. *Stop! Stop! "Shah!* Enough from you." *Insults!* He couldn't make out specifics, but knew he was being called names. The corner shut itself with a sudden *snick*.

His thirst satisfied, Melech resumed his march westward, keeping his head bowed and seemingly *daven*ing back and forth, from right to left to right to left. Eliezer held the reins in one hand, the scroll in the other, unable to let go of it. A fascinating mystery! It must have come from some ancient land whose alphabet had never been discovered, whose writings had never been deciphered. And here he was with this important piece of hidden history, unable to decode it despite all his years of study. Did he know a specialist? Someone who — if he ever returned home again — could tell him what the piece was and what it meant?

Toward dusk, they encountered a caravan — camels, donkeys, a few horses — camped out under sheets laid across high wooden frames. Eliezer entered the camp with some caution, not sure of the welcome he would receive. A few of the lounging merchants and porters looked up at him as he rode in among them, then one particularly fat one stood up and held up a flat palm. "Halt," he said. Behind him, a dozen or so women huddled: wives or trade goods? "What can we do for you, old man?" he asked, in more of a challenge than an offer.

"A chance to rest, sir, if you will allow."

"All right, all right." The man gestured toward the packs and bundles scattered about, and the much larger bales roped to the backs of the animals. "Look around, see if there is anything you'd like!" He was dressed in nice-looking robes, light blue with gold embroidery. "I am Kitte Stam."

"I am Eliezer ben-Avraham, at your service."

"For gold, you can get anything." Now, his sweeping motion included the gaggle of females as well. "Let me know if anything strikes your fancy, and we can surely negotiate a fair price."

"Of gold I have little," Eliezer said as he dismounted. "What I can offer is far more valuable."

"Indeed?" Kitte Stam eyed Melech covetously. Melech eyed him back. "What a fine steed!"

"No, he is not for sale at any price. I am a wizard."

Kitte Stam laughed. "Of course you are. And I am a king. Bow before me!" he shouted with a mock-stern look on his face.

"As you wish, Your Majesty." With a few words and hand-gestures, Eliezer created a rank of tiny courtiers floating before Stam's eyes, who all bowed abjectly and in perfect unison, then vanished.

Stam applauded with delight. "Wonderful!"

"Is there anything I can assist you with, in exchange for some supper?"

"Assist? Let me think about it. Have some bread and hard cheese and we can consider the question." Stam had one of his servants bring Eliezer a selection of stony rolls, a steel cup of water, and a wheel of cheese that one crumbled rather than sliced. He sat under an awning and made a meal of soaked bread and cheese pebbles with Stam as his attentive spectator and fellow diner. "Good, eh?" Stam boasted.

"Excellent," Eliezer lied.

"Assistance," Stam said. "I always prefer shiny metals — yellow is the best kind — but perhaps I could use some help." He tapped his short-bearded chin with a dry, wrinkled forefinger. "What's that?" he asked, pointing to the pouch that never left Eliezer's side. He sliced some salted meat off a slab his servants had provided for him.

"Personal goods." He pointed to his belly and slightly below. "For my, well, conditions." Then, as supposed explanation, he added, "An old man."

"Ah." Stam chewed thoughtfully. "Nothing else?"

Eliezer reached in for the scroll, then thought better of it, then thought better of it again. "This."

"May I?" Stam asked, reaching for it. Eliezer handed it over and Stam shoved a thumb under the end to unroll it. Eliezer shook his head. "No?"

"It is not a good idea," Eliezer gently informed him.

"Nonsense." Stam tried to lift the scroll's edge; it snapped back so violently that it took a layer of thumb-skin with it. "Ow!" Stam sucked on his wounded digit. "What did you do to this? Why did you hex it?"

"I didn't. It came this way."

"All right, what do you want for it?" Stam turned it in his fist, gazed through its tube as Eliezer had done. "A wonderful thing."

"Nothing. It's not for sale."

"Nonsense, wizard!" He cautiously tried to lift a corner, with an unbitten side of his thumb, and had to let go before it snatched another chunk of flesh. "This for your supper." He jammed meat into his mouth and ate it more quickly than Eliezer had ever seen a human ingest anything. The look on Stam's face was blissful, as if he had found God.

"No deal." Eliezer now worried about whether he should have handed it over; surely the man wouldn't confiscate it? "It is not mine to sell; I am merely returning it to its owner or owners." He smoothed some dirt before his feet and, from (his very faulty) memory tried to carve some of the marks he had seen. "There are letters like this. Do you recognize them?"

"Now, who is helping whom, wizard?" Stam leaned and twisted so that he could see the characters relatively right-side-up. "They don't look very familiar. On the other hand, maybe ... maybe ... I have travelled far and seen many foreign scripts." He shook his head. "Sorry, I can't be of assistance. But you can." He laid the scroll before Eliezer, who resisted the temptation to whip it straight back into his pouch; instead, he slowly maneuvered it toward and into its home, exhibiting a trust he did not feel. "Them." With his uninjured thumb, Stam gestured toward the women. "Can you make more?"

"More?"

"Yes. I have plenty of textiles; I'm a little low on jewelry, so some more rings and baubles would be nice; but my stock of women is especially low." To treat women like this— even to Eliezer, who understood the inherent inferiority of the feminine, this treatment of women as commodities was offensive.

"I cannot create or destroy life with my powers. I can modify it, temporarily," he added, telling a half-truth; he could do temporary or permanent, as needed, "as long as what I do does not violate any of the Commandments of my faith."

"What? That is absurd." Stam shook his head. "But we all want to be good people, eh?" He looked at the women. "Modify, modify. Does that mean you can turn a dog into a woman? And vice versa?"

"Well, yes, but—"

"Interesting."

Eliezer did not know for sure what Stam was thinking; what he was certain of, however, was that it wasn't anything good.

"And you can modify *them*, I mean themselves?"

"Within reason, yes." *Oy gevalt.*

"Their bodies?"

"No!" Eliezer rose to his feet, or tried to. His arthritis and fatigue fought him, held him in place.

"Patience, my friend, patience. No need for concern. More food?"

"Thank you, no, I have eaten enough."

But Stam hadn't; he stuffed some more meat into his maw and chewed with ecstatic delight. At least he had the courtesy to wait till his mouth was empty before saying, "I could eat this all day long! With all due respect, wizard, and I certainly don't wish to offend, but I am not used to being denied what I want. You ask what you can do, and I ask for the scroll, and I ask for help with my women, and you deny me. I am quick to anger if I am taken for a fool, to be cheated out of my food, for example. I am an important man, you know." Although seated, he seemed to tower with pride. Eliezer did a quick count. That was five...

"That is obvious." He looked around the camp. "You have spices?"

"Yes."

"I will make them spicier. You have exotic fruits and other delicacies?"

"Dried and well preserved, and delicious."

"Their flavour will be enhanced, and their preservation extended; they will not go bad no matter what the weather." He closed his eyes, which stopped Stam from interrupting him, and cast a shielding spell around anything in those packs that might need extra protection from the sun and wind. "You have strong beasts?"

"The strongest I can find."

"They will now be stronger." And so he waved his hand, recited a few incantations, and thickened muscles all around him: camel, horse, donkey, goat... and, for fun, a dog, which became so enraptured by his extended energy and strength that it would not stop running all over the camp. "You have silk? Other fabric?"

"As I said."

"They will be stronger, more lustrous, even entrancing to see. You will sell every bolt."

"Wonderful!"

"As for your women..."

"Yes, wizard?"

"They will be so charming, so alluring, so enchanting that no man will ever be able to resist them!" And with that, he did absolutely nothing to them.

"Wizard!" Stam cried in delight. "You have more than earned your meal!" He glanced over to the women, and seemed so utterly besotted as to be ready to take them all immediately. "Your magic worked! You say you are able to strengthen... you understand, I'm sure."

Eliezer bowed. "You will have no problem with stamina or performance."

"A glorious wizard! I will sing your praises wherever I go." Then he looked down at Eliezer's pouch once more. "Are you sure?"

"It is neither mine to sell nor yours to buy."

"A pity. I envy you such a treasure; you are a fortunate man." Envy: that made six out of the *goyische* list. Not a bad total; another he had met recently, he thought wryly, had won the prize for Number Seven. Melech, who had been largely silent up till now, snickered, and Eliezer couldn't help but hear a cynical edge to his amusement. "Enough small talk! Come, dine some more, rest, and sleep. I must test the powers of *your* magic," he said with a broad grin. With that, he lifted himself off the short stool upon which he sat, and headed for the gaggle of females. He would likely get little sleep tonight, but at least he'd be preoccupied and not bother Eliezer any more. One of Stam's servants led Eliezer to a clear area where the servant could fill a large sack with straw and rags and form a creditable mattress. With a few stray pillows, Eliezer had a fine place to sleep. But he held his pouch close, and no matter how bumpy or sharp its various contents might be, he kept it jammed against his side even as he drifted off.

He was awakened by violent shaking and even more violent shouting. "Wizard! Wizard!" He opened one eye and saw his host beaming down at him, as bright as the sun but far less magnificent, or welcome. "Wizard! There you are— I see you in there!" Stam laughed at his own wit. "You are a true marvel! Your magic... well, what can I say?"

Eliezer replied with a grunt.

"I can never repay you for your, well, contributions to my life!"

Eliezer opened his other eye and tried to sit up. Stam helped him to a sitting position; that immediately awoke his bladder. "I am glad to have helped. Now, if you'll excuse me. An old man, you know."

"Of course, of course." Stam stood aside, and let Eliezer get up and head behind one of the camels where no one could see. As he stumbled through bundles, some of them still-sleeping forms, he looked out for a discard-pile of spent young women, but happily saw none.

When he returned from his mission, he found his sleeping-place surrounded by bowls and plates and platters. "Dig in!" Stam told him, and Eliezer, not one to disdain a fine spread, obeyed. Stam watched him eat with disconcerting attention, smiling the whole while. Finally, he said, "I don't know how you did it, but you're a fine, fine worker of magic."

"I can only work with what I am given," Eliezer said generously, and accurately, although not in the way Stam might think it was intended. He was glad that only Melech, and not this egomaniac, could read his mind.

"I am curious— why do you not, well, do something for yourself?"

Eliezer nearly swallowed an entire flatbread at that, but literally bit his tongue. "*Oy*," he said to himself, "what I would do...."

At the end of his breakfast, Stam asked, "Will you come with us? I could use your powers, and I would make your journey among us very, very pleasant. I can assure you that you would lack for nothing."

"I am sorry, great merchant, but I have my own travels to undertake. In fact, I should be on my way even now." He gathered himself and his property together and began to move toward Melech, who stood just a few yards away. As he rose, Stam caught sight of his pouch once more, and the covetous glitter returned to his eye. "I don't know where my quest will take me, but I must surrender myself to its needs."

"Consult the Geomancer, then, wizard. He'll know."

"And who is that?"

"The Earthspeaker. We have heard of him, but no one has seen him." Stam pointed west. "He is somewhere out there. Try to find him, and he may be able to direct you."

"Thank you." Geomancer: a true wielder of magic? Such mysterious powers lay hidden in this world!

"May I at least see it once more? Perhaps I can identify the alphabet, now that I can see them with a rested brain." At the look in Eliezer's eyes, he said with excessive volume, "I may be many things, but I am not a thief!"

So Stam held out his hand, and Eliezer reluctantly withdrew the scroll and put it in Stam's palm. Before Eliezer could move, Stam whipped a knife from his caftan and slid it under the scroll's edge.

"No!"

"Nonsense!" He lifted the parchment just enough to see perhaps a line or two of text— then he suddenly screamed, dropped knife and scroll, and slapped his hands against his eyes. Eliezer knelt and retrieved the scroll, and quickly replaced it in the pouch. Stam lowered his hands from his face and blinked in Eliezer's general direction. "Damn you, Wizard! I am blind!"

"I—"

"Get out of my— leave my camp now before I have you killed!"

"So be it." Melech trotted over and Eliezer mounted as quickly as he could. They left the camp at a gallop, but despite the noise and dust generated by Melech's hooves he could hear and see Stam's rage behind him. "Fool," Eliezer mind-said to Melech.

Human, Melech replied.

Day 7

Eliezer was still shaking an hour after his flight from Stam's camp. All he could do was pray that Stam's condition was only temporary, and indeed a tiny voice, whether from somewhere in Melech's mind or perhaps the scroll's spirit, reassured him that a brief sight had led to a brief loss of it. He hoped that was so.

"Where shall we lay our weary heads tonight, eh?"

He would have loved to find something approaching a "permanent" home, meaning a place they could stay for a couple of days, as *shabbos* was coming and it would be followed immediately by Yom Kippur. His dream was to be where he could do nothing and still be fed and housed. This constant scrambling for mere room and board was simply exhausting.

"I'm too old for this, Melech." The horse informed him that that had been true for quite some time. "Thank you for the support. You're no spring chicken or foal yourself, my friend. Let me know when you detect something," he said. The horse replied in the affirmative, and raised his head every now and then to sniff the wind. A geomancer? Someone able to read the Earth itself? Maybe he could still feel wonder after all, that such magic would exist!

The day waned, and so did his energy. He thought he would have to spend *shabbos* in the desert again, but then Melech skipped a step and said, *There.* He veered toward the south and what looked like just another dune or stone outcropping, although one that was in a remarkably symmetrical conical shape. As they drew closer, he saw that it was in fact a hill of dirt that had been dug out of the ground, and from beyond, or rather within, the hill came the sound of scraping. Melech shook his head and grunted. *Let's go,* he said.

"Danger?"

Worse.

"*Who's there*?!" someone shouted from below. "Identify yourself! And don't come any closer!"

"I am Eliezer ben-Avraham, and —"

"The wizard! Oh, yes, I've heard of you and your little games! Stay away from my hole!"

"Of course."

"No tricks! Stay away or you will ruin it!"

Eliezer dismounted and found a large stone to sit on— for as long as his meagre flesh permitted. Meanwhile, the scraping continued. He peeked into the food sack and worried that he would have to ration the contents very carefully.

"Are you the great Geomancer?"

"Silence! What are you, stupid?"

"Well, I'm speaking to you…"

"*Silence!*" Melech wandered around the hill of loose sand and transmitted reassurance that he had found some edible plants. Good for him! Eliezer awaited more word from whoever was down in the hole and was not disappointed. "Are you still there?"

"Yes."

"What do you want?"

"I thought I was supposed to maintain my silence."

"Stupid! Why are you here?"

"What exactly are you doing?"

"You came to ask foolish questions? I am *reading!*"

"Ah." It was understandable, if tremendously rude. Eliezer also hated to be interrupted when he was in the middle of a good, or important, book. But when he had visitors… "Sorry to interfere with your studies, or is it pleasure reading?"

"*Idiot!*" More scraping. "Oh, I see, I see. Tell your horse my home is not a toilet!"

"My apologies. He is a mere beast."

"Hah!" Scrape scrape. "You came from the East, and you're going to the West, hm?" The voice was that of a man around Eliezer's age— well, an older gentleman, in any case. Scrape.

"I am returning an item to its owners, but I know only vaguely where to find them."

"Make me a blanket!"

"What?"

"I said, make me a blanket! Do your wizard thing, whatever you do, and make me a blanket! A *warm* one!" Scrape. "*What are you waiting for? Do you want food or not?*"

"Is that my task?"

"*Yes*, stupid!" How did the gentleman keep his voice with all that yelling? "Make me a blanket and I'll direct you to my cache. Fail in your task, and you can *starve!*"

The sun had not yet gone down, so there was still time to work before *shabbos*. He drew two skeins of yarn — one white, one blue — from the air, and motioned them to weave themselves into a long, thick blanket. "Thus the ultimate fabrication," Eliezer said to Melech, who did not respond with the hoped-for amusement.

The yarn slid in and out, through and beyond, the lifeless fibres behaving as if they had taken on a life of their own. There were many times when the creation sought to escape the control of the creator.... but in this case the warp and woof were under full control, and the *Mogen David* in the center of the blanket blazed forth in all its six-pointed glory.

"Now," Eliezer called as the final knots were tied and the fringes splayed beneath, "shall I come and hand it down to you?"

"*No!* Don't you come anywhere near here!" So Eliezer sent it flying like a magic carpet toward the hole, and then released it abruptly from its levitation spell. "Hey, idiot!" the voice cried as the heavy blanket dropped upon its owner. "Nice." After a few moments, the Earthspeaker said, "On the north side of the hill, dig three handwidths from the edge!"

Both man and horse found the spot and Melech began to dig with a front hoof. A few inches below the surface, they found a sheepskin bundle, and in that bundle was a collection of paper-wrapped breads, nuts, and dried fruit, along with a skin of amazingly cool fresh water. Eliezer made a fine meal out of these. Melech, however, had to go farther afield to find shoots suitable for his supper.

"Many thanks!" Eliezer shouted when he was satisfied. "Now, really, what are you doing down there?" Melech came by and sniffed at the dried fruit that remained.

"I told you, idiot! Reading! Reading the signs!" Scrape scrape. "A book?"

"Stupid! The Earth! I'm reading her entrails!"

Both Eliezer and Melech froze in place. Eliezer began to say something, then realized he had nothing to say. There *was* nothing to say. He'd pictured lines and charts in the sand, the dropping of piles of sand here and there, sixteen random figures and a few more mystical practices. He had not anticipated undiluted insanity.

"Rest here! It's warm!"

That was true; the ground was soft and seemed to benefit from a glow of heat rising out of the Geomancer's excavation. Scrape scrape. Apart from the occasional sound of his host's divination, there was peace here, and he could experience *shabbos* properly: in *shalom*. Peace.

Shabbat shalom.

The sun settled below the horizon at last. He opened his pouch and pulled out his *tallis*, the one his grandfather had given to him on his *Bar Mitzvah*. The scroll nearly rolled out along with it, but Eliezer stuffed it back in, overcoming its resistance to being confined. He wrapped the *tallis* around his shoulders, fingered its silken fringes, and said the blessings. But he missed the truly proper means to honor the Day of Rest: a *minyan* and a cantor and a rabbi to guide him. His only guide now was a crazy man in a hole.

Meanwhile, the scraping sound faded. "Have some more to eat, wizard!"

"Are you going to spend the whole night down there?" Eliezer asked.

"Of course, stupid! It's what I do!"

"Of course." He ate a couple handfuls of nuts. "And when do I get the answers to my questions?"

"When I'm ready! *Idiot!*"

Apparently, as long as Eliezer remained silent he also remained uninsulted. Thus, he lay down on the dark, warm sand, which seemed to envelope him in an aura of comforting heat, and fell asleep to the sound of one long, gentle, barely audible scrape.

It was a good sleep, although he dreamed without pause, or so it seemed: men screaming at him, women offering food, horses he was riding racing out of control, and stars everywhere: in the sky, around his head, covering the ground. And one little old man slapping him on the head, over and over. As he rose out of the dream he knew what was happening, and finally lost his temper with the fool. "Stop it!" he cried and flailed at the Geomancer's hand. "Enough from you, *chaleria! meshuggenah!*"

But it wasn't the geomancer. It was the scroll; it had escaped his pouch and was smacking him awake, beating him about the cheeks and forehead.

"You? I don't have enough to deal with from that *schmuck* down there?"

"Shut up!"

"You shut up!" Eliezer grabbed the scroll and shoved it once more into the pouch, then sealed the puckered opening with a spell and rubbed his face with both hands. "*Oy*, these magical maniacs. Melech!" The horse sleepily replied that he was awake— now.

"Eat something— and do it *silently!*"

Eliezer did as he was told, but only because he was hungry and didn't want to listen to any more shouted aspersions cast upon his intelligence. He aimed a series of mentally articulated uncomplimentary expressions in both Yiddish and Hebrew at the Geomancer; sadly, Melech, being the only one who could actually "hear" them, couldn't avoid bearing the brunt of his diatribe.

Eliezer spent most of the day reciting *shabbos brochah*s and attempting to suppress his impatience. If the Geomancer had something to tell him, fine— he'd wait. But there was no evidence the fool in the hole knew what he was doing, or had a sound mind to begin with. He could have been a mad hermit, a fraud, or the greatest diviner ever born.

"Idiot!" the geomancer yelled at last.

"What?" Eliezer replied, risking the implication that he was merely confirming that identity.

"Go west!"

"*What?!*" That's what he'd been waiting for? "That's your great esoteric mystery? I should go west? Like I've *been* doing?"

"You seek the home of your item. West and north: climb the hill with the jagged ridge, speak and learn, decide, and bring the text home! Thanks for the blanket!"

Eliezer waited for more, but none came. "That's it?" he asked. Scrape scrape. "I guess that's it," he said to Melech. It was noon, and he dared to go into the geomancer's stash once more. Since he heard no objections raised, he made a light meal of what he found. "Come," Eliezer said, picking up his pouch, "let's go. We have our answer, or all that we will get. And, more importantly, we had our rest." He sneered. "So why am I still so exhausted? Eh?" He lifted his pouch, but it fought him as the scroll within struggled, bounced, jabbed against the sides while Eliezer tried to tie it to the saddle. "Settle down, you *fershluggeneh*…!"

The Geomancer finally broke his silence. "Will you *shut up?*"

Eliezer asked, in a more subdued voice, "Why didn't you warn me to stay away from him?"

Melech replied that he'd tried, and asked in turn, quite reasonably, if that would have made any difference, and Eliezer had to admit that, no, it wouldn't have.

A crazy man digging holes in the desert, a crazy book refusing to lie still, a bunch of kings, princes, and mayors behaving like fools… and all demanding the ridiculous from him! It was too much. Eliezer shook his head. Was what he'd done really so bad? Had he been such a terrible person to deserve all this? He looked up to Heaven, and lifted his arms in a pleading gesture. *"Vos villst du fun mein leb'n?"* he asked. "What do you *want* from my life?"

Melech lowered himself to allow Eliezer to mount, and flashed him a look that could have meant anything from *I understand* to *Let's just get out of here* to, maybe, *Shut up*.

Day 8

They rode through the afternoon in search of the jagged hill. He hoped that whoever owned the scroll would reward them with a hearty evening meal, for *Yom Kippur* began the following night, and the fast would be difficult to endure without a full belly to start with. As he watched the sun descend before him, he found himself missing one thing above all: the singing of the *Kol Nidre* before the *Yom Kippur* service, before the start of the fast and the hours of pleas for forgiveness:

All vows, and prohibitions, and oaths, and consecrations, that we may vow, or swear, or consecrate, or prohibit upon ourselves, from the previous Day of Atonement until this Day of Atonement and from this Day of Atonement until the Day of Atonement that will come for our benefit: regarding all of them, we repudiate them. All of them are undone, abandoned, cancelled, null and void, not in force, and not in effect. Our vows are no longer vows, and our prohibitions are no longer prohibitions, and our oaths are no longer oaths.

He'd always found so much hope in that song, that tradition: maybe with that sung declaration, he could wipe his mind and memory and history free of all the old covenants and promises, and consign the entire ridiculous horde of *goniffs* and *schickers* and *meshuggenahs* and *shmegeggis* to oblivion. Leave the old to rot behind him. Such a wonderful boon! but unless he somehow found himself at a *Yom Kippur* service — a very unlikely eventuality — he would have to do without.

He ate and drank a little from his diminishing supplies, then, as the sun flattened itself against the horizon, he stopped and bade farewell to *shabbos*. All he could do was watch the stars emerge from the deepening blue above; no tasks, no obligations, no requests demanded his time and diminishing energy. On the other hand, without the Geomancer's delightfully cozy anthill, he felt a chill, and wove a blanket for himself. In the dim light cast by the moon, the stars, and a couple of steadily shining planets, he watched the threads do their weaving dance above his head.

"Do you want one, too, while I'm at it?"

Melech declined the offer with thanks.

"I thought you might want something on your back besides an old man." He heard a flapping sound, and feared some predatory night bird might be stalking them, but after glancing around a bit he saw that it was only the pouch, which lay on the ground near his side. The parchment inside was having fits. "Be patient!" Then he added for good measure, "*Stupid!*" Melech chuckled. Eliezer snatched the completed blanket from mid-air and pulled it over himself, and the *hamische* warmth began to seep into his bones. It was better than any lullaby.

He slept late the following morning, after a night of frequent interruptions from within and without. He nearly kicked the noisy pouch, but refrained from committing an indignity on his property and the Star of David that embellished it.

He mounted Melech as soon as he could, and they started on their journey, if travelling to an unknown destination could be considered a journey. The occasional cloud passed over the sun, relieving the heat for a few moments at a time; Eliezer had recourse to his waterskin too often, and worried about running out. It was urgent that they find food and water soon, and plenty of each. He let Melech follow his nose, but while the horse was useful when it came to water, the food he found suited only an equine belly. Eliezer chipped away at the provisions in his sack, all the while his cruel memory calling past feasts to mind: spiced meats, pastries, stews, a *fresser*'s Paradise, a *nosher*'s Eden.

Then Melech's head jerked erect; he gave a few snorts and turned suddenly toward the northwest. There, the horizon was bitten by a low corrugated silhouette. They rode toward it, and the ground sloped gently upward at first, then more sharply. He had to dismount, and trudged through the dirt and stones, fighting gravity and arthritis until he finally reached the jagged summit that curled away from him on either side. There, lying below him, was a vast bowl of sand, its outline perfectly round, and in the middle of it—

"No! *Oy*, no no *no!*" He slapped his hands over his face. "No, not *them!*"

What is it? Melech asked. The horse climbed up and stood to his left; Eliezer drew his hands away and looked down again; the sight remained, against all his hopes that it had been a mirage, a waking nightmare. For in the exact center of the crater stood a high thin cone of stone, its surfaces pierced with windows, and people were visible walking back and forth within.

The Rockcity of Al-Ayar, with its *meshuggeneh* priests and their *ferkakte* Holy Book!

"And so, Eliezer ben-Avraham," a female voice suddenly said in his right ear, and he nearly jumped out of his skin, "you have come full circle."

A brilliant light tickled the corner of his right eye— the sort of light he'd experienced only twice before: once, at a mad *seder*; and before that, when he'd been told of his curse and punishment. He licked his lips and turned to face the being that stood next to him, staring out over the sand cupped before them. A woman! Yet more than a woman. Not an angel, either, yet an entity made of light. "I know who you are." In all his wanderings, in all his experiences, he had been and had encountered the Masculine, except for that one Purim night... "You are Shekhinah." The Female Principle, the side of the Kabbalah he had sorely neglected. He had lacked balance— an inexcusable mistake.

The eyes she turned upon him were pure light. When she spoke, there was a catch in her voice or his hearing; words faded, blurred with ambiguity. Fool that he was, he had not properly accommodated her, and could not hear her properly as a result. "I have come from the [your?] Father," she said.

He tried not to hope. He did not dare to hope. "What is your message?"

"It is time to come [go?] home."

He couldn't speak, couldn't answer, except to say, "I am an old man, and I'm very tired." He blinked away the burn in his eyes. "Is this true? Is this decreed?"

"It is the [your?] choice."

"Choice?" To go home: it could not be true, it was too good to be true— a demon had come to deceive him, raise his hopes.... And yet... had he not atoned enough for his sins, for many years and every day of his life, even beyond the hours of *Yom Kippur*?

"No more wandering?" To rest at last!

"No more."

"And my powers?"

"No more."

"I see." A fair price. And he felt something drain from him, knowledge and energy all at once.

"No more ludicrous tasks to perform for *meshuggeneh goyim*?" All those good deeds he'd had to do, to use his powers just because others asked him to.

"No more."

"*S'gehert*?" he asked Melech, who had wandered away and was sniffing the ground. "You heard?" It took all his strength to keep the relief and joy from his voice. No answer; the horse remained silent, perhaps letting him have this moment. A wave of peace enveloped him, as if his blanket had flowed over him, warming him. "What do you think of that, Melech?" Still no reply. "What's the matter? Cat got your tongue, or some other beast? Eh?" He addressed Shekhinah once more. "No more *mitzvahs*?" As soon as the words were out of his mouth he knew how absurd they were, how foolish.

She did not reply. He looked over and saw Melech, who had turned his back and was eating some shoots he'd found— in a very horsey manner....

"Oh." Only once before had he felt a pain so sharp: when he'd looked back and seen his village for the last time, when he'd watched everything he'd known and loved shrink away behind him. He swallowed, and continued watching his old friend, unable to take his eyes off Melech even as he spoke to her. "What you offer me, Spirit," he said, "is a false choice." Melech swished his tail against a fly that was bothering him. "Old fool that I am, I understand. The obligation to do *mitzvot* is not my curse, but my birthright. It comes not from being a sinner but from being a man." He licked his dry lips and faced her once more, because he could no longer bear to see Melech, because he could no longer stand the silence in his head. "And my powers made me able to do even more than others." For such was his burden, and such was his boon. So was he supposed to feel blessed, not cursed? He nodded his head at the full truth of it. "And because I can, I must. Some choice." She stared at him without expression. "Is that the message you bring from my Father?" Now, he shook his head. "Then you know my answer."

"Be well, Eliezer ben-Avraham," she said. Then, literally in a blink, she was gone.

Once again he looked over at Melech. The horse still munched away at his find. Eliezer was afraid to try, but inhaled and steeled himself anyway. "Melech?"

The horse raised its head. *I'm here.*

Eliezer let out his breath: *danke Gott!* "What have I done? To both of us?"

The sun was much closer to the western horizon than he would have expected— how long had he and Shekhinah chatted? Eliezer held out his hand, and Melech trotted over; as he did so, the blue pouch hanging from his side jounced around and the *Mogen David* embroidered on its side glittered in the waning light. The slope leading down to the Rockcity was gentler than the rise to the summit of the rim, so Eliezer prepared to climb into the saddle. Then he realized what he was doing, and flushed with shame.

"*Oy.* Where's my head?" He took a deep breath. "So, my friend, what do *you* want to do?" He didn't dare consider the possibilities....

Melech replied by lowering himself as far as he could to accommodate Eliezer.

The relief that flooded over Eliezer was almost unbearable. He mounted and said, "Come. At least something should go home today."

He let Melech choose his pace. As they descended toward the city, he heard a female voice singing the *Kol Nidre.*

A nice touch.

The scroll grew more eager to end its journey, jumping around like a maniac; Eliezer decided to restrain himself no longer, and swatted it with immense satisfaction. "Why can't these people keep their words in their books, and their books in their volumes?" He began to detect figures around Al-Ayar: people had seen them coming, and were emerging from their stony home. "I'll insist that we be well rewarded for returning their property to them. We're going to be well fed this evening if I have anything to say about it."

Good thinking, Melech said. *For a human. You're talking sense at last.*

Our titles are available at major book stores
and local independent resellers who support
Science Fiction and Fantasy readers like you.

EDGE Science Fiction
and Fantasy Publishing

www.edgewebsite.com

Our titles are available at major book stores and local independent resellers who support Science Fiction and Fantasy readers like you.

Alphanauts by J. Brian Clarke (tp) - ISBN: 978-1-894063-14-2
Apparition Trail, The by Lisa Smedman (tp) - ISBN: 978-1-894063-22-7
As Fate Decrees by Denysé Bridger (tp) - ISBN: 978-1-894063-41-8

Bad City by Matt Mayr (ebk) - e-ISBN: 978-1-77053-093-5
Bedlam Lost by Jack Castle (POD) - ISBN: 978-1-77053-109-3
   Bedlam Lost by Jack Castle (ebk) - e-ISBN: 978-1-77053-105-5
Beltrunner by Sean O'Brien (ebk) - e-ISBN: 978-1-77053-102-4
Black Chalice, The by Marie Jakober (hb) - ISBN: 978-1-894063-00-7
Blood Matters by Aviva Bel'Harold (tp) - ISBN: 978-1-77053-073-7
Blue Apes by Phyllis Gotlieb (pb) - ISBN: 978-1-895836-13-4
   Blue Apes by Phyllis Gotlieb (hb) - ISBN: 978-1-895836-14-1
Braided Path, The by Donna Glee Williams (tp) - ISBN: 978-1-77053-058-4

Captives by Barbara Galler-Smith and Josh Langston (tp) - ISBN: 978-1-894063-53-1
Children of Atwar, The by Heather Spears (pb) - ISBN: 978-0-88878-335-6
Chilling Tales: Evil Did I Dwell; Lewd I Did Live edited by Michael Kelly (tp)
   - ISBN: 978-1-894063-52-4
Chilling Tales: In Words, Alas, Drown I edited by Michael Kelly (tp)
   - ISBN: 978-1-77053-024-9
Cinco de Mayo by Michael J. Martineck (tp) - ISBN: 978-1-894063-39-5
Cinkarion - The Heart of Fire (Part Two of The Chronicles of the Karionin) by J. A.
   Cullum - (tp) - ISBN: 978-1-894063-21-0
Circle Tide by Rebecca K. Rowe (tp) - ISBN: 978-1-894063-59-3
Clan of the Dung-Sniffers by Lee Danielle Hubbard (tp) - ISBN: 978-1-894063-05-0
Claus Effect, The by David Nickle & Karl Schroeder (pb) - ISBN: 978-1-895836-34-9
   Claus Effect, The by David Nickle & Karl Schroeder (hb)
   - ISBN: 978-1-895836-35-6
Clockwork Heart by Dru Pagliassotti (tp) - ISBN: 978-1-77053-026-3
Clockwork Lies: Iron Wind by Dru Pagliassotti (tp) - ISBN: 978-1-77053-050-8
Clockwork Secrets: Heavy Fire by Dru Pagliassotti (tp) - ISBN: 978-1-77053-054-6
Clockwork Trilogy Boxed Set by Dru Pagliassotti - **COMING IN SPRING 2015**
Coins of Chaos edited by Jennifer Brozak (tp) - ISBN: 978-1-77053-048-5

Danse Macabre: Close Encounters With the Reaper edited by Nancy Kilpatrick (tp)
   - ISBN: 978-1-894063-96-8
Dark Earth Dreams by Candas Dorsey & Roger Deegan (Audio CD with booklet)
   - ISBN: 978-1-895836-05-9
Darkness of the God (Children of the Panther Part Two) by Amber Hayward (tp)
   - ISBN: 978-1-894063-44-9
Demon Left Behind, The by Marie Jakober (tp) - ISBN: 978-1-894063-49-4
Devil Will Come, The by Justin Gustainis (tp) - ISBN: 978-1-77053-089-8
   Devil Will Come, The by Justin Gustainis (ebk) - e-ISBN: 978-1-77053-090-4
Distant Signals by Andrew Weiner (tp) - ISBN: 978-0-88878-284-7
Dreamers by Donna Glee Williams (POD) - ISBN: 978-1-77053-112-3
   Dreamers by Donna Glee Williams (ebk) - e-ISBN: 978-1-77053-096-6
Dreams of an Unseen Planet by Teresa Plowright (tp) - ISBN: 978-0-88878-282-3

Dreams of the Sea (Part 1 of Tyranaël) by Élisabeth Vonarburg (tp)
- ISBN: 978-1-895836-96-7
    Dreams of the Sea (Part 1 of Tyranaël) by Élisabeth Vonarburg (hb)
    - ISBN: 978-1-895836-98-1
Druids by Barbara Galler-Smith and Josh Langston (tp) - ISBN: 978-1-894063-29-6

Eclipse by K. A. Bedford (tp) - ISBN: 978-1-894063-30-2
Elements by Suzanne Church (tp) - ISBN: 978-1-77053-042-3
Europa Journal by Jack Castle (tp) - ISBN: 978-1-77053-106-2
    Europa Journal by Jack Castle (POD) - ISBN: 978-1-77053-104-8
    Europa Journal by Jack Castle (ebk) - e-ISBN: 978-1-77053-091-1
Even The Stones by Marie Jakober (tp) - ISBN: 978-1-894063-18-0
Evolve: Vampire Stories of the New Undead edited by Nancy Kilpatrick (tp)
- ISBN: 978-1-894063-33-3
Evolve Two: Vampire Stories of the Future Undead edited by Nancy Kilpatrick (tp)
-ISBN: 978-1-894063-62-3
Expiration Date edited by Nancy Kilpatrick (tp) - ISBN: 978-1-77053-062-1

Fires of the Kindred by Robin Skelton (tp) - ISBN: 978-0-88878-271-7
Forbidden Cargo by Rebecca Rowe (tp) - ISBN: 978-1-894063-16-6

Game of Perfection, A (Part 2 of Tyranaël) by Élisabeth Vonarburg (tp) - ISBN:
978-1-894063-32-6
Gaslight Arcanum: Uncanny Tales of Sherlock Holmes edited by Jeff Campbell &
Charles Prepolec (tp) - ISBN: 978-1-8964063-60-9
Gaslight Grimoire: Fantastic Tales of Sherlock Holmes edited by Jeff Campbell &
Charles Prepolec (tp) - ISBN: 978-1-8964063-17-3
Gaslight Grotesque: Nightmare Tales of Sherlock Holmes edited by Jeff Campbell
& Charles Prepolec (tp) - ISBN: 978-1-8964063-31-9
Genius Asylum, The by Arlene F. Marks (ebk) - e-ISBN: 978-1-77053-111-6
Green Music by Ursula Pflug (tp) - ISBN: 978-1-895836-75-2
    Green Music by Ursula Pflug (hb) - ISBN: 978-1-895836-77-6

Healer, The (Children of the Panther Part One) by Amber Hayward (tp)
- ISBN: 978-1-895836-89-9
    Healer, The (Children of the Panther Part One) by Amber Hayward (hb)
    - ISBN: 978-1-895836-91-2
Hell Can Wait by Theodore Judson (tp) - ISBN: 978-1-978-1-894063-23-4
Hounds of Ash and other tales of Fool Wolf, The by Greg Keyes (tp)
- ISBN: 978-1-894063-09-8
Hydrogen Steel by K. A. Bedford (tp) - ISBN: 978-1-894063-20-3

i-ROBOT Poetry by Jason Christie (tp) - ISBN: 978-1-894063-24-1
Immortal Quest by Alexandra MacKenzie (tp) - ISBN: 978-1-894063-46-3

Jackal Bird by Michael Barley (pb) - ISBN: 978-1-895836-07-3
    Jackal Bird by Michael Barley (hb) - ISBN: 978-1-895836-11-0
JEMMA7729 by Phoebe Wray (tp) - ISBN: 978-1-894063-40-1

Keaen by Till Noever (tp) - ISBN: 978-1-894063-08-1
Keeper's Child by Leslie Davis (tp) - ISBN: 978-1-894063-01-2

Land/Space edited by Candas Jane Dorsey and Judy McCrosky (tp)
- ISBN: 978-1-895836-90-5
    Land/Space edited by Candas Jane Dorsey and Judy McCrosky (hb)
    - ISBN: 978-1-895836-92-9

Lyskarion: The Song of the Wind (Part One of The Chronicles of the Karionin) by J.A. Cullum (tp) - ISBN: 978-1-894063-02-9

Machine Sex and other stories by Candas Jane Dorsey (tp)
- ISBN: 978-0-88878-278-6
Maërlande Chronicles, The by Élisabeth Vonarburg (pb) - ISBN: 978-0-88878-294-6
Making the Rounds by Allan Weiss (tp) - ISBN: 978-1-77053-118-8
  Making the Rounds by Allan Weiss (POD) - ISBN: 978-1-77053-116-1
  Making the Rounds by Allan Weiss (ebk) - e-ISBN: 978-1-77053-115-4
Milkman, The by Michael J. Martineck (tp) - ISBN: 978-1-77053-060-7
Milky Way Repo by Michael Prelee (ebk) - e-ISBN: 978-1-77053-092-8
Moonfall by Heather Spears (pb) - ISBN: 978-0-88878-306-6

Necromancer Candle, The by Randy McCharles (tp) - ISBN: 978-1-77053-066-9
nEvermore: Tales of Murder, Mystery and the Macabre
  edited by Nancy Kilpatrick and Caro Soles (tp) - ISBN: 978-1-77053-085-0

Occasional Diamond Thief, The by J. A. McLachlan (tp) - ISBN: 978-1-77053-075-1
Of Wind and Sand by Sylvie Bérard (translated by Sheryl Curtis) (tp)
- ISBN: 978-1-894063-19-7
On Spec: The First Five Years edited by On Spec (pb) - ISBN: 978-1-895836-08-0
  On Spec: The First Five Years edited by On Spec (hb)
- ISBN: 978-1-895836-12-7
Orbital Burn by K. A. Bedford (tp) - ISBN: 978-1-894063-10-4
  Orbital Burn by K. A. Bedford (hb) - ISBN: 978-1-894063-12-8

Pallahaxi Tide by Michael Coney (pb) - ISBN: 978-0-88878-293-9
Paradox Resolution by K. A. Bedford (tp) - ISBN:978-1-894063-88-3
Passion Play by Sean Stewart (pb) - ISBN: 978-0-88878-314-1
Professor Challenger: New Worlds, Lost Places edited by Jeff Campbell & Charles Prepolec (tp) - ISBN: 978-1-77053-052-2
Plague Saint, The by Rita Donovan (tp) - ISBN: 978-1-895836-28-8
  Plague Saint, The by Rita Donovan (hb) - ISBN: 978-1-895836-29-5
Pock's World by Dave Duncan (tp) - ISBN: 978-1-894063-47-0
Puzzle Box, The by The Apocalyptic Four (tp) - ISBN: 978-1-77053-040-9

QUISTA - BOOK ONE: DANAY by Aviva Bel'Harold (tp)
- ISBN: 978-1-77053-108-6
  QUISTA - BOOK ONE: DANAY by Aviva Bel'Harold (ebk)
- e-ISBN: 978-1-77053-107-9

Railroad Rising: The Black Powder Rebellion by J. P. Wagner (POD)
- ISBN: 978-1-77053-099-7
  Railroad Rising: The Black Powder Rebellion by J. P. Wagner (ebk)
- e-ISBN: 978-1-77053-098-0
Red Wraith, The by Nick Wisseman (ebk) - e-ISBN: 978-1-77053-095-9
Reluctant Voyagers by Élisabeth Vonarburg (pb) - ISBN: 978-1-895836-09-7
  Reluctant Voyagers by Élisabeth Vonarburg (hb) - ISBN: 978-1-895836-15-8
Resisting Adonis by Timothy J. Anderson (tp) - ISBN: 978-1-895836-84-4
  Resisting Adonis by Timothy J. Anderson (hb) - ISBN: 978-1-895836-83-7
Rigor Amortis edited by Jaym Gates and Erika Holt (tp)
- ISBN: 978-1-894063-63-0
Rosetta Man, The by Claire McCague (ebk) - e-ISBN: 978-1-77053-094-2

Salarian Desert Game, The by J. A. McLachlan (tp) - ISBN: 978-1-77053-114-7
　　Salarian Desert Game, The by J. A. McLachlan (ebk) - e-ISBN: 978-1-77053-113-0
Shadow Academy, The by Adrian Cole (tp) - ISBN: 978-1-77053-064-5
Silent City, The by Élisabeth Vonarburg (tp) - ISBN: 978-1-894063-07-4
Slow Engines of Time, The by Élisabeth Vonarburg (tp) - ISBN: 978-1-895836-30-1
　　Slow Engines of Time, The by Élisabeth Vonarburg (hb)
　　- ISBN: 978-1-895836-31-8
Stealing Magic by Tanya Huff (tp) - ISBN: 978-1-894063-34-0
Sticks and Stones by Angèle Angèle Gougeon (ebk) - e-ISBN: 978-1-77053-110-9
Stolen Children (Children of the Panther Part Three) by Amber Hayward (tp)
　　- ISBN: 978-1-894063-66-1
Strange Attractors by Tom Henighan (pb) - ISBN: 978-0-88878-312-7
Stranger King by Nadia Hutton (ebk) - e-ISBN: 978-1-77053-100-0

Taming, The by Heather Spears (pb) - ISBN: 978-1-895836-23-3
　　Taming, The by Heather Spears (hb) - ISBN: 978-1-895836-24-0
Technicolor Ultra Mall by Ryan Oakley (tp) - ISBN: 978-1-894063-54-8
Ten Monkeys, Ten Minutes by Peter Watts (tp) - ISBN: 978-1-895836-74-5
　　Ten Monkeys, Ten Minutes by Peter Watts (hb) - ISBN: 978-1-895836-76-9　.
Terminal City (Book One in the Terminal City Saga) by Trevor Melanson (tp)
　　- ISBN: 978-1-77053-083-6
　　Terminal City (Book One in the Terminal City Saga) by Trevor Melanson (ebk)
　　- e-ISBN: 978-1-77053-084-3
Tesseracts 1 edited by Judith Merril (pb) - ISBN: 978-0-88878-279-3
Tesseracts 2 edited by Phyllis Gotlieb & Douglas Barbour (pb)
　　- ISBN: 978-0-88878-270-0
Tesseracts 3 edited by Candas Jane Dorsey & Gerry Truscott (pb)
　　- ISBN: 978-0-88878-290-8
Tesseracts 4 edited by Lorna Toolis & Michael Skeet (pb)
　　- ISBN: 978-0-88878-322-6
Tesseracts 5 edited by Robert Runté & Yves Maynard (pb)
　　- ISBN: 978-1-895836-25-7
　　Tesseracts 5 edited by Robert Runté & Yves Maynard (hb)
　　- ISBN: 978-1-895836-26-4
Tesseracts 6 edited by Robert J. Sawyer & Carolyn Clink (pb)
　　- ISBN: 978-1-895836-32-5
　　Tesseracts 6 edited by Robert J. Sawyer & Carolyn Clink (hb)
　　- ISBN: 978-1-895836-33-2
Tesseracts 7 edited by Paula Johanson & Jean-Louis Trudel (tp)
　　- ISBN: 978-1-895836-58-5
　　Tesseracts 7 edited by Paula Johanson & Jean-Louis Trudel (hb)
　　- ISBN: 978-1-895836-59-2
Tesseracts 8 edited by John Clute & Candas Jane Dorsey (tp)
　　- ISBN: 978-1-895836-61-5
　　Tesseracts 8 edited by John Clute & Candas Jane Dorsey (hb)
　　- ISBN: 978-1-895836-62-2
Tesseracts Nine edited by Nalo Hopkinson and Geoff Ryman (tp)
　　- ISBN: 978-1-894063-26-5
Tesseracts Ten: A Celebration of New Canadian Specuative Fiction
　　edited by R.C. Wilson and E. van Belkom (tp)
　　- ISBN: 978-1-894063-36-4
Tesseracts Eleven: Amazing Canadian Speulative Fiction
　　edited by Cory Doctorow and Holly Phillips (tp)
　　- ISBN: 978-1-894063-03-6

Tesseracts Twelve: New Novellas of Canadian Fantastic Fiction
edited by Claude Lalumière (tp)
- ISBN: 978-1-894063-15-9
Tesseracts Thirteen: Chilling Tales from the Great White North
edited by Nancy Kilpatrick and David Morrell (tp)
- ISBN: 978-1-894063-25-8
Tesseracts 14: Strange Canadian Stories
edited by John Robert Colombo and Brett Alexander Savory (tp)
- ISBN: 978-1-894063-37-1
Tesseracts Fifteen: A Case of Quite Curious Tales
edited by Julie Czerneda and Susan MacGregor (tp)
- ISBN: 978-1-894063-58-6
Tesseracts Sixteen: Parnassus Unbound edited by Mark Leslie (tp)
- ISBN: 978-1-894063-92-0
Tesseracts Seventeen: Speculating Canada from Coast to Coast to Coast
edited by C. Anderson and S. Vernon (tp)
-ISBN: 978-1-77053-044-7
Tesseracts Eighteen: Wrestling With Gods
edited by Liana Kerzner and Jerome Stueart (tp)
- ISBN: 978-1-77053-068-3
Tesseracts Nineteen: Superhero Universe
edited by edited by Claude Lalumière & Mark Shainblum (tp)
- ISBN: 978-1-770530-87-4
Tesseracts Q edited by Élisabeth Vonarburg and Jane Brierley (pb)
- ISBN: 978-1-895836-21-9
Tesseracts Q edited by Élisabeth Vonarburg and Jane Brierley (hb)
- ISBN: 978-1-895836-22-6
Those Who Fight Monsters: Tales of Occult Detectives
edited by Justin Gustainis (pb) - ISBN: 978-1-894063-48-7
Time Machines Repaired Whie-U-Wait by K. A. Bedford (tp)
- ISBN: 978-1-894063-42-5
Triforium, The (The Haunting of Westminster Abbey) by Mark Patton (ebk)
- e-ISBN: 978-1-77053-097-3
Trillionist, The by Sagan Jeffries (tp) - ISBN: 978-1-894063-98-2

Urban Green Man edited by Adria Laycraft and Janice Blaine (tp)
- ISBN: 978-1-77053-038-6

Vampyric Variations by Nancy Kilpatrick (tp) - ISBN: 978-1-894063-94-4
Vyrkarion: The Talisman of Anor (Part Three of The Chronicles of the Karionin)
by J. A. Cullum (tp) - ISBN: 978-1-77053-028-7

Warriors by Barbara Galler-Smith and Josh Langston (tp)
- ISBN: 978-1-77053-030-0
Wildcatter by Dave Duncan (tp) - ISBN: 978-1-894063-90-6